Arielle Immortal Quickening

The Immortal Rapture Series
Volume 4

Lilian Roberts

Cover Design by Shari Ryan
Edited by Jacy Mackin

Previously self-published as *Arielle Immortal Quickening*, 2013

This is a work of fiction. Names, characters, places, brands, media, and incidents are either the product of the author's imagination or are used fictitiously. Any resemblance to similarly named places or to persons living or deceased is unintentional.

ISBN 978-1-945415-11-1

Library of Congress Control Number: 201490

Chapter 1

ARIELLE STOOD FROZEN. The hotel room lost its brightness, and the air thickened. When she tried to inhale, her lungs refused to expand. Her heartbeat pounded painfully in her chest, leaving her faint. The fear was so deeply rooted it held her like a vise. With her eyes squeezed tightly shut and her lips pressed together, she listened to the stony silence that had fallen as Sebastian gave her time to gather her thoughts. The feelings of helplessness and loss draped over her like a heavy curtain while she tried to absorb his last words…

His soft voice had been composed, tainted with a hint of wretchedness. She wasn't ready to accept bad news about any person she loved. Her head throbbed, her self-awareness was in full alert, and she literally felt sick from fear and uneasiness. Her knees buckled underneath her, and she practically collapsed on the floor, drowning in a huge range of intensity and emotional instability. Falling back on the bed, she rolled over and buried her face in the pillow. This wasn't going to be good. Sebastian's expression spoke volumes.

He sat beside her on the bed and ran his hand up and down her back with tenderness and understanding. He was quiet, waiting for her to say something.

She remained unmoved, wordless, her mind wandering aimlessly. *Is the bad news about someone I love?* she wondered anxiously. Finally she pulled herself up and sat on the bed, hugging her knees to her chest as her thoughts turned dark. She took a shuddering breath and gazed into Sebastian's eyes. An unsettled glimmer spread across his eyes, and he pinched the tip of his nose.

Arielle's mouth went dry, and her chest rose and fell anxiously as she stifled a gulp. Unless her mind was deceiving her, Sebastian only pinched the tip of his nose when he was extremely uncomfortable or worried about something or someone. She noticed a flash of anguish crossing his eyes. She was afraid to hear what he was about to tell her; she was sure that her facial expression read with dread and despair. She was trembling. Her misery didn't escape Sebastian.

He reached for her and gathered her to him as close as possible. She laid her head on his chest, looking for reassurance. His voice was soft, but she could hear a hint of distress.

"Arielle, did you hear me, baby?" he asked. She looked up to meet his gaze, unable to speak. She was afraid to ask any questions, knowing any negative information would be painful.

"Arielle, please, I don't like to see you this way. You need to hear what I have to say," Sebastian's voice was velvety soft.

She tried to analyze each and every word in his sentence but was unable to accept the thoughts that invaded her head. The news could not be about her parents, because she had just finished talking to her mum on the phone. *Mother said everything at home was fine.* It wasn't about their friends either, because her mother would have phoned her. Who was all this about? Could it be one of their immortal friends? She knew that eight of their friends had been hunting down Annabel ever since they'd tried to kill her and Eva at St. Jean de Luz. But if this were about their immortal friends, why would Sebastian be so reluctant to discuss it openly with her? Nothing really made sense. Why was Sebastian so upset? Sucking in a deep breath she went for it.

"Who was involved in the accident?" she asked in a hollow whisper.

"Our best friends," he replied in a guarded tone.

Her shock was evident as fright took her over and weighed down every one of her limbs. She realized that the worst feelings that had invaded her mind earlier were right now becoming a reality. Her first thought was denial, but she had to push that into the back of her mind, because she needed to find out the details. Suddenly she was conscious of the tears streaming down her face and her uncontrolled trembling.

"What happened?" she murmured, keeping a blank face as she

felt a lump climbing and closing her throat.

For a moment, he didn't reply, and she looked up into his eyes. His face was pale, and his expression strained. "It's Gabrielle," he muttered. Her eyes went wide with horror, and she felt the muscles of her chest tighten. She didn't really seem to hear his answer. She thought her mind was tripping into a state of shock as bad feelings were now settling inside her very core, taking completely over her senses. She felt his arms pulling her even closer, his fingers lifting her face up, and her eyes piercing hers. She tried to decipher his look, but she found herself unable to do that. Sebastian remained silent, as she looked on bewildered, her face soaked with tears, and her heartbeat hammering her chest uncontrollably. She shook her head in denial and rubbed her temples with her fingertips as she pressed her lips together harder. He took her hands and placed them flat on his chest and covered them with his.

"Please, Arielle, say something," he pressed on in a soft voice.

Silence stretched and suddenly she looked up at him with horror in her eyes.

"How bloody bad was it? You are freaking me out!" Her voice was louder than she expected, but the desperation held her in a tight grip.

Sebastian visibly started at the tone of her voice. After a brief hesitation, he reached toward her and took her face between his hands. "Gabrielle is in the worst condition. Troy says she's in intensive care, and they don't know if she'll make it. Right now, she is in a coma with a fractured skull, a broken leg, several broken ribs, and fifty stitches in her left thigh."

Arielle tried desperately to swallow the lump wedged in her throat. "Oh, My God... Oh. My. God!" she whispered, slumping down onto the bed. Distantly, she felt Sebastian pull her up into his arms, holding her tightly against him. Without thought, she buried her face in his shoulder and sobbed.

He didn't interrupt, allowing her time to grasp the truth. However, her need to know more about the accident finally broke through and calmed her. Worse, a niggling feeling told her that she didn't know all of it yet. "Did Troy tell you what happened? What did the doctors say?" she asked into his shirt, desperate to hear that Gabby would be all right.

"No one knows yet, but they are hoping that she'll pull through. The surgeon told her parents that the next few days would be critical. Hopefully, she will regain consciousness without any long-term damage. He assured them that she was healthy and strong before the accident and that her body is still fighting to heal." He hugged her tighter. "Everyone except Ian and Eva are by her side."

Arielle curled her fingers into the fabric beneath her palms, frantically trying to calm the quick inhalations and exhalations that left black spots and the words "dead dead dead" before her eyes. "What happened to them, Sebastian? Tell me."

"Both of them escaped with bruises, cuts, and a couple broken limbs. Overall, they are extremely lucky. Troy says they'll be released sometime tomorrow."

"Thank God," she praised. For a moment, she closed her eyes and concentrated on breathing. Once the spots disappeared, she kissed Sebastian's cheek and continued. "How did it happen?"

Sebastian half-smiled down at her, the strain of everything weighing heavily in his expression. "The vehicle overturned on their way back home from a dinner party at the Polo Club." Arielle waited for him to continue. "Troy and I purchased six tickets to a fundraiser there before you and I decided to take this trip. Originally, it would have been us, Troy and Gabrielle, and Ian and Eva. Since Italy seemed more important, I suggested Troy invite Paul and Loren to use the tickets.

"What happened to Paul and Lauren?" The panic pushed at her.

"They are fine. They went to the function in their own car, so they left separately," he assured her.

"Good," she murmured. "God, what happened?"

"The four of them left the dance quite late with Gabrielle driving and Troy in the passenger seat. The roads were wet from some light showers and slick. Gabrielle insisted on driving, and, as you know, Troy is happy to let her do whatever makes her happy. Gabrielle swerved to avoid hitting something in the middle of the road, and the car flipped several times before smashing against a concrete wall that stretched along the road. They didn't have seatbelts on. Troy saw everyone being ejected out of the car." Sebastian's voice was despondent.

Immediately, Arielle knew that they had to get back to Brighton.

Gabby and Eva were her friends, her sisters, her family! Words failed her as her mind raced. Decision made, she exhaled.

"Arielle, what's going on in there?" Sebastian pointed at her head.

"I want to go home," she whispered, anxiously.

"I knew you would. I'll make the arrangements, and we'll be on the first flight out." She held on to Sebastian, refusing to let go as she cried silently and prayed for her friends. He took her face in his hands again and kissed her softly.

"Don't worry, Arielle; I'm right here. Remember that I love your friends very much. They are part of my life now, and they'll always be," Sebastian's voice was comforting. He was watching her carefully, making sure that she was okay. He smiled softly. "We have to let others go through their own journey while we stay on ours. We can love them; we can be there for them, but don't forget that we have to be here for *us*, too. You have to accept this accident and let the wallop subside in order to be strong for our friends and give them the support they will need from us."

He gave her a pointed look, pushing her gently away and meeting her eyes. "What are you thinking?"

"I feel so shattered, and you're so strong, so incredibly amazing. I'm thankful I have you." Without hesitation, she pulled him close again and wrapped her arms around his neck.

His lips caressed her ear. "There is one lesson that I've learned while walking the long, miserable, immortal road for over five centuries. If we live our lives at its fullest, then we can't stop the bad--or good--experiences from happening." The bitter smile he gave her didn't fit with his beautiful profile.

And knowing that he was right didn't disperse the hurt she felt at being so far away from the people she loved while they needed her. "I feel so helpless," she added in a muffled voice. "I want to do something, but I am unsure what that might be."

"All we can do is go back home and be with them. We are going to do that as soon as possible," he reassured her, trying to calm her. "I'm here, Arielle. Please don't wallow in the negative; you can't help them if you make yourself ill." *If I can just help her process what I've already told her, she'll be able to handle the rest of the news soon.* The hurt in her eyes was tearing him apart, but nothing he could do would make her pain go away.

"Arielle, call your mother while I make the flight arrangements; she might have some more details." He pressed his lips to her forehead and walked out of the room.

She picked up her phone, and her mum answered on the first ring.

"Mum, did you hear about Gabby and Eva? They were involved in a car accident last night." She desperately needed to hear something comforting.

"Yes, dear, I just found out a few minutes ago. Gabby's mother called me a couple minutes ago; she and John are devastated. They spent the night in the ICU waiting room, because the doctor told them that Gabby's condition is extremely critical. I called Eva's mom once I hung up. Madeline said she stayed beside Eva's bedside the whole night. Apparently, Eva and Ian were pretty lucky." Arielle heard shuffling in the background.

"Your dad and I are getting ready to go to the hospital to be with them for a bit. Unfortunately, there isn't anything else we can do right now."

"Was it in the news there?" she questioned, hoping more details had been released. *Like what caused Gabby to swerve.*

"Katherine told me that they splattered it all over the front page in the morning paper, and we just got through reading the details. Good Lord! Arielle, if you saw the picture of the car, you wouldn't be able to comprehend how anyone came out of it alive!

"The accident investigators and the police officers on the scene were stunned. They couldn't explain how Eva and Ian could escape with minor injuries. The back of the car was completely destroyed. The amazing part is that Troy was unscathed. The paper called it a miracle. If those kids didn't have guardian angels, they'd be dead!"

"I'm glad it turned out the way it did, Mum," Arielle said softly. "Sebastian and I are praying for Gabby. We're coming home with the first flight out, and we should be there soon. I love you, Mum. My heart is breaking over this accident." Thinking about it brought tears back to her eyes.

"Arielle," she heard her mum's voice, strong and reassuring. "I'm sure it'll all work out. She's under God's care now, and I know she'll come out of this soon. I love you, dearest, be careful!"

"I love you, too, Mum."

Setting the phone back on the receiver, she wished she could take away the agony her friends and family were feeling. She lay across the bed, waiting for Sebastian to return.

Chapter 2

ARIELLE CLOSED HER EYES, and her mind drifted to Brighton. Mentally shaking aside the accident and the bad thoughts whirling in her head, she tried to recall happier times and better days that warmed her heart. Most of those dreams were shared with the two women who were lying in the hospital.

She accepted the thought that something good would come out of this whole thing. Inwardly, she scowled. She had a strong feeling that something had changed, but she wasn't sure yet. Pondering the possibilities, she dozed off until she heard someone enter the room.

"What did your mum say, baby?" Sebastian asked as he entered the room with a soft smile on his face.

Arielle raised her head and drew herself up onto her elbows. "She said the investigators were fascinated with the outcome of one of the worst accidents in Brighton history. They are sure something extraordinary took place last night. All of our friends should have died. At least, everyone except Troy, who can't die. The car was completely destroyed."

"I'm glad about the outcome," he contradicted, and she could sense something unusual in his behavior, but she couldn't quite grasp it. "I made the flight arrangements, and we're leaving in the morning. That is the first flight out," Sebastian said, as he pulled her in his arms and pressed his lips to her forehead.

"I love you, Arielle," he murmured. "Everything will be all right. We'll all be together shortly. Gabrielle will be fine, and we'll pick up where we left things before the accident. Please trust in me." He sounded so sure and confident that she felt more at ease, especially when he suggested that they cancel their afternoon outing and spend the time together without distractions instead.

Curled up with him on the bed, Arielle grinned as she remembered a plan that she made with her friends. "Eva, Gabby, and I had a wild idea."

"What about?" he asked.

"We want to get married on the same day. We thought that would make our wedding day a magnificent event. Don't you think it would?" She chuckled softly as tears welled up again. She gazed at his face with a bitter smile, and she noticed a brief shadow crossing his beautiful emerald eyes. "A wedding for three couples," she mumbled again, as she detected a half smile teasing the corner of his mouth.

"I'll be happy to be your husband, any day, any time, any way you choose," he said and laughed softly. He gazed deep into her eyes, and she felt as if she was sinking in the passion of his soul. Jaw set, he stated. "If I had my choice, we would be married by now."

Arielle blinked, surprised. "Oh, why?"

"Why?" Sebastian couldn't believe she was asking him that question. He seemed shocked. "Arielle, I love you," he stated. "I feel like I've know you all my life." His voice was filled with emotion.

"Sebastian, please! You have been on this earth for over five centuries, and you have known me for a little over a year," she snorted, pinning him with her gaze.

He closed his eyes, and his jaw muscles shifted. A feeling of tenderness washed over him. "My life began when I met you," he said quietly. The look he gave her was full of promise and pleasure. "I want to be your lover and your best friend for eternity." His voice was mesmerizing, soothing every part of her body and soul.

God... she thought to herself, *how can he be so perfectly faultless?* She heard his quiet laughter and flinched. Certain she'd thought aloud again, she glanced at him and saw his eyes filled with amusement. Suddenly bashful, she bit her bottom lip and stared down at her hands with a small smile.

"You are my lover; you're my private dream," she said sincerely. "I want to marry you, but I also want to be out of school before we get married. I thought you were okay with that," she said, gazing into his beautiful eyes.

"Yes, I know, baby, but that doesn't stop me from wanting to marry you now. I want the world to know that you're mine."

"They do!" she said, utterly surprised. "Everyone in *my* world knows that we are engaged to be married, and I mean everyone!"

Sebastian sighed, nodding in agreement. He then reached for her, and she fell into his arms, letting relief lap about them. Their eyes locked, and his lips came down on hers in a warm and passionate kiss.

"I just want you to be my wife more than anything I have ever wanted in my life," he whispered. Arielle's heart swelled at the thought of this man being her husband; sharing her life, her heart, and her dreams. This man that she considered a mere dream not long ago, a desire that might never come true. She choked back tears and reached up to press her lips against his. Arielle basked in the strength of Sebastian's mind and body, and she let out a loud sight. Sebastian nuzzled her hair and drew her tighter in his embrace.

"What are you thinking?" he asked, his brows creasing.

Arielle chuckled. "Oh, my thoughts are mostly about you," she murmured, and Sebastian grinned.

"That's what I want to hear. I want to be the center of your universe, the only man in your life," he said, and his voice cracked.

She pulled back, and their gazes met and locked. Her lips curved teasingly.

"Am I the center of your universe?"

"I'm sure I have told you that before, but in case you didn't hear me or don't remember, you are that. And much more."

"How much more? How can there be more?"

"Arielle, you're the very core of my soul. Without you, there is no me." His voice was soft and sincere, his statement mind-blowing.

She drew a deep breath and sank deeper into his embrace. Putting a finger under her chin, he lifted her face as his lips came down on hers with passion that was set to explode into something beyond rational thought, beyond anything he could comprehend. The kiss fed the fire that already sweltered in his veins and increased the confusion that swept through his thoughts. *Why does my body respond to hers, like a thirsty man at the sight of water or a hungry man at the sight of food?* he wondered and shuddered. Sebastian was at a complete loss. The same question had recurred since he first laid eyes on Arielle. The feeling grew stronger with passing time until he couldn't breathe without her by his side. That was a truly startling revelation for someone like him, a strong, unbreakable, and resilient immortal.

Realization brought his equilibrium back under control. It would be unconscionable to act on his desires for her while she was in this state of mind. She ached for her friends, so he paused and prevented his impulse from penetrating this part of his mind.

The thick sweet scent of freesia filled Sebastian's nostrils, and he inhaled deeply. He nuzzled Arielle's hair again and rejoiced at the fragrance that was as familiar to his senses by now as the very air he breathed.

Sebastian rested on the bed and put his arms around Arielle; he pulled her to his chest and sheltered her. They lay in a calm silence for a very long time, as deep emotions coursed through them. Sebastian smiled faintly and drew in a shaky breath. Despite the muddled thoughts about the situation, Sebastian gave the appearance of a man in complete control, a man who knew exactly how to handle each and every situation. But the truth was entirely different. Sebastian was nervous about what was to come when they finally went home. How was he going to divulge the truth to Arielle and when would be the right time to do that? He cursed inwardly in frustration.

Arielle was resting in the solace of his embrace with her eyes closed, and she seemed to be calm but for a few dry sobs that shook her body lightly here and there.

The sun went down slowly, and the light in the room faded away, shading every piece of furniture. Arielle was asleep and Sebastian didn't want to move; he didn't want to wake her up. Suddenly, a sob shook Arielle's body, and she moaned lightly. Sebastian sucked in a huge breath and tightened his embrace. She was shivering, so he held her closer and rubbed his hand up and down her back, wanting to protect her from whatever haunted her sleep. His mouth set in a straight line and his chest muscles tightened, as joy surged thought his body.

She was his to have and protect, and he would give his life to do just that. He placed a soft kiss on her temple and placed his face in the crook of her neck.

Arielle opened her eyes slowly and blinked several times. The room was dark now, and she tried to bring the ghostly shadows in the room into focus.

"What time is it?" she whispered.

"I don't know, Baby, but it's getting late." He breathed the words and placed a tender kiss on her temple once again. She turned and pressed a warm kiss to his lips as she pulled away from his embrace and stretched, trying to gather her thoughts.

"How long have I been asleep?" she asked.

"Oh, it has been about a couple of hours. You were exhausted."

She eased off the bed and set her feet on the floor. She stretched and smiled down at Sebastian.

"I'll be right back," she said, walking into the bathroom to wash her face and brush her teeth. When she came out, Sebastian was still lying in bed, his hands behind his head while watching her carefully. Arielle's lips curved, and he smiled back. Turning she walked to the balcony doors and pulled them wide open. It was now twilight, and the air felt warm as a light breeze brushed across her face and made her shiver lightly. She stepped outside and took in a lungful of air. She could smell the ocean, and it made her smile, reminding her of Brighton and her two best friends.

The thought of Eva and Gabrielle made her frown, and tears welled up. Her eyes scanned her surroundings and her breath hitched when she saw the magnificent sliver of the moon peaking at the end of the horizon. She watched mesmerized as the moon started to climb slowly over the ocean and spread its silvery light across the dark waters. It looked like a huge pearl suspended from the dark, unending surface of the sky.

Tuscany's beauty was mesmerizing. Several boats with their shimmering lights were moving slowly, casting streaks of bright illumination across the waves. She wrapped her arms around her body and stood utterly unmoved. She felt his warmth radiating toward her just before his arms snaked around her waist and pulled her possessively flush against his body. He nuzzled her hair and pressed a soft kiss on her shoulder.

"What are you thinking, my love?"

Arielle bit down on her lower lip and placed her hands over his. There were so many questions and so many emotions that were whirling in her head; she couldn't differentiate which ones were more important that the other. Turning around without leaving his embrace, she looked up into his beautiful eyes. "I was thinking that school is starting in a couple of months," she said and swallowed hard. "How is this going to work for Gabby?" A tone of despondency coded her voice. "Do you think that she will be able to come out of this well enough?"

Sebastian listened carefully, searching her eyes, but he remained silent.

"God, I love her so much, I can't imagine what she is going through," she furthered, tears threatening to escape her eyes.

He didn't say anything again for a short period of time. Finally he pressed a soft kiss on her lips and whispered, "Everything will go back to normal before you know it." His voice was so comforting.

There he goes again, Mr. Positive, my Darcy, and my life's miracle, she thought. She snuggled even closer to his embrace and wrapped her arms around his neck, rising to her toes and pressing his lips with her tongue.

Sebastian moaned as her touch resonated through his bones. Pressing his hands to the small of her back, he pulled her even closer and their lips met. They stood there holding each other, lost in their thoughts.

Exhaustion weighed down every part of her body, and when they finally went to bed, she snuggled up to Sebastian in need of his warmth and comfort. Closing her eyes, she laid her hand flat on his chest, and he gathered her into his embrace. She took a deep breath and tried to sort through the worrisome emotions that were invading her head. Her body trembled, and Sebastian tightened his hold. "Go to sleep, baby. I'm right here," he murmured.

Sebastian watched her uneasiness as she attempted to sleep. He pressed his lips to her cheek and pulled her even closer, as he knew she liked to sleep that way. Two hours passed before he finally felt her relaxing and drifting off to sleep. His mind was working double time as silence closed in around him. He mulled over all the details of the accident and his conversation with Troy. Troy had averted such devastation! But how were they to explain the truth to Ian and Eva? The situation would be both terrifying and difficult for them to understand.

The subject would have to be approached delicately, but that problem was for another day. More important was figuring out who the woman was that caused the accident by standing in the middle of the road. While on the phone with Troy, his mind had immediately gone to Annabel, but his friend reassured him that she looked exactly like a woman the group had encountered earlier the night of the accident at the club. She'd handled the seating arrangements.

Immortal vision was flawless. Despite the darkness and the rain, Troy had to be believed. The woman was not Annabel, as bizarre as it sounded. Of course, Annabel had always known Sebastian and Arielle's whereabouts, so why would she create this accident if Arielle hadn't been in the car?

Who was the stranger Troy had seen? What had motivated her to attempt to murder their friends? Neither he nor Troy had thought of a good reason, and rage surged through him as he gritted his teeth in frustration.

Arielle would have to be told about Ian and Eva soon. One of her many superb characteristics was the ability to alleviate the stress of other people and temper their emotions. If only she could do it for herself. She was the most amazing person he had ever met, and he had met an immeasurable number of people in the last five centuries. She was the only woman that gave him knee-weakening intoxication, filling his existence with warmth and tenderness. She was the one and only bright star in his world, and they were perfect for each other. They fit together like hand and glove.

He chuckled at the thought and pulled her even closer. He didn't like to see her unhappy, and he absolutely hated to see her cry. However, he needed to tell her the truth. He had a little time ahead of him, and he was going to find the right moment to discuss this sensitive matter.

He watched her sleep peacefully in his arms, and she looked beautiful, relaxed, and untroubled. Watching her cry was the worst experience, leaving him powerless and shattered. All he wanted to do was turn the clock back to when they left for Italy and alleviate the hurt and the pain that was consuming her.

Sebastian's recollection of his transformation from human to immortal was the strongest memory he held of his human life. Ian and Eva's transformation would take four days; then, it would no longer be a secret. Their needs would completely change. They would become immortals and incredibly physically powerful-- beyond any human imagination. Immune to harm of any kind, there will be no need for doctors or hospitals, since every injury would simply regenerate. Their heart would stop beating, and their tear ducts would dry up. Human food would no longer be their preference as they would need the immortal drink of salve to nurse and sustain their bodies.

Glancing down at her sleeping, her head cushioned on his shoulder, he realized he had been frowning for the past hour. Ian and Eva's immortality lurked at the back of his mind, not allowing him to focus on anything else. The frown returned to his face and his lips twisted in frustration. Through the shadows of the room he gazed at the ceiling and decided not to allow his mind to dwell on tomorrow. Pressing a gentle kiss on her hair, he closed his eyes.

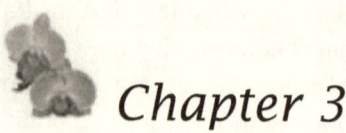

Chapter 3

THE FLIGHT TOOK OFF EARLY, and they touched down in Brighton a little before noon. Only stopping at their house long enough to drop their luggage off and freshen up, they made it to the hospital in record time. When they arrived at the hospital, they made their way into the ICU waiting room where they met Gabrielle's parents, as well as Eva's mother. The three parents were sitting together, talking in low voices. The physical and emotional trauma of the situation was obvious in the fret lines carved into their faces and the exhaustion they wore like a mantle around their shoulders.

As they approached, Dr. Taylor stood up and greeted them warmly. He hugged her with one arm and shook Sebastian's hand with the other. Arielle hugged him back as tears welled up. She loved him just like a father, and she sobbed in his embrace. She knew perfectly well that his heart was shuddering.

"I'm so sorry," she murmured, her voice was breaking.

He patted her tenderly on the back. "I know, dear, and we're really glad that you, and Sebastian, escaped this nightmare."

Sebastian hugged Katherine and Madeline. After exchanging warm regards, he walked over to sit next to Dr. Taylor. Arielle leaned down hug Gabby and Eva's mothers affectionately.

"Weren't you on vacation, dear?" Mrs. Taylor asked.

"Yes, we were in Italy. We came back as soon as we heard," Arielle apologized, downheartedly.

"Oh, honey, you didn't have to do that," Mrs. Winters assured.

"We most certainly did. Gabby and Eva are like sisters to me. I love them dearly."

"There...there...there," Mrs. Taylor said, patting her hands lovingly. "The girls will be all right; I'm sure of that."

Excusing themselves shortly after, Arielle and Sebastian went to visit Gabby. A nurse buzzed Arielle into the ICU, only allowing her to enter as someone else was already in the room. Without an argument, Sebastian pressed her hand softly and turning away he went back to sit and talk with Mr. Taylor and wait for her. Arielle entered the ICU and the sight of her dearest friend unmoving on the hospital bed sent a wave of wretchedness through her. Gabby looked worse than Arielle had imagined. A tube that was inserted into her mouth helped her breath, and there was an intravenous line hooked to her right hand. The largest cast wrapped her left arm from shoulder to wrist, another covered her left leg from just over the knee to her ankle, and the smallest protected her right foot. An apparatus around her neck appeared to be to prevent Gabrielle from moving her body. Her head was covered in thick gauze, except for her beautiful face. Beneath the bandaids and bruises, she looked pale; her lips were dry and gray. In response, Arielle's body quivered, as if ice water ran through her veins. Her knees began to quiver at the proof that lives could be instantaneously changed.

Troy looked exhausted. He had been leaning forward, his arms bent and elbows resting on his thighs, when she entered. Hearing her, he raised his chin from where they rested on his interlocked hands. The look they exchanged was filled with nervousness over their friend's health.

A faint smile painted his lips momentarily, and he stood up, reaching for her. Her eyes filled with tears as she took his hands and saw that his beautiful face was distorted by anguish. His gaze was deeply distressed, and she knew he was in extreme pain. If he had a heart, it would be broken, so she put her arms around him and kissed him softly on the cheek.

"She's going to be all right," she murmured. He shrugged his shoulders briefly and motioned for her to sit at the chair next to him without letting go of her hands. Here was this amazing immortal in need of her touch, a simple human, and she was more than happy to accommodate him.

"I'm so glad to see you." He glanced at the empty doorway. "Is Sebastian here?"

"Yes," she replied. "He is talking with Mr. Taylor in the waiting room."

He nodded as his gaze turned back to Gabrielle, and Arielle knew that if he could cry he would be crying right now. She sat still for a few moments as she squeezed her eyes tightly shut to hold in the tears. Finally unable to take it, she stood and walked around the bed. With one hand on the bed rail to support herself, she leaned in to kiss Gabrielle's chin… the only part of her friend that didn't have a bruise or cut.

"Gabby, I know you are listening. You need to know that I love you more than you'll ever know. Troy and Sebastian and your parents are all here. We are waiting on you to heal and wake up." Wiping the tears from her cheeks, she patted Gabrielle's hand before moving to sink back into the chair beside Troy. The sobs caught her as her butt touched the seat cushion. The strain of the stress of the past few days was causing her to feel sick. Troy reached over, cupped her chin, and turned her face toward his. He held her until she met his eyes. His features were composed and serene, but she knew he felt anything except calm. "Thank you, Arielle." His voice broke on her name. "Thank you for being here."

"I'm so sorry, Troy," she said sniffing and swallowed hard. "I wish this hadn't happened."

Troy leaned over and kissed her cheek. "Me too," he replied, in a hoarse voice.

Arielle smiled weakly at Troy as she reached across his lap to take the tissue box from the windowsill. Pulling a tissue out, she wiped her tears away and quietly stood up. "I'll send Sebastian in," she whispered, and Troy inclined his head. She could feel the blood pounding in her veins as she slipped out of the room. Her legs ached painfully, and she leaned against the wall outside the ICU waiting room, sobbing uncontrollably. She wasn't sure how long she stood there alone. She saw Sebastian approaching with his smooth walk and a magnificent calmness that covered the planes of his beautiful face. He took her face gently in his hands and wiped her tears away with his thumbs. She wrapped her arms around his neck and rested her face in the crook of his neck.

"She looks pretty bad," she whimpered. She tried hard to stop crying, swallowing back her tears and forcing the salty liquid down her throat.

"Arielle," he murmured, nuzzling her hair. "It's going to be okay."

"I told Troy you will go in."

"Yes, I was heading that way." He kissed her gently on the lips, and he walked through the unit's doors. She stood there waiting for a little while, and when he came out, he looked shaken. He took her hand, and they walked back into the waiting room. She took a deep breath before she reached out and hugged the Taylors and Mrs. Winters again with sincere affection. She could see the pain and the stress that they were experiencing at having their daughters in the hospital. Mrs. Taylor's eyes were red and swollen from crying, and her face was white.

"I know it will take time, but she will be all right," Arielle whispered. She looked over at Dr. Taylor who was now sitting in the corner by himself, lost in his thoughts. Here was this accomplished surgeon unable to do a single thing to make his little girl feel any better. She leaned closer to Mrs. Taylor and asked quietly. "How is Dr. Taylor holding up?"

"He has fallen completely apart," Mrs. Taylor cried, her voice faltering. "I'm having a horrible time consoling him. I'm so lost that I'm in no position to provide that kind of emotional support for him," she added.

Arielle wished she could find the right words to ease their pain, but she couldn't. Nothing would until Gabrielle was awake. She shut her eyes and prayed that this was all just an unpleasant dream.

"We are so thankful Troy was there to get her help right away," Mrs. Taylor added. Her words brought Arielle back to reality. "She's not out of the woods yet, but the doctor thinks that she'll come around soon. We're hoping that there will be no permanent injuries." Her voice was breaking.

"I'm so sorry."

"We are extremely thankful, Arielle, that she didn't sustain any lasting injuries," She added with a deep sigh. Arielle hugged her warmly. Mrs. Winters approached, and she heard her shaky voice.

"Arielle, if you saw the car you wouldn't believe that anyone survived that crash. The front seat was pushed into the back seat. It was a miracle that both Eva and Ian escaped with small injuries. They could have died!" she said with a strained light in her eyes. "The amazing thing is that Troy was completely unscathed." Gabrielle's mom glanced over. "I'm really happy, Mrs. Winters, that Eva didn't get seriously hurt." Eva's mother didn't seem to hear a word Mrs. Taylor said.

"Nobody, including the police investigators, could understand this type of outcome from such a horrible accident. It was a miracle that they survived!"

"I'm so glad they survived," Arielle said pressing Mrs. Taylor's hand softly. "Now all I want to think about is their speedy recovery," she added.

"Yes, that's what we are praying for," both mothers murmured simultaneously.

"I wish I had been here," Arielle said with a shaken voice. "It was hard getting the news over the phone and not knowing the details."

Their expressions became alarmed. "We are glad you weren't here." Mrs. Winters voice was unyielding as she reached over and took Arielle's hand in hers. "What if you were in the same car? No... no... we're glad you weren't here."

"I feel awful; they are my best friends, my sisters," Arielle mumbled, and the words trembled in her throat.

"They love you, too, Arielle. You girls have been inseparable since you were little girls," Mrs. Taylor said. Arielle gave her a sweet smile. Both ladies reached out and took her in their arms, and their eyes welled up with tears once again.

Arielle glanced between the two of them, and her expression became thoughtful. "I spoke to my mum on the phone before we left Italy, and she told me that she would be coming to be with you."

"Aaa...Both your mum and dad were here yesterday. They spent several hours with us, and it was very comforting. In fact, they were here when the doctor told us that Gabrielle is very strong, and she will recover quite well with time."

"That's excellent news!" Arielle remarked. There was a long pause.

"Eva and Ian will be going home the day after tomorrow," Mrs. Winters broke the silence. Arielle smiled in obvious pleasure.

She hesitated a few more minutes, and then she glanced in Sebastian's direction, trying to get his attention. He had taken a seat next to Mr. Taylor, and they were conversing quietly. Sebastian finally looked up, and their eyes locked. His expression spoke volumes; there was warmth in his eyes, and she smiled. He stood up slowly and politely took his leave from Mr. Taylor. He crossed the room in a slow stride and came to stand right next to her.

"Sebastian," she breathed, and took his hand. "We should go and visit with Eva and Ian before we go home."

"Yes," he said, "I had the very same thought." They said their goodbyes and walked away.

"Thanks for coming, Sebastian. I'll treasure our talk." Mr. Taylor's clear voice startled her. She gazed back toward him, and he was watching Sebastian with a grateful look. She was completely amazed at the extraordinary appeal Sebastian projected around him. She stared at the most striking man on this earth as he walked next to her and held her hand. Her eyes rested on his gorgeous face one more time.

"Let's go see Eva first," she said. He nodded in agreement. Bending down, he brushed his lips across her forehead.

Eva looked remarkably well. A wide smile spread across her badly bruised face when she saw them walking in.

"Hey, Arielle! Hey, Sebastian! I'm so happy to see you both," Her voice was weary and extreme emotion haunted her expression as tears rolled down her face. Arielle was pleased that all she could see was a large cast on her right leg and several black-and-blue bruises on her face. She also saw bruises on the part of Eva's body where the hospital gown left her skin exposed. Sebastian bent down and gave her a warm hug, and Eva squeezed him tightly.

"Hey, you handsome man! I missed you and your dazzling eyes." Her remark made Sebastian chuckle as he released on her a good dose of his dazzling power. Eva immediately went numb; she tried to open her mouth, but she was unable to speak. Arielle heard her gasping for air as her head fell back on the pillow, unable to hold herself up. Sebastian broke out into soft laughter as he looked away from Eva's eyes. It was but a few minutes later when they heard her sigh under her breath. Shaking her head, she mumbled, "That's not fair Sebastian; that's just not fair." For a moment, it seemed like the accident had never happened.

"I'm so happy to see that you came out of this without major injuries," Arielle said. Her voice was jubilant, and her heart was full of joy for Eva's wellbeing.

"Oh, Arielle, me too. It must have been a horrible accident! I haven't seen any pictures, and I just can't remember a thing!"

"It was…it was a pretty bad accident," Sebastian said.

"I saw the paper, and I'm so happy about you and Ian escaping with a few broken bones and some bruises," Arielle added.

"Poor Gabby!" Eva murmured. "My mum said that she's in bad shape, and my heart is breaking. Have you seen her?"

"Yes," Arielle replied. "I just did. She's still in ICU in a coma, so she didn't know that I was there. Troy looked devastated."

"We are all thankful that Troy was indestructible, because he saved our lives," Eva whispered and let out a soft sigh. "I know that his immortal speed had everything to do with getting help quickly. I know that he saved Gabrielle's life."

Arielle smiled and bent down to give her a kiss. "I'm so happy that you weren't badly hurt," she said, palming her cheek. "Can you remember anything at all?" she asked, searching Eva's face and struggling to read her thoughts.

Arielle ran her fingers through her hair and blew out an exasperated breath. She turned to look at Sebastian, a perplexed look spreading across her face. Her special gift of being able to read her best friend's thoughts was not working. Sebastian's eyebrows furrowed quizzically. Arielle flinched and fixed her gaze back on Eva.

Eva's eyes widened. "What is it?" she asked, noticing Arielle's odd facial expression.

"I'm really puzzled. I can't read a single thought in your head. This is the first time in seventeen years that all I get is complete silence."

"Really!" Eva said, seemingly relieved. "How about that? Maybe that's a good thing. Now I can keep my thoughts to myself," she added and chuckled. Reaching over, she took Arielle's hand and pressed it softly. "I'm only joking, Arielle; maybe it's temporary, and maybe it has to do with the accident. Or the medicine, the hospital, who knows?"

Arielle nodded in agreement. "Yes, maybe you're right. Try and see if you can remember anything at all about the accident."

Sebastian was standing right behind her, and he stiffened at her words. *Yes, I do believe this is going to be a rather ghastly blow to Arielle, Eva, and Ian,* Sebastian thought. He closed his eyes, trying to elude the painful thoughts about the upcoming encounters. Things were going to turn terrifying, painful, chilling. All three had to be told in the next two days. Eva's voice brought him out of his private struggle, and opening his eyes, he felt that he was moved by a profound reality. *God, how am I going to tell them?*

 *Chapter 4*

DESPITE ARIELLE'S BURNING CURIOSITY, she remained silent, waiting for Eva to say something, and she did.

"Like I said before, I don't remember anything about the accident," Eva said, pressing her lips together. "But I do remember having a strong scary premonition about the party the night before. At first, I didn't want to go, but I finally agreed because Troy and Loren were going to be there to keep us safe if something were to happen. As it turned out, we had an incredible time. The food was delicious, and we danced way past midnight." She smiled distantly. Arielle remained silent as Eva continued, "I do remember a peculiar incident at the club that bothered me a bit." Eva's blue eyes narrowed to slits.

"What was that?" Arielle asked inquisitively. Arielle was a little surprised by the amount of eagerness in the tone of her own voice. She noticed a deep crease across Eva's forehead trying to remember, but eventually she just shrugged her shoulders, giving up.

"Oh, please, try to remember, Eva; it is important!" she said. Even Sebastian appeared curious about the details.

Eva remained silent for a very long time, trying to collect her thoughts about that night. She finally gazed between Sebastian and Arielle, and began slowly, "Arielle, do you remember the feeling I had before Savanna showed up at your birthday party?" Her face twisted in disgust, and Arielle felt a strong jolt at the sound of the name.

"Yes... I do," she replied as her body went very still. Sebastian edged closer. "What are you trying to say?" Arielle asked impatiently.

Eternity passed before Eva's voice continued, a bit eerie against the silence. "I got the exact same feeling at the club when an exceptionally beautiful young woman came up to our table and introduced herself as Miss Willington. She said that she was in charge of the sitting arrangements for the night," Eva said slowly.

"What happened then?" Arielle insisted.

"Well, she said that she was trying to balance the attendance sheet she was holding with the actual people that showed up for the fundraiser. The questions that followed didn't seem so strange except that her presence was creating a feeling of pure terror for me."

"What did you do?" she asked.

"I reached under the table and touched Troy's leg, making him look at me. I was sure that he noticed the anxiety that was starting to spread across my face, because he put his hand over mine and pressed softly."

"Then what happened?" she heard Sebastian asking as he stared at Eva.

"The woman's next statement was not very strange either, but my anxiety was getting stronger."

"What was the next statement?" Arielle could hardly wait for a reply.

"She asked us to give her our names, so she could check them off the sheet. She did ask quite politely. We gave her our names, and she looked as if she was putting a checkmark next to each name.

"The tone of her voice was still very professional and very polite, but there was something repulsive about her. Her next question made me wonder why she was so persistent. She said that she showed two more names, and she was wondering if they were going to be attending the dinner."

"Arielle's and mine?" Sebastian questioned, sure of her reply.

"Yes, we knew that the names on the sheet were yours, but we didn't think it was important for her to know that you were not going to be there. We didn't think it was important for her to know that the tickets were given to Loren and Paul instead. I guess our thought was that as long as tickets were purchased for six it would make no difference what the six names were on that sheet. Paul and Loren were about forty minutes late, and Miss Willington was back at our table asking if the other two people were going to show up. Her voice had grown agitated. Troy was composed and polite as he explained that the other two should be there shortly, as they had encountered car trouble. Strangely enough, she gave us a half a smile and walked away. I still had a terrible feeling about her presence, and I was very worried about her being in close proximity."

"Ian was pretty aggravated. He wanted to know 'what in bloody hell' it mattered if the party was two, four, or six. The entire table was paid for, so the club shouldn't care if a couple people didn't show. Troy remained unruffled, and he went to see the club manager. We were all watching, and he had the strangest expression on his face as he walked back to our table."

Eva paused, swallowing. The story was drying her mouth. Arielle spotted the glass of ice water on the dinner tray and handed it to her friend. After sipping cautiously, Eva rested her head on the pillow for a minute and closed her eyes. Though she was obviously exhausted, they desperately needed to hear if the rest of the story gave them any answers.

"Gabby wanted to know what Troy said to the manager. I remember Troy's eyes narrowing and him pinching the tip of his nose, shaking his head in perplexity. He told us that the Club Manager was in charge of the personnel roster, and he had never hired a Miss Willington." Eva stopped talking and gazed again between Arielle and Sebastian. Arielle looked over at Sebastian and caught a glimpse of anxiety in his eyes. He clenched his jaw for a brief moment. Eva's voice distracted her, and she turned to look at her friend as she continued with the recollection of that night's events.

"I remember all of us speculating about who Miss Willington was and why she created such an episode. I watched Troy's eyes fixed straight ahead, and I was sure that his thoughts were exactly like mine. Shortly after the incident, Troy asked me to dance and we had a chance to talk. I told him that I had the same feeling about this woman as I did about Savanna at your birthday party, and he was also sure that she was an immortal that was sent by Annabel."

Arielle gasped out loud, and her body shivered. Sebastian moved closer and put his arm around her; he held her tightly to his side.

Arielle collected her thoughts and now she wanted to know everything Eva could recall. "So what happened next?" she asked in a trembling voice.

"Next thing I remember Troy was dancing with Loren, and then they were both gone for a very short time." She smiled softly.

"What's so funny about that?" Arielle asked.

Still smiling, Eva continued. "I knew that the short time they were gone would have been long enough for them to go to another country and back." She laughed again while shaking her head in amazement.

"Where did they say they went?" Sebastian asked.

"When they got back, they told Ian and I that they went to look for the woman that called herself Mrs. Willington, and they checked every inch of the building, as well as the surrounding fields and strictures, but she had vanished."

"What about Paul? What did he think about all that?" Arielle asked.

"Paul and Gabrielle were dancing, so Paul never noticed that Loren was gone for that brief time. I'm sure that it would have been hard to explain why Loren would go with Troy to look for a stranger."

Arielle hugged herself, unable to believe the lengths Annabel would go to make sure that Sebastian never had a chance for happiness. She was never going to forgive him for initiating the annulment of their marriage over 500 years ago. The immortal woman would never forgive his rejection to consummate the marriage and the revulsion she saw in his eyes every time they crossed paths. Arielle was sure that Annabel would spend every waking moment trying to make Sebastian miserable.

Sebastian felt her torment and squeezed her tighter and pressed his lips to her cheek.

"Don't worry, baby," he murmured, before pressing on. "Did you leave the club after that?"

"No, not after that. Shortly after Troy and Loren came back, the music and the fun expunged the incident from our minds, at least for that night. We stayed late and left around two thirty in the morning. Gabby was insisting on driving. Troy let her drive, because she was completely sober. Her choice of beverage the whole night had been water," she added. "We had an amazing time, and we were quite animated on the ride back home. Ian and I were kissing in the back seat, and I can't remember anything after that."

"Eva, do you remember what the woman at the club looked like?" Sebastian asked. His voice was quiet with a hint of concern.

"Yes, she was incredibly beautiful just like all the immortal women I've met so far. She had long brown hair and icy blue eyes. Her voice was velvety soft at the beginning, but it turned cold and scary by the end of the conversation. I knew she was another crazy immortal, and so did Troy."

Arielle stiffened and swallowed hard. Aggravated and sickened once again by Annabel, she tried to fight the anxious feeling in her gut. She drew in a deep breath and lifted her eyes. Searching Sebastian's face, she wondered if it could possibly be true. "Do you think it was Annabel?" Collapsing into the chair next to Eva's bed, she fought to keep her voice steady.

He was pinching the tip of his nose, and the crease on his forehead deepened.

"I don't know." His eyes now blazed with irritation.

"Why would she want to kill our friends?" Arielle kept probing.

"I don't know, Arielle. I'll have to talk with Troy; I need to get the details," Sebastian said. She nodded and, despite her fear, held herself in check. Deep inside, she couldn't let it go.

"I have a strong feeling that she was sent by Annabel." Eva said quietly. Arielle looked up at Sebastian, trying to decipher his thoughts, but she couldn't. Sebastian, however, was seriously weighing Eva's words in his mind, trying to draw his own conclusion about the incident.

"Annabel seems to be able to ruin every occasion for us," Eva continued, forcing a smile. "Don't you think?" The question was directed to Sebastian. He closed his eyes momentarily in frustration and nodded in agreement.

"I have to agree with you," he said bitterly.

"I'm glad that Paul and Loren came in their own car and weren't involved in this mess." The relief was evident in her voice.

"Yes, I'm very happy about that. Have they been here to see you?" Arielle asked.

"Yes, they were here yesterday, along with your parents." Eva answered with a smile.

"When are you going home?"

"The doctor believes I'll be ready the day after tomorrow, and I can't wait. I hate being in here."

Arielle caught a hint of anticipation in her voice. She was trying hard to read Eva's thoughts, but she heard only silence. In and of itself, the lack was extraordinary. In all the years the women had known one another, it had never happened. Something had happened during the accident; otherwise, she couldn't understand the quietness of Eva's mind.

"I think we should go and visit Ian for a little while," Sebastian suggested thoughtfully and clasped Arielle's hand.

Eva nodded, reaching a hand toward Arielle. Arielle clasped it, moving to give her friend a long hug and a kiss on the cheek. When they reached the door, Sebastian send a caring looked at Eva.

"You take care!" His voice was calm with a hint of tenderness.

"Tell Ian that I love him," she called out as the door closed behind them.

When they reached Ian's room, Arielle stopped and took a deep breath. She sighed inaudibly and moved closer to Sebastian just before they stepped inside. She thought about the strange, beautiful woman that was now creating an unavoidable and quite troublesome concern in her head. Sebastian sensed her apprehension, and his arm encircled her body pulling her even closer. He knew that his embrace was Arielle's comfort zone.

"What's the matter, baby?" he whispered in her ear. His gaze was profound and powerful, boring right into her eyes.

"Nothing," she murmured. He lifted her face to his and pressed his lips against hers with true passion.

"I love you, Arielle... don't push me aside. I want to know what's bothering you." She smiled, grabbing hold of his shirt and pulling him softly down to her, and she kissed him back with the same passion.

"I'm sorry, baby, I love you, too, but let's talk about this when we get home." A warm smile urged him to agree, and they walked into Ian's room.

Ian looked pretty much the same way Eva did. Bruised all over with a cast on his left arm, he maintained a great mood. She hugged him with excitement as Sebastian shook his good hand.

"We're so happy you didn't get badly hurt," Arielle said. Her voice was exuberant. He seemed to be really pleased to see them.

"Have you talked to your parents? Do they know you are in the hospital?" Arielle asked softly.

"No, I didn't want to get my family all upset, since I seem to be doing well. I'll be out of the hospital in a day or so," Ian said.

"It's the best thing to do under the circumstances," Sebastian noted.

"Have you seen Gabrielle?" Ian asked, his voice dropping to a whisper. "She's not doing well, is she?" He looked wretched.

"No, not yet, but she's expected to recover," Arielle said. She made a great effort to keep her voice from trembling as she gazed at Ian, holding back her tears. She pressed her lips tightly as a vision of Gabby in ICU flashed before her eyes.

"Troy's totally devastated," Ian mumbled sadly. "He hasn't moved away from Gabrielle's side since they brought us here." Misery spread across Ian's face, and he gave a half-hearted shrug.

"I understand that," Arielle agreed, struggling to keep her voice steady. She turned to meet Sebastian's gaze, looking for his support like a thirsty person staring at a glass of water. He smiled softly and moved even closer. Arielle turned back to look at Ian.

"I'm really sad that you all had to go through such a horrifying experience," she murmured.

"It was just an accident, Arielle. Nobody can prevent accidents from happening. I don't think anyone expected things to turn out this way."

She watched Ian intently, utterly puzzled again. She didn't hear a single thought coming from Ian's mind. *Ian had always been an open book to me, so why the silence now?*

Sebastian carried the conversation with Ian, while Arielle mulled over the hush of Ian and Eva's thoughts. She wondered if she was losing her gift or if it was simply a frightening coincidence. A considerable amount of time passed as they hashed over the series of events before the accident before it was time to go.

"I think we should be going," Arielle said, looking at Sebastian. "We'll come back to see you tomorrow." She bent down and gave Ian a kiss. Sebastian shook his hand again, and they walked to the door.

"Oh, by the way, Eva said to tell you that she loves you," Arielle said with a grin.

A wide smile spread across Ian's face. "I'm happy to hear that," he replied. "I wouldn't know what to do if she didn't."

Arielle chuckled at his statement. "Is that a true revelation, Ian?"

"Yes, it is," he replied, pride in his voice. "She means everything to me." Sebastian pressed Arielle's hand and gave her a meaningful look.

"I'll see you tomorrow, Ian," Arielle assured with a wave.

"Thanks for coming," Ian called as the door closed behind them.

"I feel the same way about you," Sebastian whispered and pressed a kiss to her temple.

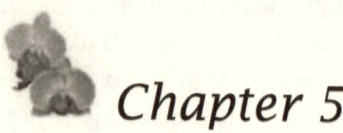

Chapter 5

THEY WALKED DOWN the long hospital corridor in complete silence. Arielle thrust her hands deep into her jean pockets in frustration. Sebastian gave her a side look. The expression on her face was that of irritation.

"Are you going to tell me what's bothering you?" Reaching over, Sebastian pulled her hand out of her pocket and laced his fingers through hers, patiently waiting for a reply. Arielle's thoughts were whirling wildly in her head. She was trying to understand why she couldn't read Eva and Ian's thoughts, and she exhaled on an audible sigh. Sebastian pressed her hand softly; when she looked up, their eyes locked. He was watching her patiently, waiting for her to say something, anything, but she remained quiet, trying to unravel the mystery in her own mind. She slowly lowered her gaze from his face and looked back toward Ian's room. Sebastian followed her gaze, and his eyes narrowed to slits.

"Arielle, please. Baby, what's wrong," Sebastian questioned, anxiously. She finally shook her head and released an exasperated breath.

"Sebastian, I'm really troubled."

Sebastian stopped and turned her to face him. He arched his eyebrows and waited. "Are you going to tell me? Or do I need to take that necklace off and read your mind?"

"No, you don't need to do that. I think that I've lost my ability to read minds. I couldn't hear anything coming from Eva's mind, no matter how hard I tried. The same thing happened with Ian," she mumbled. "I just can't figure it out. Their thoughts used to be like an open book, but not anymore."

The sudden flash of alarm followed by a troubled expression across his typically composed features warned her that she wouldn't like what he was thinking. "What is it?" she asked, extremely curious.

Before he had a chance to say anything, she saw a couple of nurses coming down the hall. She reached out to see if she could hear their thoughts, but she again heard complete silence.

"Well, never mind." Irritation filled her words.

"'Never mind' what?" Sebastian asked again, utterly calm.

"I couldn't hear a single thought from those two nurses, either.

"Maybe they don't belong in that special group you told me about," Sebastian said, trying to reassure her.

"Well, you may be right or I could be losing my so-called gift." She chuckled bitterly as they continued down the corridor.

Sebastian needed to talk to Troy before they left the hospital. Turning the corner towards the entrance to the ICU, they came face-to-face with the doctor who was leaving Gabby's room. They excused themselves and stepped aside to let the physician walk by them. Arielle turned to face Sebastian with a wide smile on her face. Sebastian's eyebrows rose quizzically.

"I could hear the doctor's thoughts," she said. "The doctor was thinking about how tired he was and that he was glad Gabby was his last patient for the day." She grinned and pressed his hands from the overflow of excitement, but it immediately changed to a frown.

"What is it, baby?" Sebastian asked.

"I still have the ability to hear people's thoughts, so why can't I hear Eva and Ian's thoughts anymore?" She looked up at him casually, and she noticed that he was disturbed. He opened his mouth to say something, but he closed it again; they had reached the ICU.

"I need to talk with Troy before we go home," he said. She felt that her last statement about Eva and Ian had drifted right over his head, completely unnoticed. His arm cradled her as he pulled her to him and pressed his lips on hers.

"I'll be right back. I know you are tired." His lips curved up in that special smile that made her body tingle with excitement. She watched him stride into the ICU with that so familiar seamless walk, and she smiled, thinking of how stunning he was. She chuckled under her breath as she thought of all those gorgeous women he could have from his undying world, but he chose to love her. She shook her head in awe, unable to understand his attraction to her, and she went back to say goodbye to Eva.

Eva smiled wide at her entrance. "Did you tell Ian that I love him?" she asked quickly.

"I sure did," Arielle said with a loud chuckle.

"Well, what did he say?"

"He said that he was glad about that, because he wouldn't know what to do if you didn't love him."

Eva's eyes welled up, and she beamed appreciatively. "I miss him, Arielle, and I'm so grateful that he didn't get badly hurt. He's my whole life."

"I know, Eva, I'm very happy for both of you." She leaned over and gave her a big hug. "I love you, Eva, and my heart aches for all of you, especially for Gabby. She's really hurt." They held each other, thinking about their best friend.

Trying to ease the mood, Arielle engaged into a long conversation with Eva about her trip to Tuscany and school coming up. It seemed that they were both trying to stay away from the accident issue. The stillness of Eva's mind was still a big mystery to her, but she really thought it might be a temporary thing caused by the shock. It had been about twenty minutes, and the nurse came in to give Eva the required medication plus something to help her sleep. She told Arielle that visiting hours were over. Arielle kissed Eva.

"I'll be back to see you tomorrow."

"If you see my mum out there, please ask her to come in," Eva said. Arielle nodded and smiled tenderly. "I love you, Arielle, and I'm happy that things didn't turn out as bad for Ian and myself."

"I love you, too, Eva," she said. "I'm going home, because you need your rest. I'll see you tomorrow." She walked out of the room and found Mrs. Winters, who was still sitting in the waiting room with a cup of coffee. They hugged each other one more time.

"I'm so happy that Eva wasn't badly hurt."

"Thank you, darling. Me, too."

"Eva just asked for you," Arielle said. She smiled at Arielle affectionately and turned toward Eva's room.

Arielle walked back to the ICU looking for Sebastian and peeked inside the door. The Taylors were around Gabby's bed, but Sebastian wasn't there. Neither was Troy. She walked back toward the waiting room, thinking she might have missed them, but they were not there either. Her steps brought her to the entrance, and she gazed outside through the huge glass swivel doors. She was surprised to see Sebastian and Troy standing close together in the parking lot, engaged in deep conversation. She watched them for a few moments, deciding that she didn't want to intrude. Instead, she stood in silence and waited.

She lifted her face to the sky and watched the few scattered clouds reflecting the bright glow of the sun that was slowly dipping below the horizon, turning the evening sky grey. Arielle was completely exhausted, mentally and physically. They had been up since early in the morning, and after the flight home, they had spent several hours at the hospital. Arielle felt quite tired. She could hardly keep herself upright. She was ready to go home and crawl into bed. Sebastian was never tired. His energy was unparalleled, and she could never keep up with him. He was indefatigable.

She could tell that whatever they were discussing was quite important. From the expression on their faces, she knew something was wrong. Right now was not the time to ask questions, so she waited… and waited…and waited. Finally, she gave herself a mental shake and wrapped her arms around herself, reluctantly deciding to go back into the waiting room. She collapsed down on a large sofa, placed her elbows on her knees, and intertwined her fingers. Her chin rested on her hands, and she lost herself in her thoughts.

Her memories took her back into the ICU, and she drew in a sharp breath at the vivid memory of her best friend's broken body. She closed her eyes, trying to wipe out the dreadful images. Moisture dripping through her fingertips made her aware that she was quietly weeping, tears running down her cheeks.

"Hey, baby! Are you ready to go home?" Sebastian's soft voice startled her.

"Yes, I am." She glanced up at Sebastian, and his face fell. Time suspended between them, and for a brief moment, he was lost.

Finding his voice again, he stammered, "W-What's wrong?" His jaw was set in a straight line. "Why are you crying, sweetheart? Are you in pain?" he asked as he reached down and hauled her into his arms to hold her close.

"No, I'm not in physical pain. I was thinking about Gabby," she replied and drew a shuddering breath.

"Gabrielle will be all right," he whispered and pressed her warmly against his chest.

She was surprised to find that it had been over an hour since she walked into the waiting room.

"Let's go home," he said. Taking her hand, he laced his fingers through hers, and they walked out. Her eyes were still tearing, and her heart was overburdened with sadness. She remained silent until they reached the car. Sebastian squeezed her hand gently as he held the door open for her. Just before she slipped in the passenger seat, he leaned in and kissed her tenderly on the lips.

"I love you, Arielle," he murmured. "I'm right here. Don't shut me out," he added with a soft smile. He slipped in the driver seat, and reaching over, he took her hand in his and held it tight. She looked over, and their eyes locked.

"Sebastian, I love you. I couldn't go through this day without you," she whispered, "You're my sanctuary."

They drove home with their fingers intertwined in complete silence. He didn't seem to want to intrude in her thoughts, but he knew they were lingering between Gabby, Ian, and Eva. The sky was turning darker, and a light mist hit the windshield. They barely missed the downpour as they pulled into the garage. Arielle took a warm bath before she got in bed, and he was there to hold her and make sure she slept feeling safe, encircled in his warm embrace.

Arielle woke up in terror, drenched in sweat. She was shaking and sobbing at the same time. Sebastian switched the light on and pulled her in his arms, trying to comfort her.

"It's only a dream...it's only a dream?" he murmured softly in her ear.

"Oh, Sebastian, it was the worst dream ever!" She pulled herself as close to him as possible in a desperate attempt to forget her freakish nightmare. She started to sob again as he held her closer.

"Do you want to talk about it?"

"Oh. It was horrible! Horrible!" She shut her eyes and bit down on her lower lip hard as her body started to shiver. She felt her heart hammering against her chest. She was sure he could hear the pounding. She gazed at him while trying frantically to take a breath.

"It's only a dream, baby!" he whispered with his arms securely fastened around her, searching her face with eyes full of love and warmth and also concern. She drew in a shuddering breath and felt a bitter taste lingering in her mouth that was sending sick waves across her body. She compressed her lips and took several deep breaths, pushing back tears.

Her high-pitched, timorous voice startled her.

"I dreamed that Gabby and I were driving home when we noticed that we were being chased by a faceless person in a black car. The chase became frantic as I swerved through small winding roads, unknown locations, and thick foliage, just trying to get away from the car that was chasing us. We ended up in a cemetery with no way out and nowhere to go. We bolted out of the car and started running with the stranger right on our heels. I tripped and rolled down a small hill. When I stood up and looked around, Gabby was nowhere to be seen."

Sebastian could feel her blood pounding in her veins, and her body stiffened with fear. He tightened his hold on her and nuzzled her hair, trying to calm her down as her voice came out utterly stress-filled.

"I was ready to get up and start running again when I heard Gabby screaming my name. I took a quick look back, and I saw a man with no face in a dark trench coat pulling Gabby up to the top of the hill. She had stretched her arm out towards me, looking desperate and screaming for help. I started running after them, climbing back up the hill, but when I got to the top, there was no sign of either one of them. I kept calling her name as I was running between the graves, sensing an unseen presence beside me. I took another fall, landing on top of a freshly dug grave." She shivered at the thought, and she must have looked completely terrified, because he was looking at her with worry.

"What did you see?" His voice sounded hollow.

"I pulled myself up, and I was a hair width away from a huge headstone that read 'Gabrielle Taylor'." She started to sob as she forced herself to take lungfuls of air. She tried to slow the pulse hammering her neck and wrists, making it painful to breathe.

"Arielle, baby, it was only a dream. Anytime people go through deep emotional events as you did with your friends, they have those types of dreams. Dreams are free and harmless, and you need to find the strength to accept what happened and just be there for your friends."

He put his finger under her chin and pulled her face to his. His hand pushed the hair away from her face, and he wiped the tears away with the other hand while pressing his lips softly against hers.

"Please lie down and try to sleep. I'll be right here with you. There's nothing to be afraid off."

She lay back down, and he switched the light off. They rested in each other's arms, and she felt a surge of love course through her body. She softly touched the hollow at the bottom of his throat, and he moaned in satisfaction. His lips trailed her cheekbone, and he pulled her even closer.

Her nearness was stimulating him to a physical pain. His mouth moved against hers, and she moaned with desire. Her lips parted, and their breaths fused in a scorching kiss. He swallowed hard, and his hands moved to her lower back and pulled her flush against him. His lips moved lower and pressed against the slow beating pulse of her throat. Her breathing slowed, and her head fell back against the pillow. Sebastian lifted his head, and his eyes widened as he stared at her beautiful face. He groaned in sheer frustration, realizing that Arielle had drifted off to sleep, consumed by exhaustion.

Sebastian lay with eyes wide-open, feeling overwhelmed with desire. He tried to relax following the heated moments just before she fell asleep, and he groaned once again, completely annoyed. He knew she was physically and emotionally tired, and he wanted her to sleep, but the heat of her body's nearness was driving him mad. He could feel her breath caressing his face, infusing his very core as he zeroed in on the rhythm of her heart. He wished his heartbeat hadn't stopped beating over five centuries ago.

It had been over a couple of hours, and he finally got out of bed, giving up on sleep. Sebastian moved quietly to the next room and heard the rain pounded the huge window. He picked up a book and sank down in his favorite recliner. He recalled his conversation with Troy, and suddenly he was consumed by anxiety. He knew that Arielle didn't have the complete truth about the accident. Earlier today, Troy had agreed that both would talk to Ian and reveal the astonishing facts.

Ian's life would be turned completely upside down, but it had to be done. They were hoping the revelation wouldn't make him fall apart. The next person would have to be Arielle. She possessed the gift of making people feel safe and secure, something he adored about her. Arielle would be the person to help them reveal the truth to Eva. How were they going to explain something so mindboggling, so bewildering? Sebastian knew they had to reveal the truth in the next two days, because it would soon become obvious to Ian and Eva that something implausible was happening and would change their lives forever.

Chapter 6

SEBASTIAN AND ARIELLE ARRIVED at the hospital around ten o'clock in the morning on the third day after the accident. As they stepped off the elevator on the floor of ICU, they noticed an unusual commotion around Gabby's room. The Taylors were standing outside her room talking in low voices. A nurse and doctor hurried passed the parents and entered Gabby's room. A few seconds later, Troy walked out of the room with a wide smile highlighting his face.

"She is awake! She held my hand! She smiled!" Troy exclaimed, just like a little boy. His voice was jubilant, and he hugged Mr. and Mrs. Taylor. Her parents were crying, and Arielle burst into tears of joy. She was startled when Troy turned, pulled her up in his arms, and planted a huge kiss on her cheek. She laughed out loud, caught in his enthusiasm, as tears of joy rolled down her face. The doctor came out smiling and told them that Gabby was going to be fine.

Eva and Ian were released from the hospital around two in the afternoon on the same day, and Eva's mother took them home. Gabby was to be moved out of ICU and into a private room the next day. The staff wouldn't allow many visitors, but they all got to see her and that was wonderful. She wasn't completely alert, but she was aware that the people who loved her were by her side. Everyone felt exuberant even though they knew she was still a long way from recovery. They stayed with her for a couple of hours, as her need for rest was evident.

Working her way around all the tubes and casts with great difficulty, Arielle gave Gabby a loving hug. She felt a weight lifting and elation taking over her whole existence. Her best friend was on her way to healing. They left for home around three-thirty, and it was in the parking lot that she wrapped her arms around Sebastian's neck and pulled him down to her, crushing his lips with hers in exhilaration.

"Mmmmm... what's this for?" he purred, without breaking the kiss.

"I just simply love you," she said, breathlessly. "Do I have to have a special reason to do that?" Sebastian laughed in bliss, a flash of excitement caressing his eyes. He pressed her softly against the car, and she saw a soft smile curve the corner of his mouth upward. He was astonishingly, breathtakingly, beautiful. She wound her arms around his neck and stretched up on her toes. Her lips closed over his in a kiss full of sexual delight. He broke the kiss and drew in a deep breath.

"Be careful," he warned her with amusement in his voice. "I'm still trying to recover from last night."

"Last night? What happened last night?" Her brows lifted inquisitively.

"Nothing happened last night; that's exactly my point," he said humorously. "You fell asleep before you finished what you started." A beautiful smile still lingered on his moist lips.

"Sorry," she murmured. "I was so tired. I couldn't help it." He opened the car door, and she slipped into the passenger seat. He walked around the car without taking his eyes off of her, his lips curved up in that amazing smile that elevated her pulse. He got in the driver's seat, and she couldn't help pulling him close and pressing her lips against his with extreme passion one more time.

"Mmmmmm... Be careful you are getting to a dangerous place." Reaching over, he took her hand and held it tightly. "I'm expecting a supreme performance tonight." Her body was tingling with excitement and worship for the most beautiful man on this earth that loved her. They drove home, and she talked nonstop about everything that flooded her mind. He was willing to listen with no complaints. He laughed with that jovial laugh he used every time she ran her mouth uncontrollably.

"Do you know how happy you make me when you do that?"

"Do what?" she asked. He was gazing into her eyes, releasing all his dazzling power. She immediately lost her train of thought, and her throat grew hotter and tighter, making it hard for her to breath. She did hear him laugh again as he looked away, giving her time to recover.

"I hate when you do that and I'm not prepared," she scolded him. When they walked in the house, Sebastian still held a glorious smile on his beautiful face. He walked into the kitchen and poured a glass of salve from the fridge.

She stepped in the shower, reaching and turning the faucet on. Before the water made contact with her body, his arms were tightly fastened around her. She shrieked and then broke out in a hearty laugh, amazed at the speed he possessed. She turned around without leaving his embrace. Reaching up, she asked for a kiss, and he was more than happy to please her.

"I love you!" he whispered. His breath was warm against her face, and she inhaled his amazing, immortal scent in delight. Their kiss was feverish, and she realized that she missed their scorching encounters. The last three days had been consumed solely by the accident.

His hands glided down the length of her spine. Reaching her lower back, he lifted her up, and she wrapped her legs around him, pressing him closer to her aching heat. His lips found the pulse of her lifeline at the bottom of her throat and nibbled passionately. She moaned, and the sound resonated through his bones. She raked her fingers through his hair, and he groaned. She placed her hands on either side of his face and crushed his lips beneath hers.

Sebastian deepened the kiss, and Arielle thought she was going die from pleasure. Her lips parted, and his tongue slipped into the softness of her mouth. *Oh, God, she tastes like pure honey!* He dove into the kiss like a wildcat after its prey. His hands stroked her silky skin, sending ripples of heat across every nerve in her body. The toe-curling kiss made Sebastian groan deep in his throat, and Arielle felt it to the core of her soul.

Sebastian lost control, joining them in a swift, calculated move. Arielle groaned into his mouth, lost in her passion. When they reached the crest of rapture, their bodies combusted in a blistering inferno. They held on to each other as their minds returned from the journey to oblivion. Wrapping herself in a bath towel, she lay in bed utterly exhausted, happy and sated. Sebastian pulled her in his arms, and she closed her eyes in bliss.

Later in the afternoon, Troy showed up to pick up Sebastian. When she glanced at the clock, she saw it was after five-thirty.

"Where are you going?" she asked, unable to hide her shock.

Sebastian had never said a word about Troy coming over or mentioned that he had plans to go out. She sensed something going on as she watched them glance at each other with guarded expressions. Their lips moved in the immortals' special way, and she knew they were talking to each other, but she couldn't hear or understand the exchange.

"It's important that we talk to Ian this afternoon. This is something that can't wait," Troy said. His voice was low and very cautious.

"Why Ian? What's up?" She could see that he was struggling to find the right words to provide some kind of explanation, but he was unsuccessful.

"Arielle, I promise we'll discuss this when I get back," Sebastian said. She was sure that her incredulous expression didn't escape him. He moved closer and gathered her to him, locking them into a tender kiss.

"Trust me," he whispered. Arielle met his eyes and nodded briskly.

"Miss me," he whispered close to her ear. His lips brushed her cheekbone, making her shiver. Then, he was gone. They were halfway out the door when Sebastian's mobile phone rang. He answered in a low voice and kept walking toward Troy's car.

She stood at the doorway watching them. The phone conversation seemed to be quite important, because Sebastian didn't get in the car. He paced back and forth on the pavement and chatted for a long time. She tried to read his expression, but he was looking down. He finally stopped pacing and turned, facing away from her. He put his free hand on the car and leaned against it, remaining completely still for the next several minutes. She saw Troy observing him warily, and she knew that Troy—as an immortal— could hear every part of that conversation. She noticed that Troy's face lost the smile he'd been carrying when he walked out the door.

She panicked. Stepping outside, she started to walk toward them. It was the moment she reached Sebastian that he shut the phone and turned around. He was surprised to see her standing right behind him.

"What's wrong, baby?" he asked.

"What is going on? Who was on the phone?"

Sebastian cleared his throat. "Oh, don't worry, it's nothing personal. It's just business," he said, forcing a smile, but it didn't escape her. She knew him better that he thought she did. She knew something was terribly wrong, but she had to wait until they were alone. He reached over and pulling her closer, he pressed his lips on hers.

"I'll be home soon, baby; please don't worry."

She turned around and walked back to the house. The car doors slammed shut. The engine revved with intensity and sped away, leaving her surrounded by total stillness. She sucked a deep breath and let the front door shut behind her. Standing in the middle of the foyer alone, speechless, she was unable to understand what could be so important that had to be handled tonight. And what about the phone call?

She pressed her lips together in confusion, and she finally shrugged her shoulders. She had to trust in Sebastian if she didn't want to go out of her mind. He would tell her the truth when he came home. Picking up a pear from the fridge, she sank her teeth into it and walked into the bedroom, looking for her journal.

Arielle had thought a great deal about her journal in the last few months, but she never found the time. She always felt healing when writing down her innermost thoughts. The book revealed her private reflections of the special moments in her life. Reading back was like looking through the mirror of her soul.

Climbing onto the bed she leaned against her pillows, and pulled her legs up, so she could balance her journal on top of her knees. Flipping through the pages, she stopped at her last entry and was shocked to find that her last entry was made in St. Jean de Luz. There was so much she wanted to capture in those pages, so she grasped this time, while Sebastian was away to reflect her deep thoughts. The pen started to glide on the blank sheet.

June 17th,

"It has been quite a while since I brought my life's deepest thoughts to you. You have let me bring my passions, my dreams, and my wishes to your pages, and you have embraced each and every thought, without passing any judgment, without making me feel humiliated. So I'm back, bringing some extraordinary emotions that have blossomed from the incredible love between Sebastian and me. However, other things took place that have literally shaken up my world and turned it upside down.

I have been absolutely stunned as to how my life and my friends' lives changed in a blink of an eye. While Sebastian and I were in Italy on a summer holiday, a horrible accident almost took Gabrielle's life and landed Ian and Eva in the hospital. I had no resources to deal with the stress that had consumed every bit of my existence.

Gabby and Eva are two people that I love dearly. They are my best friends and my secret sharers. Literally, they are two of the most important people in my life. This was beyond my control, even though I was overwhelmed by the desire to fix everything and get our lives back to what they were prior to the accident. How was I going to deal with the anxiety I was feeling?

I was thinking about Gabby and her terrible condition. I was feeling completely stressed viewing her physical injuries and knowing the imperceptible emotional trauma that would become part of her life, apart from the actual physical harm she endured. I couldn't accept the fact that a person I loved was lying in ICU fighting for her life. I am happy to report that she is out of danger now and on the way to complete recovery.

Eva and Ian are going home from the hospital with just a few bruises and a couple of broken limbs. School will be starting in a couple of months, but Gabby will not be returning with us. She will be attending school for a few weeks from home via the Internet. I will miss her terribly, but I'm sure that we will all be together again soon.

There is something that I find very strange and has been bothering me quite a lot. When I visited Eva and Ian at the hospital, I couldn't hear their thoughts any longer. I find that very bizarre, because I had been able to hear Eva's thoughts ever since we were little girls. I was also able to hear Ian's thoughts since we first met. To me, their minds and their thoughts were like open books. So why do I get complete silence from both minds? What happened to change all that?

I don't think it's me, because I still get the constant noise and the weird thoughts that pour in my head daily while out and about among people. It has to be something else, but what? Sebastian has been my steady rock, my sanctuary. He has supported me and saved me from an emotional breakdown. I don't think I would have been able to make it through if he wasn't there to extent his solid support. Our love has grown, and I know that I couldn't live without him. Once I figure out what happened with Ian and Eva, I will come back and share with you all about it, my dear, faithful, silent friend.

Arielle closed her journal and put it away. She picked up her book and decided to read until Sebastian came home.

Troy pulled away, but he kept a watchful eye on Sebastian.

"Is this the same issue as last year?" he asked.

Sebastian gritted his teeth and cursed under his breath. "Yes, it's exactly like last year, and it's the same bunch of scums and lowlifes that are willing to do whatever it takes to get the job done." Sebastian growled his anger.

"Do you know who those people are?" Troy asked again.

"No, I've no idea. There are many of them, and they have cells in every country that we have buildings and laboratories. One thing I'm sure of is that they are either connected to the Russian mafia or they *are* the Russian mafia. One person is seated at the very top and pulls the strings, moving these lowlifes in whatever direction he decides to send them, like puppets." An angry firestorm was churning deep in his soul. He cursed again, only this time out loud. "I'm sure that they are trying to place cells inside every company building and every laboratory around the world."

"I thought that you took care of those cells last year," Troy said, his gaze sweeping over Sebastian's anxious face.

Sebastian swore again. "That is what I thought, but Interpol dropped the ball last year. They failed," he snapped and shifted in his seat. "They were supposed to get to the man who created this issue, but they never did." The tone of his voice was held disgust. "Nathan and I spent five weeks removing every mole from every building around the globe. Our security is unbreakable, but I was sure they would find another way, and they might have." Sebastian's concern was evident.

"Who was the man on the phone?" Troy asked.

"Oh, that was Dylan Jamison, the head of the British intelligence. He is a nice guy but not very dynamic. Nathan and I met him last year, and we actually handed him several of the men involved in last year's incident. We never heard anything about the outcome."

"Are we going to meet with him soon?" Troy asked.

"Not exactly. We have to wait. Dillon said he is in the process of gathering important documentation. He has set up some kind of surveillance, and he'll let me know as soon as he has all the necessary data," Sebastian said. "I'll call Nathan to make sure that he keeps an eye for anything strange that might come up."

Troy knew that Sebastian was upset. "We have to concentrate on Ian and Eva right now, don't you think?"

Sebastian looked back at him and nodded in agreement. "I don't want you to worry about my business. You need to spend time with Gabrielle. She needs you right now; Nathan and I can handle anything that might come up." Reaching over, Sebastian patted Troy on the back. A smile crept slowly over Troy's lips.

"I think we are going to have our hands full with Ian and Eva tonight."

"Yes, you're right, but we'll handle it," Sebastian grumbled.

 *Chapter 7*

TROY HAD PLACED A CALL to Ian earlier in the day from the hospital. He had asked him if he could meet with Sebastian and him to discuss something very important.

"Are you both okay?" Ian had asked, his curiosity elevated.

"Yes, we're fine, but we need to talk, and it can't wait." Troy's voice had been urgent.

There had been a long silence over the phone, and Ian had finally replied hesitantly. "I don't understand. It sounds like something is terribly wrong."

"Ian, we must talk, and we would prefer that Eva is not present. Can we come and pick you up?" Troy had asked, urgently.

After another long pause, Ian had asked, "When?"

"I'm at the hospital with Gabrielle, but when I leave here, I'll go pick up Sebastian, and we'll swing by your place," he had said.

"Sure, come on over around seven," Ian had replied. Troy couldn't see the tension in Ian's body, but he could sense it in his voice.

Troy and Sebastian drove to Ian's house feeling extremely anxious and apprehensive. They tried to design an all-encompassing plan on how to navigate through the next chapter of the issue. They were not sure of how they would be able to eliminate much of Ian's anxiety and stress while he received the details of the accident. How were they going to explain to Ian what happened that night? How could they tell him he was going to be a different person when he woke up tomorrow?

"Troy, for someone who fears no one and nothing on this earth, I must say that I'm a little nervous about this. How about you?" Sebastian's voice was somewhat strained as his gaze swept over Troy's worried face.

"I've been anxiously waiting for this moment," Troy said. "I've no choice. You know by tomorrow evening, it'll all become completely evident to both Eva and Ian."

Sebastian nodded in agreement.

"I'm not sure that I'm ready to talk to Ian, but I'll do it since there is no other avenue." Troy grimaced and paused. He pinched the tip of his nose, truly bothered by the whole thing. "This is something that will not go away, and I hate having to face Ian straight on with such a huge issue." He looked bewildered as he continued. "I have pondered this in my head over and over again, and I'm sure that if I had to do it again…" His voice trailed. "I'd do the exact same thing,"

A wide grin dismissed Sebastian's apprehension as he shook his head vigorously. "I believe you would."

Troy turned and looked at Sebastian. "I'm very fond of Ian and Eva, and I couldn't let them die, Sebastian. I also know how much they mean to Gabrielle, so I had no other choice," Troy mumbled. His voice was full of concern. He looked over again, needing Sebastian's approval.

"Troy, if I were there, I would have done the exact same thing. You had two choices and two choices alone. One was to give them life, and the other would have been certain death for both of them."

Troy nodded thoughtfully.

"Troy, don't overthink this. It was the right choice," Sebastian said assertively.

"I know," Troy said, looking glum. "Every day since that awful night, I keep reminding myself that it was unavoidable, and I couldn't let them die. So now, I have to tell them." Troy looked determined as they reached Ian's house. Ian was waiting for them, and he got in the car consumed with curiosity. He loved both Troy and Sebastian, and their friendship was very important to him.

"Hey, guys, how is it going?" he asked with a happy smile on his face.

"We are good; how about you, Ian? How is your arm?" Sebastian asked.

"Every day is getting better. It's much easier for me than for Eva. She is having a hard time getting around, but we manage. Her mom has been wonderful; she comes over, makes dinner, and picks up after us, making it much easier to get through the day." Ian stifled a chuckle.

"We're glad to hear that," Troy and Sebastian said simultaneously. They smiled with true compassion for Ian and Eva. They drove to Hove by the beach, and to Ian's surprise, they took a seat at a picnic table.

"What are we doing here?" Ian asked. He had a startled look on his face.

"Ian, we have to talk to you about something very serious, and we need to be alone. Are you comfortable being here with us?" Troy asked.

"Yes…I'm fine, I'm just a little surprised, as I thought we might go somewhere to have a drink," Ian smiled.

"We can do that after we finish talking, and only if you are up to it," Sebastian said with a chuckle.

"Oh, I'm now very curious as to what you have to say," Ian said, as his eyes darted from Sebastian to Troy, and then back again.

Troy sucked a deep breath, knowing that he would have to start with a few open-ended questions.

"What do you remember from the accident?" Troy asked, watching Ian's face very carefully. Ian's eyes narrowed to slits, and he pressed his lips together. He looked as if he was searching his mind for any information he could recollect from that night's events.

"That's the most maddening thing that ever happened to me," Ian said. "I can remember walking out of the club and getting into the car. I remember part of the drive, as Eva and I were making out in the back seat," he said, and laughed softly. A grin of sheer mirth painted Troy and Sebastian's faces, and they broke out into a hearty laugh, along with Ian.

"I can't remember anything past that particular moment," Ian continued. "I've looked at the car, and I'm absolutely amazed that I'm alive."

"Ian, that is exactly what we need to talk to you about, the fact that you are alive," Troy said. A serious but tormented look spread across his face.

"What do you mean?" Ian was unable to decipher the look in Troy's face.

Troy paused for a short period of time. Finally, he looked straight in Ian's eyes and asked. "If you were presented by the choice of becoming an immortal like Sebastian and me or dying a human, which one would you choose?" Troy asked with a quivery voice. The straightforwardness of the question took all of them by surprise, but Ian was completely clueless as to where Troy was going with that question.

"Well, that's pretty easy to answer. I'd rather be alive than dead. I can't imagine anyone would choose to die." He stifled something like a snigger.

Ian threw a glance between Troy and Sebastian and blinked. They were not laughing any longer, and their look had turned grave. Ian's face fell, and his smile faded. "Why are we talking about immortality?"

A stony silence fell between them. Then, Troy rose to his feet, straightening up to his full height, and held Ian's gaze with his.

"Ian, something happened during the accident, and it can't be reversed now," Troy said. His eyes were searching Ian's contemplative face with agitation.

"What? What happened?" Ian asked.

Troy was obviously distressed as he pinched the tip of his nose again, something immortals did when they felt stress. He looked at Sebastian for encouragement. Sebastian smiled and motioned to go on. Ian was gazing between the two of them, not understanding what Troy was trying to tell him.

This time, Troy's voice came out soft but firm.

"Ian, there is no easy way to say this." He drew a sharp breath and continued, "The night of the accident, you and Eva— knocked on Death's door." Troy uttered the words with a clenched jaw.

Ian looked at him, trying to grasp the meaning of the words. Suddenly, his body went rigid, and his mouth fell open. He gasped, unable to breathe. Sebastian moved over and sat next to him, putting his hand on the younger man's shoulder, trying to ease his stress. Fear and terror had spread across Ian's face as his body started to quiver. His eyes blinked in quick succession before he hauled in a huge breath. He looked as if he had just watched the fall of the atomic bomb.

He was reacting to the unknown like a trapped animal.

He raked a hand through his blond hair and let out a low, throaty sound that evoked dread. Leaping to his feet he walked away from the table, keeping his eyes toward the ocean. His face had tightened with grief and terror at the same time. He remained absolutely unmoved for several long moments. Finally, he turned and held both Sebastian and Troy with a flat stare, then shook his head and coughed several times trying to find his voice. His eyes welled up with tears, something that made Sebastian and Troy quite sad. They knew that after tomorrow, when Ian's transformation was complete, he would never be able to tear up again.

"Oh, God! Oh, God!" Ian whispered. Troy propped his chin on his hand and glanced at Sebastian cautiously. They both remained silent, giving him time to grasp the fact that he and Eva had died. Ian walked back to the table. Dropping down on the bench, he covered his face with both hands and sobbed like a little boy, unable to stop. Sebastian and Troy remembered going through the exact same emotions and the exact same fear when they had discovered their new identities, centuries ago. They each pressed softly on Ian's shoulders letting him know that they were both there. They were his friends and ready to support him with any questions he would now have. Ian was still sobbing quietly, trying to absorb what he had just been told.

Finally looking up, he opened his mouth to say something, but he closed it again. He couldn't get his voice passed the lump that was wedged in his throat, and he couldn't get any air into his lungs. He remained silent, as fear clouded his eyes. His guts were reeling, and his heart sank into despair. Troy and Sebastian were startled by Ian's high-pitched voice.

"I'm an immortal?" He was still gasping for air.

Troy drew a deep breath. "Yes. Well, by tomorrow you'll be just like Sebastian and me."

Ian was now completely alert, and he was starting to understand that he was in fact going to be an immortal, and there were no mismatches between perception and reality.

Forty-five minutes passed before Ian quieted down, but he had not lifted his head up to look at either one of his immortal friends.

"Ian, how are you feeling, buddy?" Troy asked in a soft voice, filled with despondency. Ian finally raised his head and stared directly into Troy's eyes, clearly sad.

"Ian, you have to understand that I couldn't let you or Eva die. I'm fond of you, and you both mean a lot to the rest of us. I'm tired of losing people I care about," Troy's voice was clearly stressed.

"Now what do I do?" Ian's shaky voice sounded desperate.

"You don't have to do anything," Sebastian said. "There will be some changes that will become quite evident to you and Eva by tomorrow evening. Troy and I think that you and Eva need to go somewhere for a little while, like a vacation, to avoid questions from people around you."

"What kind of changes? What kind of questions?" Ian asked clearly shocked.

"Ian," Sebastian began calmly, "your bruises, the scratches, and the cuts will disappear overnight. Your arm and Eva's leg will heal, and you will have no need for the casts. You can keep the cast on, and nobody will know you've been healed. However, you can't disguise the fact that your bruises will disappear. And those are some bad bruises. It'll become utterly obvious to everyone around you that something is going on."

Ian remained silent, pondering Sebastian's words in his mind. "What else?"

"Your appetite will change. You can eat anything you want to keep the human façade. However, regular food will not be enough to sustain your body's required energy," Troy added.

"I don't understand. What are you implying?" Ian asked totally surprised.

"Salve is what immortals drink to sustain their energy. Using salve will give you what you need to function just like the humans around you. They will never know that you are different from them."

"I know you guys drink salve. Does it taste awful? How often do I have to drink it?"

"It does have an inimitable taste but it is quite tasty. You will need salve when you feel tired. Human food will not satisfy your hunger, and water will not satisfy your thirst. Salve will be what your body will desire, and what will sustain your strength."

Ian kept taking deep breathes, eyes wide-open, full of tension and incredulity.

"I'm scared to ask, but I need to know details."

"Your looks might change a little, but not by much. Fear will have no part in your mind. You'll be stronger than any human around you. You'll possess extreme speed and will have the ability to heal yourself from any type of injury. You'll never get sick, and you'll never die. By tomorrow evening, your transformation will be complete, and you'll be an immortal. Your powers will be incredible. You'll be healthy in body and mind and will belong to the immortal world. We all belong to a secret immortal society that demands the highest moral and ethical standards among us." Sebastian stated in a matter of fact voice.

"Remember, Ian," Troy whispered, "the woman that you love and are going to marry will be exactly like you by tomorrow evening. You'll never have to see her get sick, get older, or die. You'll now have the chance to love each other for eternity."

"Oh...my... God... Eva! I forgot all about Eva... What is she going to say? She'll be horrified," Ian shrieked, totally distressed.

"Well, Ian, we thought that the best thing to do would be to tell Arielle first. She'll help and support Eva when we talked to her. They are best friends, and they have shared a lot together," Sebastian said.

"Ian, this has to be done by tomorrow noon," Troy added.

"I believe that telling Arielle first will be the best way to go about it. It's so scary and so exciting at the same time," Ian murmured, with a faint smile.

"Ian, do you remember in St. Jean de Luz when you told us that you wished you were an immortal?" Sebastian asked.

"Yes, I do remember." Ian stared at Sebastian.

"Well, here you are. Your wish has come true." Troy and Sebastian were happy to see a faint smile touch Ian's lips. He was still pretty scared, as his voice was breaking every time he spoke.

"What else do I need to know?"

"Ian, we are going to be by your side and support you and Eva every step of the way. There are gifts, and there are drawbacks," Troy said.

"What kind of drawbacks?" Ian asked alarmed.

Troy paused and ran his tongue over his dry lips a couple of times. Standing up, he turned to face the ocean. He pursed his lips and looked back at Ian. "Your heart will stop beating, and you'll not be able to cry or dream any longer. You'll have to watch people you love around you get older and die while you remain unchanged for centuries to come," Troy admitted. He stopped talking and gazed over at Sebastian. Sebastian held a soft smile on his face.

"What will the gifts be?" They heard Ian ask eagerly.

"Besides all the things we already told you, you'll be able to learn things much faster than any human. You'll retain every little bit of information you receive just as if your mind was a hard drive. You'll need to understand your strength so you don't hurt your human friends."

"Oh...God... What about my parents?" Ian now looked anxious.

"Statistically speaking, you don't need to worry about your parents. They'll never realize the change in you. Based on the path of human life, they'll pass away way before they notice that you are not getting any older."

"What about my sister? Oh...God!" Ian's voice was trembling. "I don't mind telling you that I'm scared out of my mind."

"Ian, we do understand," Troy said. "Sebastian and I had to deal with the exact same difficulty a long time ago. We had to do it on our own, but eventually we found friends that showed us how to adapt to our new life. We are here for you and Eva. And as time goes by, you'll find a way to tell your sister the truth. She loves you; therefore she won't stop loving you when she finds out that you're an immortal." Ian stared back at Troy, a million questions, whirling in his mind.

"Humans would give anything to be able to achieve immortality, and you now have it," Sebastian added.

Ian was looking down at his hands again, going through the turmoil that Sebastian and Troy were very familiar with.

"Ian, are we good?" Troy asked wanting to make sure that Ian was okay.

"Yes, I think I'm fine," Ian replied with his voice trembling, hands shaking, body quivering.

"I'm obviously scared of the unknown, but I'm more scared when I think of the alternative." Nervousness had spread across his face, and a half a smile appeared on his dry lips.

"I should thank you for giving us both the gift of life," Ian said, looking at Troy. "I'm worried about Eva, but I'm happy she will be with me for eternity. I would never want any of this without her."

They stood up and shook hands, fully committing themselves to support one another. Sebastian and Troy said something to each other that was not transparent to Ian, at least not today. Tomorrow he would be one of the immortals, and there would be no secrets left between them.

Sebastian and Troy were surprised as to how receptive Ian was; terrified but receptive. They were ready to walk back to the car when they heard Ian's voice.

"I do have one more question."

"What is it?" asked Troy, turning back to look at Ian.

"Where should we go? I don't have a vacation place or anywhere I can go that people wouldn't know Eva or me." He glanced eagerly between Troy and Sebastian.

"Don't worry, Ian," Sebastian said. "Troy and I have homes in Italy, and you can use either one of our homes; however, I have an immortal housekeeper that I think will take care of you while you're going through the transformation. We still have over two months before classes begin, so you can stay away for a short period of time," Sebastian added with a smile.

"We think that the best and safest thing will be to have Eva call her mother tomorrow and tell her that you both have decided to spend some time together away from here. Give her the excuse that you both need time to get over the accident trauma and heal without interference from friends coming in and out of the house everyday," Troy said.

Ian nodded. "Thank you both. That sounds like a good plan."

"When you get back, you'll both be healed, and the bruises will be gone. No questions, no strange looks, and no worries." Troy was now smiling, pretty pleased with the idea.

"I would have never thought of that, but I like it." Ian's smile was still a little apprehensive, but less fearful.

"Do you want to get a drink, or do you want to go back and talk to Arielle?" Sebastian asked.

"I think I'd like to get this over with, if you don't mind." Ian looked determined to resolve this in a hurry. They agreed, and they walked back to the car feeling optimistic, each one of them for their own reasons.

"So I'm now just like you guys?" Ian laughed quietly.

"Well, you'll be by tomorrow evening," Sebastian answered Troy laughed out loud as he stepped on the gas.

"Wow...amazing. Will I feel any different?"

"No, you'll not feel any different; you will still be Ian. The things that will change in your body and mind will be completely undetected by the people around you. You and Eva will be the only ones that will recognize your differences. You'll have to be careful around humans though, as your powers will now become exceptional," Sebastian stated.

"Will I enjoy a beer after this?" Ian asked, chuckling.

"Not exactly as you do now, but you will," Sebastian snickered again.

Chapter 8

IT WAS AFTER TEN that night when they got back to the house, and Arielle was still up reading her book. She was startled to hear all three of them walking in. She put the book aside and walked into the study.

"Hey, Ian! I didn't expect to see you," she exclaimed. "How are you feeling? How are you getting along with that cast?"

"Hi, Arielle. I'm fine, the arm is fine, and I'm really happy to see you." He walked up to her with a big smile on his face and kissed her on both cheeks. She hugged him, smiling with true pleasure.

"How is Eva?"

"She is fine, a little confined in the leg cast but always happy," Ian replied with a smile, and Arielle was sure he was thinking of Eva.

Sebastian came close and pulled her into his arms, pressing his lips softly on hers and he let his finger ran up and down the planes of her back, making her shiver with excitement.

"Hi, baby…" She heard his velvety voice, and he kept her in his arms. He was peering at her with a strange look in his eyes.

"What's up?" she asked, as she had been waiting to hear what the heck was going on since the moment they had left.

"Arielle, we need to talk to you, baby," Sebastian said.

"Oh! Did something happen? Does it have something to do with the phone call you received before you left?" she asked, sure that something was terribly wrong.

"Arielle, I told you that the phone call was just business. This is a little different, and we feel that you need to be involved," he murmured.

She noticed trepidation between the three men in front of her. She left his arms and took a seat, overwhelmed by curiosity. She stared in his beautiful eyes in wonder.

"What is it?"

They took a seat across from her, and Sebastian reached over. He took both of her hands in his and smiled with that amazing grin that kept her captive. His voice was soft but serious. "If you were an immortal with the power to control life and death, would you let a loved one die in a car accident knowing you could keep them alive?" His question took her by surprise. This was definitely not what she expected.

Arielle remained silent, a little shocked. "What?"

"What would you do?" he pressed on. Her smile faltered under his penetrating gaze, and her body went into full alert. Something told her this was not a hypothetical question. She knew Sebastian extremely well. He would never ask her this kind of question unless this was a situation in hand. Her mind was now working double-time. *What happened in the last few hours to bring this up?* Her eyes were piercing through to his soul, trying to decipher his thoughts. *What is he insinuating?*

"Arielle, did you hear me?" Sebastian asked again. She noticed that the three of them were watching her carefully, emotions flashing in their eyes.

"Yes, I did hear you," she muttered with a thoughtful frown. "But I'm scared to ask what you are implying. Sebastian, I know you better than you think I do. Why don't you just come out with it?"

"No, I need for you to answer my question first. What. Would. You. Do?" he accentuated each one of the four words.

She pursed her lips before she replied. "I would keep them alive," she said without blinking. "So now let's hear what you've got to say," she said. She looked at him with a frown, but not without reservations.

Sebastian's eyes flickered between Troy and Ian, but they said nothing. After a few seconds, he raised his hand and cupped her chin. His eyes held hers. "It's about the night of the accident," Sebastian said. His voice was slow and quiet. "I told you part of what happened. I didn't think you were ready to hear the whole truth."

She examined every thought in her head, and she couldn't think of a single thing that would be news to her. She knew all about her friends and their injuries, as well as the fact that two of them were already home recovering. So what could possibly be the big secret?

"Arielle, stay with me," Sebastian said.

"I'm listening," she said awkwardly. Sebastian was still holding her hand with one hand and her chin with the other while leaning forward. Their faces were centimeters apart, and his eyes were locked on hers.

"There's only one way I can say this."

"Oh, my, God. Sebastian, spit it out," she ordered.

"The night of the accident, Ian and Eva didn't survive the impact," he said, gently.

Her eyes narrowed, and she stared at Sebastian in total disbelief.

She looked over and her eyes rested on Ian's handsome face. He didn't look like a dead person. It took but a minute, but she burst out into a hearty laugh. They were playing some kind of game. She was not going to fall for it.

"Oh...my...Gosh. That's way too funny, Sebastian!"

Sebastian let go of her chin and her hand and leaned back on his chair, watching her, giving her time to calm down. She noticed that he was tapping his fingers on the leather chair intensely. "I'm not joking, Arielle," Sebastian finally said. She looked past him at Ian and Troy, and they were not laughing. Her eyes settled back on Sebastian's face. His expression was serious, and his lips were pursed tightly.

A small gasped escaped from her tight lips. "What are you saying?" The laughter died. She looked again passed Sebastian trying to decipher the look on Troy and Ian's faces.

"Arielle, I'm trying to tell you that Ian and Eva were killed the night of the accident. They are alive because Troy couldn't let them die," Sebastian pressed on, but she had stopped listening. He stared at her, and she met his nervous gaze with hers.

She was going into a panic mode; she didn't like where the conversation was leading. She bit down on her lower lip, and she shut her eyes, getting ready to absorb what he was telling her. She felt his lips pressing against hers and him asking her to look at him. She opened her eyes, and he knew by the alarm he saw there the strain she was feeling. She was tired of bad news and bad situations; it was always the sweet and the bitter mixed together when it came to Sebastian and his undying world.

"Do you mean...?" She couldn't finish her sentence because fear traveled like lightning across her body, and her eyes rested on Ian. He forced a smile, and she was frozen in place. She was now completely alert, and she knew exactly what Sebastian was saying.

"Oh...my...God! Oh...my...God! Oh...my...God!" She forgot every single word in the dictionary except those three words. She felt that she was locked in a hollow tube, unable to get any air into her lungs. Her eyes welled up, her body went limp, and her head fell back on the chair. She was unable to keep her body upright. Sebastian stood up quickly, pulled her up into his arms, and held her securely.

"Arielle, Ian is happy with the outcome."

"Ian knows?" She fastened her gaze on Ian, and she saw a wide smile spread across his handsome face.

"Ian!" She shrieked in sheer shock. "Is this true?" She said staring at him. Ian was strangely calm.

"Yes, Arielle, it was hard to believe that Eva and I died that night, but thanks to Troy here we are." Ian said, peacefully, trying to hide the emotion that solidified his voice. Sebastian helped her sit back down, pressed his lips on her forehead, and took a seat right across from her. She forced herself to concentrate, but her mind was churning wildly. Eva's beautiful face had become the center of her thoughts. *Eva, an immortal! That is bloody outrageous.*

"Arielle, please stay focused," Sebastian's voice shook her out of her daze. "I'll explain everything."

"I'm sorry, Sebastian," she murmured. "I'm a little nervous; I always have a hard time when it comes to the unbelievable world of yours." Her voice cracked. "I should be used to bizarreness by now, but somehow I still find myself consumed with fear."

Sebastian smiled and took her hands in his again before he continued. She stared at their hands and traced the top of his hands with her thumbs.

"Arielle, are you all right?"

"Sure," she replied in a cynical voice. "I just found out that two of my best friends died, that they could have been taken away forever." she said, She then looked up and met his gaze. "What would make you think that I'm not bloody all right?"

Sebastian winced at her statement, pursed his lips, and remained silent. She noticed despondency crossing his eyes, and she immediately felt dreadful for lashing out at him.

"I'm sorry, Sebastian," she said. She pressed his hands softly, and she saw his eyes softening as a smile teased the corner of his beautiful lips.

"Arielle!" She heard Ian's voice and she looked up. "I'm very thankful to be alive. But we need your help."

"What could I possibly do for you?" she asked, looking completely at a loss. "You are now a powerful immortal, and I'm a simple human. How could I possible help you?"

Ian seemed to disregard her remark.

"We must talk to Eva tonight, because by tomorrow evening, we'll be completely healed, and it'll become obvious and quite strange to everyone around us."

"Oh...my...God!" She whispered eyes wide open. "She'll be terrified."

"Arielle," Troy's voice was hard, shaking her out of her own thoughts. "Would you rather be attending two funerals right now, or have Ian and Eva right here with us alive and well?"

She stared at him, realizing how unfairly she was acting. She bit her lower lip hard and exhaled in utter frustration.

"Troy, I am glad they are alive," she said, gazing in his eyes. "It's just so hard to comprehend something so huge. Please understand this isn't an everyday event in a human life." She truly was happy to have them alive. However, she could not help feeling strange about the news.

Her clear blue eyes flickered to Sebastian's direction. She leaned forward and cupped his face with her hands. "So...are you saying that our little group of eight is made out of three humans and five immortals?" she whispered.

"Yes," he replied, smiling. "But, Arielle, you have this whole thing wrong."

"Oh, how so?" she asked, still holding his face.

His lips curved at the corners. Their faces were very close. His breath caressed her face, and she closed her eyes, enjoying his immortal scent. "You aren't just any humans; you are the people that gave meaning to our miserable existences," he murmured. "I know that

I'll love you for eternity."

Troy and Ian were smiling, and she knew Sebastian was right. *How will this ever work?* She thought to herself. *I am going to die, and he will remain behind for centuries to come.* She didn't realize she was thinking out loud until Sebastian's voice shook her out of her trance. "Arielle, this is your destiny. I'm not going to go through eternity without you. You might be human right now but that will change when the time is right." Sebastian smiled as he leaned in and pressed his lips on hers.

"Eternity...." she murmured and chuckled under her breath.

"Yes, eternity. You are part of me now, and I'm part of you, and this is our destiny." His voice was firm. She forced a smile; leaning in, she kissed him back. Rising to her feet, she walked over to Ian and wrapped her arms around his neck.

"I love you, Ian, and I'm so happy that you are alive and well. Immortal or human, you are still Ian, and nothing has changed," she said. He was looking at her with a warm smile, and she could see moisture in his eyes as he wrapped his good arm around her and hugged her tightly. She could sense that he was thankful for the encounter.

"I love you, too, Arielle; I'm extremely thankful for Troy's gift," Ian said unpretentiously. "I now have eternity to spend with Eva, something I never dared to even dream about. I feel completely freaked out thinking of that both of us actually died on that dreadful night."

She nodded. Next she walked over to Troy and wrapped her arms around him and kissed him on both cheeks.

"Thank you for keeping my friends alive. I love you, Troy, for many reasons, but this one is huge." She chuckled as he smiled and picked her up to twirl her around the room, making all of them laugh out loud. As soon as her feet hit the floor, she turned and fell in Sebastian's arms and held him tightly. *I'm so lucky to be loved by him. And how wild is it that Ian and Eva are now immortals? I would never have thought that in a million years*, she thought. She heard Sebastian's soft voice one more time, and his arms tighten around her.

"Arielle, focus, baby," Sebastian said with a soft chuckle. "We can't change the past, so we need to move on."

She nodded, as she knew that he was right. She had to keep telling herself that she had to accept this type of life. She had fallen deeply in love with an immortal. Her life was part of his undying world, and she shouldn't be shocked or upset by the changes that would take place as they moved on. There was no world that she would accept to live in without Sebastian, and she was sure Gabrielle felt exactly the same about Troy.

"How funny is it that Eva was my protector, using her mind and her incredible visions? As an immortal, she will be able to protect me physically against anyone that Annabel would send my way in the future, and I'm sure she will send plenty."

"Arielle, I need your help," Ian said.

"Anything. Just name it," she replied.

"I want you to come to the house in the morning with Sebastian and Troy. We are going to tell Eva about her new identity, and your support will be essential."

"Don't worry, Ian, I'll be there," she replied instantly. He smiled with a serene look on his face.

"Thank you."

Troy and Ian left the house around eleven, and she was so exhausted that all she wanted to do was go to sleep. Sebastian walked into the bathroom and shut the door behind him. She undressed and slipped under the covers. She stretched, closing her eyes and flexing her muscles, trying to relax. She heard the water running, and the thought of Sebastian in the shower made her skin ripple with excitement. The sound of the water faded away while vivid memories of his touch made her body quiver. She shut her eyes in pleasure while his face filled every corner of her mind.

It seemed eons later when she felt Sebastian's arms encircling her and pulling her flush against his muscled body. His speed was something she couldn't and wouldn't ever get used to. She giggled with sheer pleasure. She reached up and pulled him down to her, and their lips met in a deep, passionate kiss. His immortal breath was sweet, the scent intoxicating and the taste mesmerizing. She moaned with raw desire and her fingers twined through his soft sandy hair. Sebastian groaned in response, and lowering his head, he let his lips travel slowly down the column of her throat and felt the steadfast beat of her pulse. He snaked his arms around her body, and rolling over her, he pulled her closer. The heat of his breath on her throat made her whimper with pleasure. His mouth moved back to hers and the kiss turned scorching hot. His tongue pressed her lips apart and plundered the softness of her mouth. They felt the heat of the kiss all the way to the marrow of their bones. His hands cupped her breasts and skimmed over the hard nipples with both palms. She arched her body against his hands and she gasped, the pleasure was incredible.

"I want you," he whispered against her mouth.

"Mmmm," she managed to say. Sebastian laughed, against her mouth and she shivered. His hands moved skillfully on her thighs and stroked her soft flesh. His tongue found its way back into her mouth, and she moaned her appreciation. She felt his erection against her thighs, and her knees parted as he pulled her hips up and found his way into his heaven. Her breath hitched as ecstasy ripped through her body and moaned. Soon their bodies found the rhythm, and raced toward the heat of the sun. His guttural moan pushed them over the brink. Their release fused their bodies and they surrendered to the exquisite delight.

She felt him roll over and lower himself next to her, pulling her into his arms. He pressed a gentle kiss on her lips, and she let out a satisfied sigh. She was happy and sated. Even though she tried to stay awake, her eyelids became heavier and heavier, and she felt herself drifting away.

Sebastian felt her body go limp, and he knew she was asleep. He chuckled under his breath and squeezed her softly. She was the most important person in his life. The feel of her body next to his was overwhelming. His desire for her was unbelievable, even though they had just made love.

He closed his eyes and smiled, his excitement evident. He felt her moving into him and was startled when her lips pressed softly against the hollow at the bottom of his throat—the most sensitive spot on his body. His excitement elevated to its highest level. She moved around a couple more times, and then she was quiet again.

His fingers skimmed over the planes of her back ever so lightly, trying not to wake her up, and he felt fire sweeping through his veins burning his thoughts and feeling him with nothing but want for her love. He took a few deep breaths and moved away from Arielle trying to cool off. *God! How am I ever going to go through eternity with such an overwhelming desire for this girl. She is my lifeline, my one and only need for happiness.*

He slipped out of the bed quietly and jumped under the cold shower. He sniggered, feeling his whole body burning up. It was about an hour later when he felt his pulse receding. He slipped back under the covers, encircled her quietly, and closed his eyes. He knew she was sound asleep.

He felt her body relaxing in his arms. He smiled and nuzzled her hair, breathing in that so familiar aroma of freesia. A feeling of contentment spread through his body. He knew that this beautiful girl would be his for eternity. He just couldn't understand why it took so many centuries to discover this amazing feeling. He still couldn't understand the wonderful familiarity of her eyes. He had spent hours upon hours trying to distinguish this peculiar feeling. Why did he have this extraordinary sensation that he had looked into those eyes before? How could that be possible? He chuckled softly, knowing that was a complete and utter impossibility. Now that he found her, she seemed to be his sole purpose for roaming the earth for over five centuries. She changed his miserable existence and gave meaning to his life.

When he woke up, the room was still dark. He rolled on his back, and he heard her moaning softly. He could see the clock on the nightstand showing ten minutes to seven. It was still quite early; Troy was not going to be there until nine. He stared at her beautiful face, wanting to wake her up. He wanted to make love, but he stopped his desire again and tried to focus on the issue on hand. This morning, they would have to explain to Eva the details of the accident and her new identity.

He was completely lost in his thoughts when he heard her sleepy voice. Ripples of heat spreading across his body as her hand caressed the muscles of his bare chest. "Good morning!" she whispered. His arms immediately encircled her, and his lips found her mouth as he pulled her closer.

"Mmmm... good morning, baby," Sebastian's voice came out filled with anticipation. "I've been waiting for you." His hands were caressing her silky skin, sliding from her back to her hips and up again. She moaned and pulled herself even closer; he was excited and this time wasn't going to let her go back to sleep.

"I wan..." He stopped midsentence and gasped. She had rolled on top of him with a swift movement that left him outright speechless. He growled with need as heat seared his skin and desire replaced every sense. His mouth moved slowly to the side of her neck, brushing her skin softly, stopping when he reached her breasts. He moaned as he tugged on the hard buds, giving her a rapturous feeling that brought tears to her eyes. He locked his hands behind her back. Moving his head up again, he took her mouth and locked them in a ravenous kiss. She kept her eyes closed as an intoxicating desire spread across her body, making her skin burn with longing for him. She hauled in a deep breath, dragging air into her lungs, and merged them together. She started to move with passion, moaning and whispering his name, leaving him astonished and utterly thrilled.

"Where in the world did you learn to do this?" he gasped, totally out of breath. He knew her lovemaking experience had been very limited.

"From you," she murmured. She opened her eyes and looked into his amazing, emerald eyes. She slipped her hand under his nape. Pulling him to her, she bent down and locked them in another hot, exhilarating kiss. His lips moved beneath hers returning the passion and the heat of her kiss. Arielle gasped as she sucked in another deep breath and moved one last time, taking both of them to another level of fulfillment as they merged in ecstasy. In a voice overflowing with passion, he called out her name over and over again. She heard him groan in pleasure, and she knew that she had created the sensation that traveled through him, burning every vein and every nerve in his glorious body. She lay across his chest for a long time, unable to move in.

"When are you going to stop amazing me?" he murmured.

"Never, that's my mission in life." She laughed heartily, and he squeezed her tighter, making her gasp for air.

"What are you doing to me?" He was trying to keep his voice steady.

"Everything I possibly can." She laughed out loud again in exhalation.

She was afire at the thought that this amazing-looking man was hers. She pressed herself against his body, asking him to hold her even tighter. She wanted to feel and enjoy every inch of him.

"I missed you, baby," he murmured.

"I know, and I'm sorry, but I had a lot of things on my mind," she said. "I never stopped wanting you. I was just exhausted."

"Troy is coming over at nine," he reminded her. "You haven't forgotten that we have to go and talk to Eva, have you?"

"No, I do remember, but it's only seven-thirty, and for the next half hour, you are completely mine." She was giggling.

"Mmmmm...I like the sound of that," he said, laughing with delight.

"I surrender," he murmured. He lay flat on his back and moved his arms behind his head, stretching leisurely. "Go ahead. I'm all yours." A wide smile was spread across his face as her arms reached around his broad shoulders, pulling him into a kiss so fervent, so intense, he gasped for air. The next half hour was mind-blowing.

In the shower, Arielle remembered to ask Sebastian about his plans to disguise Ian and Eva's sudden healing. How were they going to explain something like that to people around them? That is when she found out about his decision to send Ian and Eva on a holiday.

"Have you told Ian?"

"Yes," he said. "Ian was actually very happy about spending time in a secluded place."

"Where are they going?"

"I thought they could use the house in Tuscany. Don't you think they would be happy there for a month or so? Geneva said she would be more than happy to look after them." Sebastian had a sly smile on his face.

"Oh! Sebastian, that is wonderful," she said. She wrapped her arms around him and held him warmly. She was startled when he picked her up and locked their lips in a luscious kiss. She felt like a little girl every time he did that.

"When will they have to leave?" she asked.

"They should leave today, sometime in the afternoon. I already have arranged for their tickets with the airlines. I have also arranged for someone to pick them up at the airport and drive them to the house,"

Sebastian stated. He made everything sound so easy. She sighed in amazement.

"I know they'll be happy," she murmured. "It will make their transition much easier."

"We have just one more hurdle with Eva, and then we can all concentrate on Gabrielle's recovery." He had a thoughtful look in his eyes. His lips found hers again, and their kiss brought her back to reality and ready to face another day.

Troy arrived exactly at nine, and they drove to Ian and Eva's. The closer they got the more anxious she felt. The guys were sure that she would be the one to help Eva get through this troubling and stressful moment. She knew Ian would be Eva's rock because he was the man she loved, but Eva would need Arielle there. They were not just best friends; they were more like sisters. Eva, Gabby, and Arielle had such a strong bond between them that would never break. They knew each other better than anyone else, and that included their parents.

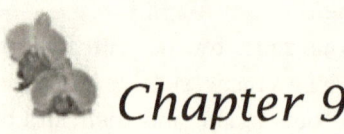

Chapter 9

THEY ARRIVED AT IAN AND EVA'S HOUSE around about thirty minutes later, and Ian opened the door. Arielle smiled and gave him a warm hug. Looking in his worried eyes, she leaned in and whispered in his ear. "Nothing has changed, Ian, you're still the same gorgeous man, and my best friend."

He grinned and nodded, but she could see stress and bewilderment spread across his face. Arielle stared into his eyes, and it took but a moment to work out the reason he was so agitated. He knew what was about to happen.

"Hey, you guys!" Eva called out cheerfully as she approached the front door on crutches. "I'm so happy to see you! What brings you this way?" she asked. "I know you aren't here to take me dancing," she snickered, pointing to the large cast on her leg. They all laughed, and Arielle reached over and embraced Eva warmly.

"No, we're not going dancing today," Arielle said, forcing a smile. She could feel her heart drumming, and her stomach churning. "Maybe tomorrow," she furthered, trying to make light of the situation.

When they all had moved inside, Arielle hugged Eva, "We've missed you, Eva," she said. "We thought it would be nice to spend a little time together. How are you feeling?"

"I actually feel great; it's just a little difficult to move around with this huge cast on my leg." She looked fondly in Troy's direction.

"Troy, you are my hero," she said. He looked a bit shocked, not being sure what she was referring to. "I'm so grateful about this outcome.

Tolerating this leg cast for a short period of time is insignificant. I can't bear to think the alternative result." Troy breathed a sigh of relief, smiled, and hugged her warmly.

"How are you, dazzling boy?" Eva said, turning in Sebastian's direction, reaching out to get a hug. Sebastian couldn't hold back a hardy laugh. A wide smile spread across his face, and leaning down, he gave her a loving squeeze. He knew how much she loved his dazzling gaze, but the smile left him as soon as realization settled in. He wasn't going to be able to dazzle her come tomorrow. His expression didn't change, but his gaze grew uneasy.

Eva seemed to notice the change in his behavior.

"Why the long face, Sebastian?" she asked. "You are always the happy one. What's bothering you?" She was very perceptive to people's feelings, human or immortal. Arielle was staring at Eva's back while she was carrying the conversation with Sebastian, and suddenly realization crushed hard into her brain, like a whirlwind twister. An overwhelming sensation of loneliness hit her like a ton of bricks. What if she could never connect with her best friend the same way they did before the accident? Abruptly, she became aware that she now knew the reason she couldn't read Eva and Ian's minds in the hospital. They were going through an immortal transformation.

Her lips tightened and deep emotions slipped stealthily into the depths of her soul. She would never have access to their thoughts again. For a moment, her breath caught in her throat. She had a strong desire to cry, but she reined in her emotions, and the need to cry dwindled away. She took a seat next to Eva and put her arm around her shoulders.

"Have you been able to remember anything more about the accident?" she asked, wanting to probe a little deeper.

"Arielle, I have tried hard to remember, but I don't seem to be able to recollect a single thing from the crash. Everything is a complete blank," she said, looking puzzled. "Did I tell you that Ian and I went to see the car after we left the hospital?" she asked her.

"No, but Ian said that he saw the car."

"We both did, and we realized that it was only a miracle that kept us alive," Eva said. Looking at Troy, a wide smile spread across her face.

"I know!" Arielle replied. "That's the first thing my mother said when I talked to her the morning after the accident. We were all sure that you had a guardian angel that kept you safe," Arielle murmured and gave Troy a meaningful look. Her voice was joyful, and Eva embraced her blissfully.

The guys pretended to be engaged in a conversation about sports. They were letting Arielle lay out the groundwork by having a casual visit with Eva.

"Arielle," Eva's voice drew her out of her thoughts. "Something strange has been happening to me ever since the night of the accident." Arielle stiffened at her words. The guys stopped talking, and their eyes were fastened on Eva's face. The anxiety spread across their faces didn't escape Eva.

"What's wrong?" she asked. "Why are you all looking at me this way?" Her gaze grew sharper as she glanced between them.

"Oh, nothing really, Eva. We were a little curious about your statement," Ian replied.

"What statement is that?"

"You said something strange is happening to you," he mumbled. "I wanted to know if there is something that you haven't told me."

"What's happening to you?" Arielle asked, waving Ian off.

Eva turned her gaze to Arielle again and added, "Ever since I woke up at the hospital, I seem to be able to have incredible visions about the future. I can see clearly that Gabby will recover with no complications at all. I can see all of us going on with our lives, as if this incident never took place. I have never experienced visions this powerful and so vivid."

"Eva, you were always extremely gifted. I'm not surprised at all," Arielle said. Silence fell for a short moment. Eva's face looked puzzled. She drew a deep breath, and her gaze darted between her friends, stopping at Arielle's face once again.

"There is a vision that I find a bit peculiar. I see Ian and me in a faraway place," she said, enigmatically. Arielle felt a tight knot in the pit of her stomach and forced a smile.

"Really?" she exclaimed.

"Arielle, I'm completely mystified. The feeling is so real, and the vision so vivid," she mumbled, pressing her lips together anxiously. After a short pause, she shook her head and continued. "But how can it be?" She turned and swept her gaze over Ian's handsome face for a brief moment, and then turned back to Arielle. Arielle noticed the fast rise and fall of Eva's chest as she tried to decipher her own thoughts. She had paused again and was running her tongue over her dry lips, incredulously. "Ian and I wouldn't think of taking a trip right now," she said suddenly and groaned. "I'm so frustrated I could scream," Eva continued. A faraway look flickered in her eyes.

They were all very quiet trying to find the right words to begin the unraveling picture when Eva presented the perfect moment with her next question.

"I'm getting a weird feeling about this visit. Is there something wrong? Arielle, what are you pondering in that head of yours?" she said and waved her hand aimlessly. "I can see the concern in your eyes. I can see that each one of you has a peculiar look on your faces, and that includes you," she said, pointing at Ian. "Is Gabby all right?" Once again, Eva looked anxiously around the room.

"Yes...Yes...Gabby is just fine. But you are right. We are here to talk about something else, something quite serious," Arielle replied.

"Oh? Let me hear it!" Eva's eyes narrowed.

Arielle paused for a long moment. She tried to collect her thoughts, realizing that communicating difficult news was a very unpleasant and stressful thing, even under the best of circumstances. She knew that receiving this type of news was going to be disturbing. The change from human to immortal would substantially alter Eva's views about her future. It would be devastating, and she was worried about her friend's initial reaction. She wanted to make sure that she delivered the news in a tender way. She didn't want Eva to go through major distress or profound sorrow about this change.

"Arielle, what is it?" Eva's voice shook her out of her reverie. "You are worrying me! What is it?"

Arielle took a seat next to her once again, keeping her eyes on her stress-filled face. She reached over and took her hand, while Ian took the seat on the other side, embracing her attentively. Sebastian and Troy walked over and sat across from her. Eva was scrutinizing their movements cautiously.

"I don't think I'm going to like this," she said through clenched teeth.

"But I'm ready to hear you," she said. She sounded like the practical Eva they all knew. She always took news better than the rest of them. Arielle smiled and leaning closer, she gave her a kiss on the cheek.

"Eva," she said astutely. "If I were dying and Sebastian could save my life by making me an immortal, would you approve?" Her eyes were watching Eva inquisitively.

"I don't understand what you are trying to say," she replied, clueless.

"Well, would you think that Sebastian was doing the right thing?" She pressed on. Eva looked a little surprised about Arielle blathering about something so uncanny. However, she did appear to be pondering her question. She finally decided to give her an answer without any reservations.

"Arielle, your question is bloody absurd," she said. "Of course, I'd prefer that you remain alive. Human, immortal it doesn't make any difference to me," she said firmly. A smiled tagged her lips. "I seem to be getting pretty familiar with immortality," she whispered. She turned away from Arielle, directing her next statement to the guys.

"Troy, Sebastian, I love you both," she said. She was holding a great big smile on her face. "You look human to me except for the fact that you are both astoundingly handsome." She chuckled softly. "But all things aside, Arielle, what's all this about?" Her voice was a little more intense this time.

Arielle drew in a breath and exhaled deeply. "Eva, the night of your accident, you and Ian did not survive the crash..." She accentuated the last words. Eva winced for a quick second. Arielle kept her eyes locked on Eva, and she noticed that she didn't blink for the next several minutes. She could actually hear her breathing elevating, picking up rhythm. She inhaled and bit down on her bottom lip. Arielle wanted to decipher Eva's trouble thoughts, but she didn't have that ability with Eva any longer. Her gaze was still locked on Eva, and she thought that she saw an inexplicable smile tighten her face. Another moment of silence, and finally Eva broke the gaze lock first. She closed her eyes, pulled her hands away from Arielle, and leaned her head back against the chair. She stood like that for a few seconds, and they all remained still, waiting for her next move. She finally opened her eyes and gave a dry gasp. Her voice cracked from sheer agony.

"What did you say?" Arielle reached and tried to take her hands in hers again put she pulled back. Her eyes flickered between Troy, Sebastian and Ian. "What did Arielle say?" Her voice was trembling, but this time she was addressing Ian.

"Eva, you know that I love you more than life," Ian said, overcome with emotion. "But what Arielle said is the absolute truth," he continued with a tender voice. He was holding her lovingly.

"But how can that be? We are here! We are alive!" Her eyes were flickering from Ian to Troy, to Sebastian, to Arielle, and then back to Ian.

"No...No... that can't be possible. Ian, I don't feel any different than I did before. If this is some kind of a joke, I don't think it is funny at all." She was now sounding pretty distraught.

"Eva, baby," that was Ian's soft voice. Something in his expression faltered, and they all knew he was extremely concerned.

Eva's eyes went wide, and she went rigid with disbelief. She swept her hair out of her eyes and opened her mouth to speak, but the sensation of a steel vice closing around her throat kept her utterly silent. She moved her hands up to her throat and looked around the room frantically.

Arielle hesitated for a moment then she reached and hugged Eva.

"Troy is the reason you and Ian are here, alive and able to love each other," she said with a warm smile.

"He didn't let us die," Ian added.

Eva's jaw dropped, her eyes welled up, and her body started to shudder. Arielle was sure the reality shock was unbelievable. Suddenly she recalled the way she felt when she found out about Sebastian. She could only imagine the way Eva felt right now.

"Ian, that's absolutely insane," she murmured, and let out a wheezing whimper. Her face was stricken with shock and her body quivered. "I can't even comprehend the possibility, of t..." she stopped mid-sentence, as if she was trying to think of the right thing to say, but suddenly she buried her face in her hands and started to sob. Ian frowned, but nobody moved. They knew that Eva was horrified, and they had to wait her out. She finally stopped sobbing. Pushing her hair out of her face, she looked up and let her gaze glide slowly over each face in the room until her eyes met Ian's gaze. Eva looked at him as if she had never seen his face before.

"No...no...no...no," she said emphatically. "I know that you are all making this up. It just can't be true. Look at us," she shouted, glancing between her friends, and moving her arms wildly between Ian and herself. "We're a mess. We're bruised up; we're in pain, I have a leg cast; Ian has an arm cast. If that were true, according to Sebastian and Troy, we wouldn't be in this condition."

"Eva, please, baby," Ian said and pulled her in his arms.

"But what do we do now?" she asked, with a tremulous voice.

"We don't have to do anything, sweetheart," Ian whispered.

Eva drew a deep breath and exhaled cautiously. "Are we immortals? Because I don't feel any different."

"No, not just yet, but we'll be soon."

"How soon?" She was still scrutinizing Ian's face.

"Troy and Sebastian said it will be later tonight," he replied, watching her intently. "Eva, please, baby," he continued. "We have to accept our fate and agree that eternity is our future." A soft smile tagged his lips. "I always dreamed of being with you forever. Well, we now have that chance. Together for eternity," Ian said, chuckling.

Eva looked up and noticed Troy and Sebastian holding a soft smile on their beautiful faces. Shock from bad news is real, and nobody in the room expected her to be delighted after getting this type of news. They were all here to support her in coping with the change. Her denial was a human trade, but in the end, Arielle knew that Eva would accept and face the reality of it. Sebastian moved closer, cupped Eva's face with both hands and softly spoke.

"Eva, we love you. Troy and I will be here for you every step of the way." He saw a faint smile tag Eva's lips, and she let out a soft sigh.

"I remember Ian telling me how much he wished he was an immortal after he returned from St. Jean." They heard her voice, soft and shaky. "That was the time you and all of your friends were going after Annabelle, do you remember?"

"How can I forget something like that?" Sebastian said. "That entire trip will remain in our memories for centuries to come," he said, and chuckled.

"Oh, Ian," she mumbled and fell in his arms. "I'm so scared."

"So am I, Eva, but this is better than the alternative. We were killed in the accident. Think about the pain that our families would have to endure. Troy gave us a second chance." Arielle nodded and kept quiet.

The next voice was the one that Arielle loved, the one that soothed her soul. It was Sebastian, and compassion was spread across his face.

"Eva, let me give you a little advice of my own experience. When I found out that I was an immortal, I assessed the degree of gain versus the loss. I used the information that I received to successfully cope with the change in my life. I'm sure that this is the best outcome of all; I only wish that you could see this now, but it may take a little time. At the very beginning of my transformation, I had absolutely no one to help me move along with my life, but you, you have all of us to support you and love you as you move on."

Eva smiled softly, thoughtfully. "Sebastian, I'm thankful that I'm alive; however, I'm scared about not understanding who I really am," she pursed her lips. "I would like to know the things I'm going to live without and the things I'll now possess. I want to know how this change will affect my relationships," Eva looked anxious again, as she continued. "My relationship with my mother and my human friends who are not aware of this amazing world you and Troy live in. That is what is freaking me out right now. It's not the immortality part of it, but the way I move on with my new identity." She looked down and rubbed her hands together in unease. "I do remember a lot from our conversation at the beach of Saint Jean de Luz, but the revelation of your immortality didn't include myself so I did miss quite a lot out of fear and astonishment."

"Eva, Troy and I gave you practically everything that we went through during our transformation at that time, but we'll be happy to answer any questions you may have," Sebastian replied with a warm, calm voice. Eva was looking at Ian who leaned in, pulled her even closer, and locked them in a warm kiss.

"Don't forget that I'm here, and I'm going to walk with you every step of the way on this unknown journey of our lives," Ian said. "I love you, Eva, and I'm happy to know that I'll be with you for eternity. I know that people that love each other as much as we do would give anything they own to achieve immortality. " Ian was lost in her eyes.

She held him tight as they locked themselves in another hot kiss, making their friends smile. She broke the kiss a little embarrassed, and smiling, she looked between the three of them and continued.

"I'm still very frightened, but ready to hear the details. What is it that I'll not be able to do or have as an immortal?"

Sebastian looked at Troy and told him something that neither one of them could hear. He got up and started to pace in front of them. He finally stopped and started to speak slowly and tenderly. Patiently, he began to recount the same things they'd revealed to Ian the night before at the beach.

"Are you saying that I'll never find a solid ground to build a foundation on this earth? Will I move into infinity without being able to attach myself anywhere?" she asked, totally animated.

*Wow...*Arielle thought, *that was a very deep question. I'd like to know the answer even though it doesn't pertain to me.*

"Eva," Troy jumped in. "If you try to grasp infinity, then you are right. We as immortals travel, always drifting in uncertainty as our lives never end. The earth moves and opens into infinity as human lives shift, slip past us, and vanish forever while we are still here."

That is the most amazing explanation I ever heard. I hope that Eva will feel the same way. Arielle thought.

"Eva, I love you and I'm here with you," Ian desperately waited for her to find the calmness and reassurance he needed so bad right now. She reached out and held him tight again as she tried hard to show that she was all right with everything that was happening right now.

"Eva, you'll have to be protected against the sunlight, because that will be the one and only thing that could kill you."

"How are you protected against the sun? I see you and Loren out all the time." Eva and Ian were now looking at both Sebastian and Troy.

"We wear a type of ring that provides that protection." Troy extended his right arm, and showed her the beautiful ring that was nestled on his hand between the middle and the little finger.

"Sebastian already acquired the rings for both of you," he said. Sebastian got up and came close as he took a small box out of his pocket. He opened it. Taking out a gorgeous, elegant silver ring, he placed it on her right finger.

"This ring is now permanently on your finger. No one and nothing can remove it, not even you," Sebastian said. Eva looked at the ring in astonishment tried to pull it off, but it wouldn't budge. She was absolutely shocked, and so was Arielle. She never really witnessed anything like this before. He then moved over and did the exact same thing with Ian. Ian's ring was larger but just as elegant and amazing as Sebastian and Troy's.

"These rings will be your protection and nothing will ever harm you again. If you get hurt, you will heal in a very short time. You'll never get sick and will never have the need for a doctor or any kind of care about your well-being." Troy said.

"Troy, how am I going to fool my mother if we are invited for dinner, and we don't eat?"

"I didn't say you wouldn't be able to eat or drink anything you want. What I said is that none of that will be enough to sustain your body's energy. You will require a special drink that is called salve, and we'll show you and Ian how to obtain it. It's an immortal secret."

Relief spread across her face as she added, "So no one will know the difference about us?"

"Did you know that Sebastian and I were different?" Troy asked.

"No, I must admit I never did. However, I always thought that you guys were amazing in a strange way."

"That was only because of your visions and the powers you possess," Arielle added in a soft voice. Sebastian gazed at her and smiled lovingly. Eva's face was calming down, but she was still having a questioning look.

"So... what are the powers Ian and I will now possess?" Sebastian was happy to give her the list.

"You will have no fear about anything or anyone. You will remain young and exceptionally beautiful for eternity. You will possess extreme strength, speed, and intelligence. You will absorb information a million times faster than any human and be able to retain everything you learn along the way. You will be able to move between places and countries without using any type of human transportation, if that is your choice. You'll be able to manifest things at will and keep them for as long as you wish. You'll become wealthy beyond belief, because

Troy and I will introduce you to many people in very high places. You'll belong to our secret society that takes care of each other and provides everything that we could possibly need to sustain us. You'll have a man who loves you beyond any reasoning and who will be standing by your side for eternity." Sebastian never took a breath during that long speech. A long stifling silence fell in the room, while his words draped over Ian, Eva, and Arielle.

Chapter 10

ARIELLE WAS ABSOLUTELY AMAZED to hear Sebastian's voice in such a matter of fact tone. She gaped at him, and her thoughts drifted to a different place. *So he is wealthy beyond belief, and he can do just about anything he wants.* Suddenly his last words about Eva having the man that loves her for eternity sent her to a painful place. She rubbed her hands together anxiously, and stared at the floor. *I won't be able to be by Sebastian's side for eternity, and that's an indisputable fact. No matter what he says, I'm human, and so is Gabby. We will both get sick and or hurt at different times, and eventually we'll both die.*

A shooting pain coursed across her nerves, and her heart sunk in despair, filled with wretchedness at the thought of Sebastian moving on, young and beautiful for eternity without her by his side. She thought of all the beautiful women in his undying world that wanted his affection and that were ready to be rid of her to get it. She winced at the thought of Sebastian sharing his love, and his bed, with someone else. That thought hurt so bad that the agony spread across her face. She swallowed hard, trying to keep tears from escaping the corners of her eyes. She pressed her lips together, and shut her eyes real tight, taking several deep breaths and shifting in her seat. She tried to concentrate on Eva's issue, but she failed miserably.

"What's wrong, baby?" Sebastian's voice was soft. Her eyes shot open, and she was startled to find him standing right in front of her. He knew she was anxious about something. He pulled her up into his arms, and his eyes pierced through hers in complete wonder. She took a few deep breaths, and shook her head trying to get rid of all the distressful thoughts that were invading her mind at that very moment. She shifted from one foot to the other and remained silent.

"Yes, what's wrong, Arielle?" Eva was now asking. She realized that her mood had become utterly obvious to all around her.

She smiled softly, and her voice came out shaken. "Oh! I was just thinking about Gabby and me."

"Oh, what about Gabby and you?" Eva insisted.

"Well, you see, we are the only humans left in our small group of six. As I see it right now, Gabby and I will get old and die someday while the loves of our lives and our best friends move on for eternity, young and beautiful forever," she said, eyes tearing.

Something inside Sebastian quivered at her words. He tightened his arms around her, and his voice reached her ear, soft as velvet. "When are you going to start trusting me?" His breath brushed her face, and she inhaled his amazing immortal scent. His warmth coursed across her skin, and she felt his calm invading her own thoughts.

"How many times do I have to tell you that we are linked together for eternity? And how many times do I have to tell you that you are not going anywhere without me?" His lips were brushing her ear as his whisper was soothing her very soul. She reached up and wrapped her arms around his neck and pulled him down to her for a kiss.

"Look at me...I love you," she heard his quiet voice. She looked up at him, and their eyes locked in a green and blue fusion. Their lips met and merged in a loving kiss. "I love you," he whispered in her ear. He broke the kiss and intertwined their fingers to keep her close to his side. "Are you all right?" he asked, sending her a smoldering side look.

"Yes," she murmured. Her body quivered under the intense of his sizzling gaze, and her breath caught in her throat.

He sensed her problem, and he grinned. Arielle embraced each and every moment in their life with passion with hunger. *Oh, God, I love her so much!* Sebastian thought, and a wide smile spread across his beautiful face.

Arielle sank back down next to Eva, still holding Sebastian's hand, lost in thought.

"Am I going to retain my gift of seeing the future?" Eva's voice brought her back to reality.

"Yes, there are many immortals that possess that gift, and many that can read minds with no exceptions at all. Sebastian has that gift." Troy said, with a chuckle.

"You can read minds!" Ian snapped, staring at Sebastian in surprise.

Sebastian cleared his throat and glancing at Ian, he said calmly. "I can read every human mind without exceptions, but I can't read immortal minds."

Ian's eyes went wide, and he let out a groan. "Holy cow..." he gasped. Taking a deep breath, he pressed his lips together and looked at Sebastian with eyes that had gone dark with shock. "You knew all along what we were thinking?"

Sebastian pinched the tip of his nose, feeling uncomfortable. He searched desperately for the right response, but the words lurched into his throat, and making a wretched face, he nodded awkwardly. "Yes, I'm sorry, Ian...I always nullify my friends' thoughts. I use my gift for things that might put someone in danger or hurt my business. So please don't feel uncomfortable."

Ian tried to keep his façade of calm. "But you can't read immortal thoughts, right?" he furthered.

"Yes, that's correct."

"Well, that's good to know," Ian said a bit relaxed.

Sebastian sat down next to Arielle, and leaning over, he gave her a quick peck on the lips.

Troy stood up from his chair, and crossing the room, he stood in front of Ian and Eva. "I hope you are not angry with me," he said, apologetically. "But, if I had to do it again, I would do the exact same thing. I just couldn't let you die." Troy brushed a hand over his eyes, as if he recalled the painful moment. Enthused by his friends being alive couldn't begin to comprise how he felt. He looked like a young boy that was waiting for consent about the decision he had made without their input.

Eva and Ian exchanged a tender look, and they both turned to look at Troy.

"Troy, we want to thank you for saving our lives," Eva said.

"We are ready to move on with our new identity. It will be an unbelievable journey, but we'll be together. We just can't grasp the meaning of eternity as of yet, but this is our destiny, and we'll take it."

Ian said. They both seemed to have a more serene look on their faces.

"Ian, did you ask Eva to talk to her mother?" Sebastian asked.

"No, not yet," Ian replied. "I was a bit anxious about telling Eva the news." He turned to Eva and pulled her closer for a kiss. "Can you call your mum, baby, and let her know that we'll be leaving this afternoon?" he murmured.

Eva's mouth dropped and looked around inquisitively. "Where are we going?"

"You are going to Italy. You'll be staying at my house in Tuscany," Sebastian said.

"We are going to Italy?" Eva exclaimed.

"That's the plan, unless you would rather not." Sebastian teased her.

"Oh my Gosh… that's amazing! I can't wait." Her face was illuminated with joy. "I'll call my mother right now," she said.

Eva stood up slowly with Ian's help, and grasping her crutches, she limped over to the bar to get her phone. Just before she pressed her mum's number on the keypad, she turned and glanced between Troy and Sebastian. "So are you saying that Ian and I will not need these casts by late tonight?"

"Yes, you'll be completely healed," Sebastian replied. "If you need anything while you are away, just call and let us know. Geneva, my housekeeper, is an immortal, so you can feel relaxed around her. She will help you with your needs and your questions. Your tickets are in order, and I've arranged for someone to pick you up at the airport and drive you to the house." Sebastian reached inside his coat pocket and pulled out two airline tickets that he handed to Ian.

"Have fun and enjoy yourselves. Come back when you feel that you're ready." Ian and Eva were smiling blissfully, eyes filled with exhilaration.

"Thank you, Sebastian…" Eva whispered, still not believing all that had transpired this morning. She turned and looked at Arielle, and she could see moisture in her eyes. Arielle let go of Sebastian's hand. Standing up, she walked to Eva and gave her a huge hug.

"Eva, like I told Ian, human or immortal, you are still my best friend, and I love you. Nothing has changed, or will ever change between us. I think this is the amazing," she said, gazing in Eva's eyes. "You protected me as a human with your premonitions, and now you can protect me physically against Annabel." They both laughed out loud, and the guys seemed to be more at ease knowing that Eva was less stressed about her new life.

"Do you want me to take you to the airport?" Arielle asked Eva.

"No, I'll ask my mum to do that, and she'll be more than happy to let us go away for a while. She wants us to get over the accident trauma and get back to our normal lives" She chuckled nervously, knowing that nothing about their lives was going to be close to normal. Eva pressed her mother's number, and they talked for a short while while Ian discussed with Sebastian a few more details about the trip.

Soon they said their goodbyes, and the three of them climbed inside Troy's car. She sat next to Troy as Sebastian took the back seat. She remained completely silent, keeping her gaze straight ahead. Her thoughts were full of questions about immortality and the world of wonder.

"Arielle, is something bothering you?" Troy asked. She turned to look at him, and he had a soft smile on his face. She was a bit stressed.

"How did you do this?" she asked Troy.

"How did I do what?" he asked quizzically.

"How did you make them immortal?"

Troy was silent for a short moment, and she could see that he was trying to find the best way to explain his actions the night of the accident. The look in the rear view mirror didn't escape her. Troy exchanged a look with Sebastian in the back seat, as if he was asking for his approval. He licked his dry lips a couple of times.

"The crash was something unbelievable. It was so dark that I was sure Gabrielle, Ian, and Eva could not see a thing. When the car stopped moving, I checked on Gabrielle, and I knew she was badly hurt, but she was breathing. However, Eva and Ian were barely alive, and I knew they had but a few seconds before they stopped breathing. I called for an ambulance, and using my speed, I went home and picked up two jars of salve and got back just in time." He took a couple of deep breaths and continued. "Their pulses surged to a safe level following the salve intake. The first ambulance arrived within a few minutes, and the paramedics provided Gabrielle with immediate care and oxygen and took her away. By the time the second ambulance arrived, Eva and Ian were well out of grave danger, but the paramedics provided great care to both of them. They were placed on the gurneys and rolled into the ambulances. The ride to the hospital was fast, and hospital staff was waiting for them to provide immediate care. That is the whole story in a short view," Troy said.

"What did they say about you being completely unscathed?" She asked again.

"They were shocked, to say the least," he said, and chuckled softly. "They asked if I needed any medical help, and I politely declined. The police officers asked several questions about the accident, and I told them that Gabrielle had swerved to avoid something on the road and lost control of the car. They asked me if I was declining medical assistance due to my religion beliefs, and I had to say yes. They told me how surprised they were that I escaped serious injuries, and I acted just as surprised." Troy stopped talking and stared out the windshield obviously upset.

"That is absolutely incredible," Arielle murmured. "I'm completely amazed at the control you have over life and death." She was truly mesmerized by that immortal ability. They were both silent, and neither one of them made any further comment. Her mind was whirling wildly.

The next time she would see Eva and Ian, they would both be part of the incredible immortal world. She laughed quietly at the irony. She was sure that they both looked at her, but they said absolutely nothing. She was so overwhelmed with thoughts and questions. She was sure they would never satisfy the curiosity that was creeping over her.

Sebastian took Arielle horseback riding for the rest of the afternoon, and out to dinner. Arielle was exhausted. They enjoyed a warm luxurious shower together and went to bed. Arielle picked up her journal once again, eager to write about Ian and Eva's immortality. Sebastian picked up the sports magazine and decided to kill time until Arielle was ready to sleep.

June 20th,

Dear friend, just a quick note to let you know about the incredible shock that sent my world off its axis once again. I found out that that my best friends Ian and Eva are now immortals. That definitely explained my struggle in understanding how I wasn't able to hear their thoughts any longer. But how wild is this? They both died the night of the accident, and Troy gave them immortality. It is hard to fathom, but it is an absolute fact. There are only three humans left in our group of eight. Gabby, Paul, and I. Everyone else is an immortal and that is just outlandish. What in the world is going on in Brighton?

Sebastian has arranged for Ian and Eva to leave Brighton for a month on a holiday to Italy. They will stay at the house in Tuscany, and Geneva will help them get through their transformation to immortality. They were both quite shocked and pretty scared, but with Sebastian and Troy's support, they reluctantly accepted their destiny. I guess we all accepted the fact that it was better to have them alive as immortals than not at all. Knowing that by this evening Ian and Eva's limbs would completely healed and their severe bruises will disappear, Sebastian and Troy decided to help them avoid the difficulties in trying to explain such an incredible outcome to the family and friends that would be visiting them at home, and especially Eva's mother.

The trip will be used as an excuse. They will tell Eva's mother that they need to get away from the terrible memories and heal. At least the time away will provide a chance for them to reflect at the changes in their lives and to accept their incredible new bodies with the new extraordinary abilities.

Arielle put away the journal, and turning around, she saw Sebastian laying back, a wide smile spread across his beautiful face.

"What?" she asked amused.

"Are you ready for bed, baby?" Arielle chuckled. She switched the light off and sank into bed, right into his embrace. Their lips locked into a passionate kiss, and she closed her eyes. Arielle splayed her hand over his chest and laid her head on the crook of his shoulder. His arm encircled her and pulled her closer, just as he did each and every night. Soon he heard her soft breathing, and he smiled serenely. He nuzzled her hair and inhaled the sweet smell of freesia. He felt peaceful, tranquil, and happy. He reached with his free hand and pulled the covers over her, affectionately. He drifted off to sleep, a soft smile on his face.

 *Chapter 11*

THE NEXT TWO WEEKS became a wonderful routine. Her mornings started very early, filled with excitement and potent emotions of exhilaration. Sebastian was her wake up call. His strong arms hauled her to him and held her tightly against his warm, exciting, muscular body. He would crash her lip beneath his in a passionate kiss, broadening and prolonging each and every moment with her in bed. They shared intensity, and desire until she could sense his heat, and she would stop breathing.

And then she would open her eyes to the most beautiful face on this earth. She loved to watch his lips curve irrepressibly, and his emerald eyes shimmer. Looking into those gorgeous eyes, she wanted to cry out to the world how much she loved him. Time would suspend and emotions would seize every single nerve of their bodies, while sensation wreathed their minds and souls. Pure pleasure was his specialty, and she reveled in it. He drove her to the highest point of awareness, until she exploded into shards of passion.

Later she would lay back and watch him kick the covers back, jump out of bed, and walk to the shower. *What a sight!*

They had a firm agreement that neither one of them would leave the bed in the morning without waking the other up. Their eyes were to gaze at each other's face first thing in the morning and last thing at night, and they did stay true to that commitment. She would go back to sleep, and by the time she would wake up again, he would be gone. A fragrant freesia was left on the pillow and a short note *"miss me"* in his very delicate sixteenth century script.

He had spent a very long time away from the office because of his deep desire to be with Arielle. Even though he had Nathan to run the everyday problems, he had to get back and run his business. Troy had joined Sebastian's team at IIRL, and they liked to leave early in the morning for the office.

Arielle spent a lot of time with Gabrielle at the hospital. Troy would stop by every day around noon faithfully and would sit with her for a while. Their love was heartwarming, and his devotion to Gabrielle was unbending. Many of their friends stopped by to cheer her up with happy news and let her know how badly she was missed. Paul and Loren came to visit several times, and she was always happy to see them, and so was Arielle.

Gabrielle was getting better every day, and Arielle could see that Gabby was looking forward to her visits. They spend a lot of affectionate and quality time together. Arielle was the one that talked most of the time, and she could see that her jokes and her stories were uplifting. She saw enjoyment spread across Gabby's face; she guessed the healing power of humor was actually true. Her mission everyday was to use the opportunity to take Gabby's mind away from her trauma and raise her spirit. She was sure that she was succeeding in doing exactly that.

Arielle understood that an overwhelming life experience triggers a frightening sense of security loss that is devastating, even if the event is perceived as unpredictable and uncontrollable. She felt agony that was piercing through her very soul, and it erupted inside her as full-blown fright.

It had been a few weeks since Ian and Eva left for Italy. They kept in touch, and she was very happy to hear that they were adapting to their new identities quite well. Arielle took advantage of Sebastian's busy schedule to also spend some quality time with her parents. Her mother prepared some of her favorite lunches, and she enjoyed leisurely walks with her father once again, in the garden. She remembered vividly the feeling of walking next to her father as a little girl, holding his hand. She was tickled to death to find that the feeling was just as warm and just as splendid now that she was grown up. She could see a little moisture at the corner of her father's eyes, and she was sure it was from just pure pleasure.

It was during one of those visits to her parents that her phone rang and she saw Eva's name on the screen. She eagerly answered.

"Eva!" she exclaimed. "How are you? I missed you so much!"

"Hi, Arielle, I missed you, too. This place is paradise. I don't think I want to come home," she said, and laughed out loud. Arielle was incredibly pleased to hear Eva's care free laughter.

"Well, tell me about you and Ian! I can't wait to hear the details," Arielle said, eagerly.

"I honestly don't know where to start, but first let me say that Geneva is amazing!"

"She is that and more," Arielle agreed. "You sound so happy!"

"Arielle, I'm very happy but a bit nervous as well. Sebastian's suggestion to come to Italy was perfect. Geneva was very helpful. I'm not sure how would have coped with all these changes."

Arielle could hear the anxieties under the nonchalant tone in Eva's voice as she continued. "Geneva became the perfect link between our human and immortal lives. She is very supportive, just as Sebastian said she would be. She provided answers to every little question that came up following the completion of our transformation," she said, apparently extremely astounded by Geneva's abilities and piquing Arielle's curiosity about details. Eva was silent for a long moment. Arielle didn't really mind the quietness; it gave her time to come up with her next question.

"Can you tell me anything about your transformation? Or is that a secret?" Arielle asked curiously.

"I'm not sure that I can give you any details, because the actual transformation wasn't anything transparent to either one of us. But I can tell you that our senses were on high alert, not knowing what to expect. At first, there was nothing unusual, but shortly before midnight I had the most extraordinary feeling that something was happening to my body, and I wasn't sure if that was a good or bad thing." Her voice was breaking up, but she drew a deep breath and continued. "I know that sounds weird, but when I looked over at Ian, he wore the same surprised expression on his face."

"What happened then?" Arielle asked intensely, trying to control her breathing.

"Well, we braced ourselves for the unknown, and what took place after that was unfathomable."

"What...what do you mean by that?" Arielle asked.

"Well, soon after that, we became aware that our limbs had healed, and we watched in astonishment as each other's bruises, deep cuts, and scrapes, disappeared. Arielle, it was as if someone waved an invisible magic wand across our bodies and wiped away every mark, every pain, every fear, and every anxiety that was overwhelming us since before we left Brighton."

"Wow! That's amazing. How are you feeling now?"

"Honestly, I don't feel any different. I actually feel great, just as Sebastian said I would. It is pretty outlandish!"

"Wow!" Arielle whispered again, utterly mesmerized. "What did you do after you healed?"

"Oh, this is the fun part," she said, and chuckled. "We didn't realize the strength that we now possess so when Ian and I decided to take off the casts, we barely got our hands around them, and they crushed between our fingers into fine white powder. It was astonishing to say the least."

"Unbelievable..." Arielle's voice trailed. This was as crazy as responses could get, yet it was factual.

"Arielle, it's the most extraordinary feeling!" Eva continued. "We are perfectly healthy, and we feel great! We would never know that we're different that we were before, but for the amazing abilities that we now possess."

Arielle heard the enthusiasm in Eva's voice and smiled wide.

"I'm so happy to hear that," she, replied, warmly. "I want to tell you one more thing about Geneva."

"What?"

"She worships the ground Sebastian walks on. This woman is blindly devoted to him," Eva said, chuckling.

Arielle didn't respond right away; she was thinking about her own blind devotion to him. He was so protective, so caring; he would never let anything happen to her or to her friends.

"Well, I can't blame Geneva for feeling the way she does. I'm pretty devoted to him as well," Arielle said, and smiled. "When are you coming home?"

"Well, we know that school is starting soon, so I guess it'll have to be sooner than we want to leave this place," she replied, regretfully.

"Well, I can't wait to see you both. I love you so much!" she said.

"We love you, too, Arielle."

"Don't do anything I wouldn't do," Arielle said, her voice filled with mirth.

Eva snorted. "I wouldn't think of it."

Arielle smiled at Eva's words right after she hung up. She was again thinking about the incredible magnitude Sebastian's existence created for every person that crossed his path.

The fourth week, she was sitting next to Gabrielle's bed running her mouth about something completely unimportant. Gabby was looking quite well compared to the first three weeks. She didn't have the bandages around her head, the brace around her neck, or the tubes that went through her mouth and nose. She could now breathe on her own, but she still couldn't eat solid foods.

She had the cast on her leg, the casts on both arms, and the bandages around her thigh where she'd needed fifty stitches. Her face looked brighter, less stressed, and Arielle could see a faint smile here and there. That smile was more apparent when Troy was there. Arielle could sense the incredible love they shared. Gabby was still under heavy medication so the soreness, the ache, and the discomfort wasn't as bad as it could have been. There were no permanent damages that would create lasting complications for her, and that was the best and most desirable result.

Gabby's abrupt question startled her. "I haven't seen Eva and or Ian? How are they?" Her eyes were probing Arielle's face for answers. Arielle wasn't ready to share with her any details about Eva or Ian at this time.

"Did Troy tell you anything about the accident?" she asked Gabby.

"Um…Troy told me that they sustained some broken bones and bad bruises, but otherwise, they faired extremely well," Gabby said.

Arielle reached over and touched her hand gently. "Yes, that's true. They both have casts bounding their limbs, and it's very difficult for them to get around. They ask about you every day, and I'll let them know when you can receive calls."

"Oh, I've missed them," she whispered sadly.

"Gabby, when they were hospitalized, they came in ICU more than a few times to see you, but you were in a coma. They were both very worried about you. By the time you gained consciousness, they were released. Right now, you need to rest, and don't worry about anything else," Arielle said and squeezed her hand gently.

"I understand," she muttered and nodded agreeably. Arielle changed the subject quickly. She didn't want Gabby to think about anything unpleasant or anything that was associated with the accident. Soon they were engaged in more happy subjects.

Loren stopped by and brought Gabrielle a beautiful bouquet of exotic flowers. Gabby was visibly pleased and gave Loren a huge hug of appreciation. Loren's gaze swept over Gabby carefully and smiled wide.

"You look fantastic!" she said.

Gabby sighed and smiled. "Thank you, Loren. I wish I could say that I feel fantastic, but I don't."

"All in good time," Loren reassured her. Reaching over, she squeezed Gabby's hands tenderly. She stayed for a little while and chatted away about some funny incidents between Paul and herself, bringing joy and cheerfulness to the room.

Arielle left with Loren around two o'clock in the afternoon, and they decided to go downtown and do some shopping. She loved Loren's impeccable taste in clothes, and they exchanged ideas and opinions on several of their purchases. They enjoyed spending time together and talking about Paul, Sebastian, and their relationships. They had just walked out of a clothing store when Arielle heard Loren's immortal velvety voice.

"Arielle, I want to thank you for something that has made a big difference in my life."

"Oh…" Arielle turned her inquisitive gaze at Loren.

"It's your friendship," she said simply. "It has brought the most amazing and the most extraordinary feeling into my life. I was never blessed with a sister, or even a friend that I could trust with my personal relationships. When I first met you, I envied the bond that you share with Eva and Gabrielle. At the time I couldn't even imagine how amazing it would be to share my inner thoughts with someone and know that I could trust them with my life." She stopped and took a deep breath. "You see, it has always been my parents and Sebastian, and there are things that I just couldn't possibly share with either one of them." She paused. "But now I have you!" she exclaimed, pointing both hands toward Arielle. "How lucky can a girl be?"

Arielle shifted to face her, and the look in Loren's face was intense.

"Well, yes, you do now have me," Arielle said, chuckling.

"Thank you," Loren murmured, sincerely. "It means the world to me." Arielle's lips curved into a happy smile as she turned and headed toward the parking lot with Loren at her heels.

"Loren, don't feel alone," Arielle said. "I remember when it was easy to talk to my mum about every thought and every problem I encountered in my young life." Arielle stopped talking for a short moment and then hmmphed. "One day, I woke up and realized that I was grown up, and things had changed. I was struggling to keep explicit thoughts to myself, unable and totally embarrassed to talk about them. That's where my two best friends Eva and Gabby came in. They became my secret sharers. Their minds became the secret vaults that kept every intimate thought I had safely locked away," she said, and sighed deeply.

They stopped walking again and gazed into each other eyes, and then they hugged warmly.

"I'm thankful to have you in my life," Loren muttered, and Arielle knew she was sincere.

"I feel the same way, Loren; would you like to come by the house for a little while? Sebastian would love to see you. He adores you!"

"I'd love to do that, but only for a short time. I'm meeting Paul around seven thirty." She giggled at the sound of his name just like a little girl, and Arielle felt happy for her.

When they arrived at the house, Sebastian was already there and in the shower. They could hear him joyfully whistling an old tune, and they both laughed out loud.

"There's salve in the fridge, so go ahead and help yourself, and I'll go in and let him know that you're here," Arielle muttered.

Loren turned and walked into the kitchen, and Arielle went into the bedroom calling his name.

Chapter 12

"HI!" SHE CALLED LOUDLY, making sure that he could hear her over his whistling and the running water. She should be used to Sebastian's speed by now, but again she found herself completely struck by how fast he could move. He was out of the shower before she had a chance to draw her next breath. He was standing in front of her completely naked, hot steam filling the room. His beautiful sandy hair was dripping water that slid down his muscled body, pooling onto the floor. Her breath held in her throat, as he was more beautiful that a mythical Greek God.

She had never heard the shower door open, and now she yelped as she found herself lifted up and into his arms. His mouth landed on hers, locking them into a kiss full of passion and hunger. Her pulse quickened, and her heart started to beat wildly. *God, will I ever get over his immortal speed?* She shot him a playful look.

"Mmm…I missed you…" he murmured against her lips as he started to walk back into the shower with Arielle in his arms, still fully clothed.

"No…no…not now," she said, and he stopped. His eyebrows furrowed.

"Why not?" She was so startled she didn't answer him right away, and he started to walk back into the shower.

"Loren is here; she wants to see you," she exclaimed with amusement, and he froze in place. He set her down carefully.

"Oh," it was all he said, looking shocked.

"Look what you've done…" she scolded him softly, looking down at her saturated clothes. "I need to change," she complained, trying to brush the water off of her blouse. "Look at me, I'm completely drenched." He just smiled.

"I'm sorry, baby, I didn't know...." He laughed again as he jumped back into the shower, and she heard his beautiful voice.

"I'll be right out," he mumbled, still laughing. She couldn't hold back a jovial laugh just thinking about his boyish looks, his extraordinary appeal, and the immense affection that filled her heart every time she was near him. She took a dry t-shirt and jeans out of the closet and dressed before walking back into the living room. Loren was standing in front of the huge window with a glass of salve in her hand, staring at the ocean and the remarkable cliffs that hovered over the blue waters.

Her immortal abilities let her know that Arielle was standing right behind her. "What a magnificent sight," she whispered.

"I know," Arielle said. "It's absolutely mesmerizing. The view is what sold me on this house, and I know Sebastian feels the same way." She moved a lot closer, and resting her eyes on Loren's astonishingly beautiful face, she searched for the right words before she asked the question that had been occupying her thoughts for a very long time.

"When are you going to tell Paul?" she finally said.

Loren stilled, silently meeting Arielle's gaze. Her bottom lip was caught between her teeth in pure stress, as her hand shook a little making the salve sway inside the glass from one side to the other.

"I've tried, but I don't seem to find the right words. I'm hopelessly in love with him, and I'm scared that the truth will drive him away."

Arielle hid her smile. *This sounds way too familiar,* she thought and pressed her lips together. She remembered Sebastian's concern about losing her, and later Troy's worry about losing Gabby. "You do have to tell him, Loren," she emphasized. "Paul loves you; he would never leave you. But he should know your true identity."

Loren stood beside Arielle and listened quietly. Mentally, she was trying to formulate the words in her mind that would soften the blow when she divulged her immortality to Paul.

Arielle gave her a side-glance, and she could almost hear her internal battle. She shook her head in frustration and turned her gaze on Arielle. "I know that Sebastian thinks that I fall in love with every guy I date, but believe me, Arielle, I don't. I've never truly loved any man in my long journey on this earth. Paul has giving a new meaning to my life. He's like a priceless gift that I don't want to live without." A long sigh escaped her, and she held Arielle's gaze steadily.

"Loren, I understand your fears, but you must tell Paul who you are," Arielle said once again, emphatically. Looking at Loren at this very moment, she saw Sebastian emotions mirrored on her face. Boring into her eyes, she continued. "Paul and I have talked about this relationship, and I know that Paul's love for you is unbelievable. Remember, Loren, that even though your undying world can be pretty scary for simple humans like us, we are determined to embrace it, because we can't live without you." She stared out the window as she sucked a deep breath. There was a long pause. Loren looked worried; Arielle reached over and took her hand, making her look at her.

"Loren, Paul loves you unconditionally. I'm sure that your true identity will not change the way he feels about you. I'll be here to support you if you need me," she said with a soft smile.

Sebastian cleared his throat, and they both turned to find him leaning against the doorframe. A wide smile was spread across his fabulous face.

"How long have you been standing there?" Arielle asked.

"Long enough." He walked up to Loren and took her in his arms.

"Hi, sis, how have you been?" he asked, and planted a kiss on her cheek, squeezing her tightly and making her giggle.

"I've been busy," Loren replied. "Arielle suggested that I stop by for a little while. I hope you don't mind."

"Mind? How could I possibly mind seeing my favorite sister?" Sebastian said. His lips curved into a startling smile. "Remind me to thank you later." Arielle heard his velvety voice against her ear barely above a whisper. The tone in his voice made her shiver with excitement. She snorted, shaking her head and left the room, letting them spend some time together. She decided to start dinner, so she kept pretty busy until she heard Loren getting ready to leave.

"I'll ring you later," she called out. Arielle walked to the door and stood next to Sebastian. He smiled at Loren and put his arm around Arielle's waist, pulling her closer. She giggled quietly and waved goodbye to Loren.

"I had a great time, Arielle!" Loren called, joyfully. She got into her car and drove off, still smiling. Sebastian pulled Arielle inside and let the front door close behind them. He leaned closer and brushed his lips against her ear, and her breathing accelerated.

"What's wrong?" he purred, and chuckled with amusement. His voice was smooth, filled with desire, making her shiver. She turned to look at his face, and their eyes locked. His gaze revealed a sizzling emotion ready to erupt at any moment.

"Stop," she said, softly. Pulling away, she walked back into the kitchen to finish making her dinner. She was making the salad when he walked in and stood right behind her. She giggled as she felt his arms around her waist, pulling her tightly against him. His warm, wet lips pressed against her neck making her knees quiver. Putting down the salad bowl, she twisted around without leaving his embrace to face him. Reaching up, she searched for his lips.

"Mmm...I missed you," he moaned, and she shivered with anticipation. She could feel the heat of his body, and all she wanted to do was soak in it.

"Me, too," she whispered. Their lips locked in a fevered kiss. His hands moved underneath her shirt, stroking her back and moving lower to caress her hips. Her body quivered under his touch and ripples of excitement ran across her skin. She breathed in his amazing scent and smiled, thinking how happy she was that a man like him wanted to be with her.

"I love you, Mr. Darcy," she murmured, against his lips.

"What am I going to do with you?" he muttered, and she chuckled. She hadn't heard that phrase for over three weeks. She was not surprised to find herself in bed before she could reach her next thought. His immortal speed was still something she was trying to get used to with no success.

"Seriously, Sebastian, you have to stop doing that." She was now lying on her back, as he pressed her down softly with his warm body.

"I don't understand what you mean," he said, and she detected his amusement.

"Your speed makes me dizzy," she gasped. "And..." Her voice trailed as his lips moved slowly down the column of her throat.

"And, what?" he murmured. His gaze intensified, and she almost lost herself in his eyes.

"I...I didn't get to prepare my dinner," she mumbled, "And I'm so hungry." She forced the words to sound nonchalant through a thick cloud of desire.

"So am I," he murmured, chuckling.

"You are?" She met his eyes feeling his gaze scorching her face.

"Yes, I'm very hungry *for you*." His look was one of sheer excitement as he bent down once again and crashed her lips beneath his in a passionate kiss that made her tingle from her head to her toes and spread heat like a tornado across every single fiber of her body. He was an amazing man, and she was happy that he was completely hers. Sebastian released her mouth, and let his ravenous gaze travel leisurely up and down her body. His eyes sparkled with excitement; his lungs locked.

"Mmmm...you are beautiful!" he whispered, and his arms tightened around her. The next couple of hours were filled with rising sensations, mind-blowing pleasure, blistering waves of passion, and thunderous eruptions of bliss. The sobs of ecstasy that escaped her lips stroked the core of his soul making him groan. He purred her name over and over again, capturing her consciousness, her essence, and her soul. They moaned with gratification as they lay breathless, gasping for air, lost in the haze of the aftermath. Sebastian cradled her in his arms, nestling her face in the crook of his arm, and she slid into a serene sleep. Sebastian tilted his head back and peered at her face. Passionate love washed over him; he drew a shuddering breath and grinned. He was happy; Arielle was the most amazing woman he had ever been with. Their love encounters were unbelievable. He pressed a tender kiss on her forehead, and resting back on his pillow, he closed his eyes.

It was twilight when she decided to get up and finish her dinner. She knew he was not going to have anything to eat, but she was starving.

She lifted her head from the pillow, and turning slowly, she gazed into Sebastian's beautiful face. He seemed to be deep in sleep. His eyes were closed, and he was breathing quietly. She let her gaze drink him in and grinned blissfully as she followed the rise and fall of his magnificent, masculine, bare chest. She shook her head trying to put aside her cravings, and gently she eased away from his embrace. She edged herself close to the side of the bed, and just as she tried to sit up, his hands fastened about her waist and he pulled her back into bed.

"Where do you think you are going?" he murmured.

She yelped, startled. "I was going to get something to eat," she whispered, as she tried again to pull away from his steal embrace. He released her reluctantly, and he immediately felt the loss of her warmth. He groaned in frustration, struggling to fight his desire to pull her back into his arms where she belonged. Suppressing the need, he just watched her as she got out of bed, and he drew in a sharp breath.

Pushing her hair away from her face, she looked down at Sebastian, and their gaze locked. She lost her train of thought, and nearly turned around and jumped back into bed, but at the last minute, she changed her mind. Pursing her lips together, she turned and walked into the shower, closing the door behind her, letting a loud sigh escape her. She heard him chuckle just before she turned the water on, and leaning against the tile wall, she remained motionless. The first warm drops hit her skin, and she quivered at the sensation. She wet her hair. Massaging a small amount of shampoo into her scalp, she let her emotions whirl wildly. She thought of how much his love had changed her life. *I don't deserve to be this happy,* she thought as she washed her face. She would never understand how he chose her over the vast amount of perfect women in his immortal world. She dragged in a deep breath and exhaled, shaking her head. It was a while later that she realized she had been standing unmoving under the water, lost in thought about Sebastian's world that she couldn't grasp.

She stepped out of the shower and wrapped a towel around her, and she picked up the hairdryer. She looked into the mirror, and she was startled to find the man of her thoughts leaning against the doorframe, watching her blow dry her hair. Her gaze swept over Sebastian's unclothed, shockingly beautiful body. Heat emanated in her stomach and spread across her skin like fire. The sight of him was quite distracting. His eyes were electric and fervent, and it was wrapped all around her. She groaned quietly and forced the feeling of desire back down her throat.

She finished drying her hair, and when she turned around, he hadn't moved an inch. He was still watching her with the same hunger in his eyes. She walked toward him, a wide smile spread across her face. His arms reached out and wrapped around her waist, pulling her flush against him. The towel dropped onto the floor, and their bodies melted into each other. Arielle threw her arms around his neck, and he moaned with eagerness. His hands stroked her naked body, and their lips locked in a passionate kiss that made her world shudder about her. He deepened the kiss, and she gasped, pressing herself even closer. She parted her lips, and he slid his tongue inside the warmth of her mouth. The sweetness of her mouth sent a delightful sensation deep into his bones. Sebastian groaned as he felt her relaxing in his embraces, and he lifted her in his arms.

She broke the kiss reluctantly and pushed against his chest softly. He let out a soft gasp, and she noticed curiosity lingering in his eyes.

"What's wrong?" he moaned, tightening his hold on her.

"Please, put me down," she murmured, "I'm hungry."

"Mmmm… so am I," he said.

"Stop it; you are always hungry," she scolded him, tenderly. He sighed aloud and put her down. Stepping aside, he let her walk past him. She picked up a clean t-shirt and a pair of shorts and went into the kitchen. She prepared a plate of spaghetti, and, as usual, she was the only one eating tonight. She heard the water running in the shower as she picked up a book and took a seat at the kitchen table. Eating and reading at the same time was something that she enjoyed immensely. She took a couple bites, pulled the book even closer to the plate, and opened it.

The book was by one of her favorite authors, Jane Austen. She was extremely satisfied, getting into the romance of "Persuasion" one more time. Anne Elliot was the heroine of the story, anguished over her enduring love for gorgeous Captain Wentworth. A warm feeling swept over her at the thought of her own Wentworth.

"What are you reading?" He was standing right behind her, his hands resting on her shoulders, his cheek flush against hers.

"Persuasion," she replied.

"Ahhh...another Jane Austin love story."

"Yes, she is my favorite author," she said with a smile.

"I'm completely aware of that," he chuckled, as he put his finger under her chin and lifted her head up to press his lips on hers.

"I know all about your favorite books and your favorite author," he whispered in her ear. "I love you a lot more than Wentworth ever loved Anne, or Darcy ever loved Lizzy," he said, and his eyes glittered. She could feel his body heat through her t-shirt, and she giggled ecstatically. He knew how to say the right thing at the right time. *What an amazing man!*

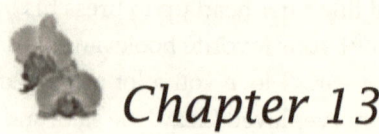

Chapter 13

CLASSES WERE COMMENCING in two weeks. This was the last semester of their senior year. The anticipation of their imminent commencement was overwhelming but also bittersweet. Arielle knew that the university was just a stepping-stone to upcoming achievements in her life. The fear and the excitement of entering the real world that would challenge her in new ways became her daily thought.

She wasn't going to let Sebastian's wealth interfere with her plans. She wanted to embark into that wonderful journey using her own abilities, just like all the other students. This would be the time for her to make a difference and to plunge into new beginnings with hunger and commitment for a better tomorrow. She was planning on reaching for the stars, and she was fixed on that course.

Gabby wasn't going to be able to attend the first two weeks of school; however, there had been an agreement between the Dean of Medicine and her parents. She could attend classes via the Internet and take her tests the same way. They were all delighted that the accident was not going to prevent her from graduating with her senior class.

Troy agreed reluctantly for Gabrielle to move to her parent's home after she left the hospital. She would remain there approximately three weeks, until she was able to care for herself with no assistance. Troy suggested getting her private help at his house, but Gabby thought it would be better this way. She would rather be at home and let her mother provide the care she needed right now.

She left the hospital five weeks following the accident and moved into her old bedroom at her parent's home. Troy was in distress. He missed her terribly. He wanted to take her home, to their home and their bed. He wanted to hold her and love her like he knew she wanted to be held and loved by him. It had been five weeks at the hospital and now another three weeks or more at her parent's home. He wasn't happy at all, and he had a hard time hiding his feelings from Gabby.

It was the second day after she left the hospital, and Arielle was with Gabby in her bedroom when Troy arrived. He smiled at Arielle as he walked by her and embraced Gabrielle, pulling her tightly against his body, locking them into a passionate and zealous kiss.

"Gabrielle," she heard his soft whisper, his lips at her ear. "I'm not going to make it without you for another three weeks. You have to come home. I need you," His voice was full of anxiety.

Gabby was trying to hold back laughter. He looked absolutely pitiful. She wrapped her arms around him and gazed into his beautiful eyes. "I love you, Troy," Gabrielle murmured. "I know that this will be difficult for both of us, but I think this is the right thing to do. I'm not strong enough to be alone, and I can't expect you to be there every moment of every day. My mum is home, and she's delighted to have me here. Take this time and enjoy your books, your work, and our friends. Time will go by faster than you think," she said, smiling softly.

Troy grunted and muttered something inaudible under his breath. He paused for a short moment. Turning, he rested his gaze on Arielle long enough to notice the amusement on her face. He started to say something and suddenly stopped. Arielle wasn't sure what he wanted from her. Eventually, he shrugged his shoulders, and his gaze found its way back to Gabby's smiling face. He leaned in and pressed his lips on hers with obvious hunger.

"I need you. I can't breathe without you," Arielle heard him murmuring in a wretched voice. Arielle chuckled quietly at the remark; Sebastian used that sentence with her, quite often.

"Troy, I'm here, baby," Gabby said trying to remain serious. "I'm not going anywhere." Gabby was having difficulty trying to keep a straight face. This beautiful, incredible, indestructible immortal looked utterly miserable. They were still looking at each other, eyes locked, and expressions fervent. Troy's arms wrapped around her, and Gabby relished the sanctuary of his solid, heartfelt embraces. Troy took a deep breath and surrendered, nodding his agreement to her decision.

"I've never experienced separation pain like this," he said, and he exhaled deeply. "First the hospital, and now your parents' home." The tone of his voice was that of misery and desire.

Listening to Troy's reaction made Arielle smile inwardly. Her attention wandered from Troy to Gabby's thoughts. She could read her mind, and she focused on the turmoil that was consuming her thoughts. She was battling her need for Troy against the need to stay the course and get better with her mother's support. She was sure that her mother's care exceeded any care that a hired nurse could provide for her.

She couldn't read Troy's thoughts, but she was sure that he wanted to protect Gabby and take care of her in their own home. However, he was being a bit selfish, not that Sebastian would react any different if she was in Gabby's shoes.

Arielle smiled. Troy was a warm passionate guy, and she loved him. He had become one of her dearest friends and, in many cases, her protector. She chuckled at the memory of all the occasions that he had saved her life from angry immortals. Both Troy and Gabby turned to look at her inquisitively. She hadn't realized that she had chuckled just a bit too loud. Trying not to cross the line between her amusement and their privacy, she cleared her throat and began a gradual walk toward the other side of the room.

Troy stayed for a while, and it was on his way out that she heard him mumbling something like, "I'll endure." When the door shut behind him, she and Gabby burst out into a hearty laugh.

Gabrielle was really coming along extremely well. Now all the casts were off her limbs, the bruises were going away, and the stitches had been removed. The four and half inches long gash on her thigh was still raw, and she was still experiencing a fair amount of pain. She was on pain pills to be able to tolerate the hurt, and she was taking antibiotics to prevent infection until completely healed.

The doctor said that the gash would mend, and the scar would fade away slowly. But for the time being, she needed to be careful and keep it clean. Her father made sure that she did the right things to become well. She needed to rest and regain her strength. She was having difficulty getting around from being in bed for all these weeks.

Arielle left around two o'clock in the afternoon, and Gabby walked her to the door.

"I thought we were getting married to unbreakable immortals and look what we are getting into." The mirth in her voice as she referred to Troy's earlier scene was evident. Arielle chuckled, nodding in agreement. They hugged, and Arielle promised she was going to visit the next day.

The days seemed to creep along, and time seemed to pass like sand dripping into an hourglass. Troy and Sebastian spent a lot of time at the office, and she spent a lot of time with Gabby at her house.

Eva and Ian were coming home at the end of the next week. Arielle was filled with excitement as she stood in front of her study window and gazed out across the ocean. She couldn't wait to see them. She swallowed hard at the thought and pursed her lips. She simply wondered what they would look like. Would she feel any different around them? Would they have maintained their human sense of humor? Or would she feel awkward around them?

She didn't feel awkward around Sebastian, but she never knew him when he was human, so she had nothing to compare. Would that make any difference when it came to Ian and Eva? She couldn't fully understand the whole thing about immortality. The immortal world was something out of a novel, not real life. But here she was thrust right into the middle of it. She shook her head and shifted from one foot to the other apprehensively.

Her next thought went to Gabby. She would have to be told about Ian and Eva's new identities once she was completely well and back at school. She felt tightness in her throat and drew in a sharp breath. What was going to be her reaction to such incredible news? The last couple months had been an implausible phenomenon. She turned her gaze away from the ocean. Picking up her book, she sat down on the sofa to read and wait for Sebastian to come home.

It was the end of the week when Troy came home with Sebastian, completely distraught. He sank into the chair and dropped his head in his hands, looking completely miserable.

"What's wrong with you?" Arielle asked, shocked by his demeanor.

"Arielle," Troy said. "I don't think I can make it for much longer, I can't sleep, and I can't breathe without Gabrielle by my side. My whole world has turned upside down, and I don't seem to be able to get out of this vicious cycle." She looked up at Sebastian, and he shrugged his shoulders as if he had already tried to get him out his misery but failed. *Here he goes again*, Arielle thought. She moved closer, and putting her finger under Troy's chin, she lifted his face up until their eyes met. She was pretty frustrated with his attitude, and she scolded him cautiously.

"Troy, I love you," she said, with lips pursed long enough to gather the right words to use. "All I can see right now is a very selfish man, a man who only cares about his loneliness and his personal emotions in an obsessive way." She took a deep breath and let go of his chin. "This is the time that you need to be supportive, reassuring, encouraging, and completely understanding of Gabrielle's needs. Don't make her feel guilty by acting like a spoiled little boy. You know that she loves you more than life," she said, clear exasperation in the tone of her voice. She paused, because she did notice that her voice was getting pretty intense, and she saw a docile look in his eyes. Then taking a deep breath, she continued. "You need to get yourself together and make her see that you are happy. Tell her that you support her decision to stay with her parents. She was in the hospital, for God's sake, for five weeks, and you never acted this way."

He was looking at her a little shocked, but she was on a roll. "Now that you both are at the last leg of this horrible experience, you are making it difficult for her. You are this incredible, unbreakable, and amazing immortal, so how come you don't show those powers you possess?" She was looking at him as if she needed an answer, but she didn't wait for one. "Just think how exciting it will be when you take her home and you can let her know how much you have missed her. Think about how scorching that moment will be and stop acting like a child."

He was now looking at her with wide eyes and a stunned look on his face. He pursed his lips. "I...I know that you are right," he said taking a deep breath. "How can a young girl like you that have barely been on this earth for twenty-one years can be so sensible?" He forced a smile, and reaching over, he pulled her down to him and planted a huge kiss on her cheek. She tried to stand up, but Troy held her gaze for a long time as if he was reading her very core.

"Sooo…what did you see in there?" she asked him, exhaling loudly.

"Arielle, you think like an old soul. Has anyone ever told you that?" he asked. She stared at him waiting for more information, but he didn't say anything.

"No…I never heard that before, but I'm open-minded," she said.

"Arielle, you are a wonderful human being, and I'm happy you are in my life," Troy said, smiling. She smiled back at him, as she shook her head and walked away, mumbling under her breath.

"Men…I will never understand you guys." She heard both Sebastian and Troy break out into a hearty laugh. Troy left around six and headed to Gabrielle's house. She stood up and started to walk to the kitchen as Sebastian reached out and pulled her back and held her tight.

"Where do you think you are going? Do you have any idea how much I love you?" he murmured.

"No, not really," she giggled, as his arms pulled her even closer and his lips met hers passionately.

"Can you help me? I need you…"

"With what?" she asked amusingly. Her tongue circled his lip line, and she heard him moan.

"I need you," he gasped again.

"For what?" She tried to hold back laughter, but she failed and he laughed with her. She knew exactly what he wanted and she wasn't wrong as she found herself off the floor and into his arms, heading for the bedroom. She did try to protest, but his mouth found hers, and her objections were muted. Her whole body quivered with excitement, as she was very familiar with his next move.

"Mmm…" She heard him moan without leaving the kiss, and she just melted with anticipation.

Eight days were left before classes would start, and she couldn't get herself motivated to get ready. Ian and Eva were coming back this Saturday, and they had asked for Sebastian and Arielle to pick up them up at the airport. She was panicking as she wasn't sure what to expect following their transformation. She was wondering if their looks

had substantially changed and if she would be getting her best friend
back with no significant differences at all.

Arielle and Sebastian made their way to the airport and waited
where Eva and Ian would be coming out once they had gone through
customs. There wasn't a single soul that didn't turn to stare at the
magnificent looking man that was walking right next to her. She smiled,
as she knew the effect of his stunning looks to human eyes. The plane
landed on time, and Sebastian was completely aware of her anxiety.
He held her close, trying to reassure her that everything was going to
be all right. It wasn't long before they were in plain view, and she knew
he heard her muffled gasp. Her jaw dropped from clear astonishment,
and she swallowed hard.

Two strikingly beautiful people walked towards them with familiar
gaits and wide smiles spread across their faces. She could hear the soft
murmurs their presence created from the bystanders. She was taken
aback by Ian and Eva's looks, but it took only a few seconds and she
reminded herself that they were her best friends. She ran to Eva, and
they held each other in a warm embrace. She could feel the strength
in her arms and the warmth of her body as tears filled her eyes and
she sobbed with excessive passion. She knew that Eva couldn't cry
any longer, and she thought she was sobbing for the both of them.
They had now joined the amazing immortal world, and they looked
like they had just stepped out of another era. Eva's beautiful blue
eyes were sparkling like jewels.

"I love you, Eva. You look absolutely gorgeous," Arielle whispered.

Eva gave her a shy smile. "I love you, too, Arielle. I don't feel
any different, but I know better than that," she whispered back and
chuckled softly. Arielle let go of Eva and fell into Ian's arms, happy
to see him. She yelped blissfully as Ian lifted her of the floor and
twirled her around, planting a kiss on her cheek.

She was not surprised that he picked her up effortlessly, but she
wanted to tease him about his immortal powers. When he set her feet
on the ground, she tilted her head and looked at Ian up and down.
Ian's eyebrow furrowed.

"What?" he asked curiously.

Arielle knew that was a ridiculous question, but she went with it.
"Am I weightless for you now?" Arielle asked suppressing laughter.

"Pretty much!" Ian replied simply.

There was laughter that followed Ian's reply, and Sebastian moved closer to hug Eva and shake hands with Ian.

Ian's looks were magnificent. He was astonishingly beautiful, just like all the other immortals she had met, and God knows, there were plenty. She snickered out loud at the thought, and lifting her head, she noticed that all three of them were watching her.

"What's so funny?" Eva asked.

Arielle shook her head in pure wonder. "You are both stunning," Arielle said. "I'll never get used to the striking immortal looks." Sebastian snaked his arm around Arielle's waist and pulled her tightly against his side, nuzzling her hair.

Arielle snuggled closer and looked up into his eyes. "Do average looking immortals exist somewhere out there?" He lifted an inquisitive brow, and she sighed, shaking her head in utter wonder. Sebastian pulled her around to face him, and peered through her eyes. Arielle gasped at his smoldering gaze and grinned quietly.

"You are stunningly beautiful, and you are not an immortal. How do you explain that?" Sebastian asked, his voice seriously indulgent. She didn't reply to his remark; she just stared, locked into his gaze. He suddenly bent down, and with a quiet groan, he covered her mouth with his, and she lost sense of time.

He finally lifted his head reluctantly and grinned, still keeping their gaze locked. Arielle shivered and tried to regain her self-control. She heard Eva and Ian chuckle, and she averted her gaze to them. She smiled wide, and taking Sebastian's hand, she laced their fingers together and pulled him closer to Eva and Ian.

"I missed you both so very much. How did you like Tuscany?" she asked wanting to know all about their trip.

"Oh Arielle... what a fabulous place! I remember you describing the view from the house over the phone, but I could never imagine the true beauty of such a place," Eva said, and turned to look at Sebastian with a grateful grin on her face.

"Ian and I want to thank you for that amazing piece of heaven you provided for us. Geneva helped us through some shaky moments with extreme care and remarkable understanding. She's a real treasure with immeasurable tolerance and an unfathomable commitment to you," she said.

Sebastian's lips curved to a wonderful smile of contentment. Arielle let go of Sebastian's hand and moved between Eva and Ian. They all left the airport with their arms wrapped around each other in total delight. She had her friends back, and Sebastian could sense her enthusiasm.

"Do you guys feel any different?" Arielle asked, glancing between them, trying to catch a true reaction to her question.

"No, not at all…" Eva said. "To tell you the truth, I'm amazed that I feel this great!" She looked happy and relaxed, completely secure with her new identity.

"And you, Ian?" Arielle turned her attention to Ian and gazed into his beautiful eyes.

"No change at all. Apart from all the extraordinary abilities that we now possess, I don't feel any different. I actually feel great, strong, healthy and utterly in love with Eva." Ian and Eva's eyes met and Arielle could almost feel the warmth, and the deep commitment to each other.

"I missed you, Arielle," Eva's voice was velvety soft, just as Arielle expected it would be.

"I did tell you that Gabby is now at home, didn't I?" Arielle asked in a soft voice.

"Yes, you did tell me over the phone, but I also called her the day before yesterday. She told me that for the first two weeks she is going to attend classes from home. Then she'll be back in class with us. She also told me that Troy is not taking this short separation very well. What's going on with that?"

"Oh… he's just being a little selfish," Arielle said and waved her hand dismissively. "But that's only because he's crazy in love with her. Whoever heard of an immortal throwing fits like a 4 year old?" she snorted and took a deep breath.

She grazed her finger over her dry lips. "I feel like there is an immortal invasion in Brighton, don't you agree?" she said, and glanced between the three of them. She did notice amusement spreading across their beautiful faces, and she flashed them a grin. "Pretty soon there will be just a few of us left," she added, and threw her hands up in the air in defeat. She kept a straight face as the three of them broke out into a hearty laugh, making people around them turn and gawp.

The ride back to their house was a cheerful one. Eva and Arielle took the back seat and never stopped talking. They were totally animated and completely engrossed in their conversation. Sebastian and Ian laughed at some of their wild statements and declarations. It was a heartwarming sight to watch Eva and Arielle lost in the warm of their friendship, that special bond that held them together since they were little girls. They were happy, serene, sitting joyfully together in the back seat.

"I have to tell you, Eva, the first few days were absolutely horrible. I missed you so much, and I was too scared to think about your transformation. I wanted you back with no changes, the same friend I had since fourth grade. I'm tickled to death to find out that you are the same Eva that left here a couple months ago." They were holding each other happily.

"I don't feel any different, and I love you exactly as I did before. You and Gabby are my very best friends. We understand each other's needs, anxieties, and difficulties."

Arielle laughed, knowing that nothing had changed. It was just like old times; they were completely aware of each other. They were comfortable just sitting and talking together.

They were halfway home when Eva edged close and whispered in her ear.

"Do you want to hear something?" she murmured.

"What?" she whispered back eagerly.

"As an immortal, I discovered that the sexual desires are highly elevated."

"How so?"

"On a scale of one to ten, I would say it is ranking at about one thousand." Arielle's eyes widened, and she tried to keep herself quiet by placing her hand over her mouth. They both grinned at each other, and finally broke out into a hilarious laughter, making the guys look back and stare at them.

"What's so funny?" Sebastian asked, but the girls didn't reply. They just kept giggling. Arielle leaned even closer and whispered in Eva's ear.

"I've been utterly fascinated with Sebastian's appetite," she giggled. She reached to the front seat and ran her finger across the side of his beautiful face. She heard him inhale a deep breath, and placing his hand over hers, he stroked the skin with his thumb, making her shiver. Silence fell between them for the next several minutes.

Eva's next statement startled her. "While in Italy, I thought about the time Annabel locked us in that room in St. Jean and left us there to die," Eva groaned.

Arielle shivered, and her smile faded at the sound of Annabel's name. She hadn't thought about her in a while. The fact that Troy, Sebastian, and their friends were looking for her fervently around the world had kept Annabel out of Arielle's mind. She was sure that Annabel would surface sooner or later, but she hoped that it would be much later. Eva paused, and her eyes searched Arielle's face.

"I can assure you that the result would be much different today, don't you think?" Eva added, and made a smooth slicing motion with her hand across her neck, let out a hearty laugh. Eva's facial expression and clenched fists told Arielle that Eva's next meeting with Annabel was going to be brutal. Images of Eva and herself locked in that small stifling room flashed through her mind and made her shiver. Eva sensed Arielle's fear, and reaching over, she clasped her hand protectively.

"Don't worry, Arielle. I'm here, and I'll protect you," she said firmly, and smiled softly. More silence followed, and all Arielle could think of was Annabel. She pursed her lips and gazed at Eva quietly.

"I'd like to cross paths with that bitch now," Eva pressed on. She frowned inwardly, but she managed to keep a smile on her face. Arielle pushed her hair away from her face anxiously and got lost in thought.

"We're here." Ian's voice broke her out of her reverie. They were in fact parked right outside Ian and Eva's home. They climbed out of the car and exchanged hugs, promising that they would be getting together and have a couple of nights out before classes begin. Ian and Eva thanked Sebastian once again for the great trip, and standing at the threshold, they waved goodbye as Sebastian and Arielle walked back to the car.

Chapter 14

SEBASTIAN HELD THE DOOR OPEN for her, watching her perch herself in the passenger seat. He shut the door and walked around slowly, keeping his gaze on her as a soft smile outlined his lips. He slipped into the driver's seat, and before he even pulled away from the curb, he started his relentless inquiries about her conversation with Eva.

"What was all that whispering about?" Sebastian pressed on.

She held up a staying hand. "Sebastian, I know you heard every word of it, so why are you asking?"

"I heard the words, but I want to hear them from your lips, and as you very well know, as long as you wear that necklace, I can't read your thoughts."

She grinned, recalling Eva's comment. She clammed up, though, refusing to talk about it. He paused for a short period of time; his gaze flicked to her several times. She was a little more than shocked to feel his hands behind her neck, ready to unclip her necklace. *God...how does he do that?* She never saw him move. Instantly, she brought both hands up, clutching her necklace tightly, pressing it against her body. She exhaled forcefully. She pushed him softly away and shook her head frustrated.

"Sebastian, please keep your hands on the wheel. You are going to run off the road. Do you want to get me hurt?" She let out a deep sigh. "Sebastian, you don't need to do this; you don't need to know every little thing I am thinking about," she said defiantly. She turned away from him and gazed out the window.

"Oh…" She heard his velvety voice, feeling the weight of his gaze encircling her. "I thought there weren't going to be any secrets between us." She pressed her eyes shut, and she knew that he was right; there were no secrets between them. That was a commitment they made to each other a long time ago. She turned, and their eyes met. He held an easy smile on his face as he leaned in and pressed his lips softly on hers. The heat of his gaze enfolded her, and the touch of his lips spread passion across her veins. He was the only man in her life that could provide this splendid desire.

"All right, I'll tell you." Their eyes met, and she wanted him to see that she was regretting the fact that she had to tell him every little detail of her conversation with Eva, and her thoughts on the subject. "Well you heard what Eva said about the infinite sexual desires that immortals have." She lowered her gaze, and she heard him laugh quietly.

She lifted her head slowly; he was grinning, waiting for a reply. "I told her that I wasn't an expert about the immortal desires; however, I was completely aware of your limitless needs." He reached over, putting his finger under her chin. He lifted her face to meet his narrowed eyes.

"Are you saying that I want you more than I should?"

She swallowed hard. "Jeez, Sebastian. Yes…that's exactly what I'm saying; however, I didn't say that I don't like it." She took his hand away from her chin and placed it over her heart.

"Can you feel my heartbeat going wild?" she asked, watching him carefully.

"Yes," he moaned, quietly.

"Sebastian, you are the only person on this earth that can elevate my heartbeat. But your needs seem astounding to a person like me." She tried to enunciate each and every word. He switched his gaze from the road to her, and his eyes scrutinized her face.

"Do you want me to change?" he murmured, piercing through her eyes.

"No…I don't want you to change a single thing about you. I love you just as you are, and for whom you are." She took a quick breath, and she noticed a flash of relief spread across his face.

"However, I do have a question," she said.

"Anything," he replied, as he pulled up to a red light and stopped.

"Does the fact that you have an unending desire for me come from being an immortal, or something else?"

"Arielle...I don't know exactly how it works," he replied, frustration etching his face. He leaned in and kissed her quickly as the light turned green, and he pushed on the gas.

"I never felt the same desire about any other woman. I just don't seem to be able to keep my hands off of you. I know I want you every moment of every day, and I would absolutely go out of my mind if I couldn't have you." He exhaled deeply keeping his eyes on the road. "It's a lot more than just sexual desire. It's the endless and passionate love I hold for you. I'm also sure that being an immortal makes the passion and the need stronger, limitless, vigorous, and unrelenting." His frustration was evident.

She let out an audible sigh and leaned in, searching for his lips. He moved the car slowly to the side of the road and stopped. He locked them into a passionate kiss. Drawing back a fraction, enough for her to feel his lips clinging to hers, he moved in again with the same passion as she was struggling to catch her breath.

"What are you doing to me?" he murmured, frustrated, without breaking the kiss, his moan full of his yearning for her. She broke the kiss and chuckled. He was amazing. He was sexy, and her tension soared, thinking that he was all hers.

"Sebastian, you have to admit that you have limitless needs," she murmured. He nodded in agreement as he pushed on the gas and merged back into the traffic. He fell quiet through the rest of the ride home as he kept his gaze fixed on the road and his hand on the wheel. She couldn't tell if he was trying to cool off or if something else was going on. She could hear him sigh several times, taking deep breathes in between. He pulled into the garage and came around to open her door. Stepping out of the car, she smiled wide and fell into his arms.

His arms snaked around her waist, and drawing her closer, his hands stroked her back gently. Her heart raced. Sliding her hands around his neck, she snuggled even closer, savoring the sanctuary of his embrace. His lips brushed against her ear, and his tongue moved from her lobe down to her jaw, across her collarbone, and settled back on her lips. His fingers tightened around her back. Tilting his head, he deepened the kiss, sending ripples of heat sensation across her skin.

He lifted his head and breathed. "Do you want me to stop?"

His breath was warm against her skin, his expression fraught. "I don't want to push myself on you, Arielle." He then pulled back and, without warning, his hands dropped to his side. Her knees gave in, and the floor shifted underneath her feet. If not for the car door, she would've collapsed onto the floor. She swayed back and forth, trying desperately to hold herself upright. She saw a flash of satisfaction cross his eyes, but it disappeared just as fast as it came.

His gaze left her face, and turning away, he walked into the house, never looking back. Arielle stayed frozen, holding on to the car door, completely numb, searching her mind for answers. *What in bloody hell was that for?* Tears welled up, realizing that he had done that on purpose. He was obviously upset with her, but why? She swallowed hard, pushing back the lump that was climbing slowly up her throat. She closed the car door and walked into the house.

What in the bloody hell? She felt moisture on her face and tasted the familiar salty flavor on her lips. She walked into the bedroom, shut the door behind her, and threw herself on the bed. Her mind was spinning; her body was feeling the aching need for his touch. The emotions of rejection and unfulfilled passion were overwhelming. She closed her eyes and tried desperately to recall details of her conversation with Sebastian. She was completely baffled as to what was so bloody bad, that had him so distraught?

When she opened her eyes, the room was completely dark except for the vague light from the digital clock on the nightstand. The eerie quietness of the house was deafening. She tried to think and realized that somewhere in the midst of her thoughts, she had fallen asleep. She wasn't sure for how long, but she knew that she needed to get herself out of bed. Suddenly, a single thought made her body stiffen. Sebastian! Where was Sebastian? She tried to listen for any noise, but there was absolute silence. Her eyes stung and her face was aching. She reached up and pressed her eyes softly with her palms and felt moisture. *Oh, my God, I've been crying in my sleep,* she thought, surprised. She wiped her eyes and pressed her hands hard against her cheeks, trying to wake up. She had to find Sebastian.

She jumped out of bed, heart thrashing, blood racing, anxiety rising. She flipped the light switch so fast that its brightness blinded her. She reached up, and she cupped her hands over her eyes and waited for a couple of minutes. She wondered where he was and why he was so upset with her. She tried to remember if she had said something that hurt his feelings, but she was sure she hadn't.

She slipped on a camisole and walked into the kitchen. The house was illuminated by a gorgeous full moon that nestled right in the middle of a lucid gray sky. She took a bottle of water out of the fridge and spotted his silhouette sitting on a bench in the garden, staring out towards the ocean. She couldn't believe that he had been out there all this time. She took a swig of water and made her way outside, stopping right in front of him. She was determined to get this issue resolved.

"Hi…" she said softly. He raised his gaze to meet hers. He wasn't smiling, and she could sense sadness that was spread across his beautiful face. She reached and cupped his face, locking her gaze with his.

"What's wrong, baby? Why are you so mad at me?" Her voice was cracking as her heart was breaking. He continued to watch her silently.

"Sebastian, I love you; you are hurting me with your silence," she whispered. "I don't know what I did to make you so upset. I need for you to tell me." She let go of his face. Taking a deep breath, she sat on his lap, wrapping her arms around his neck. He didn't put his arms around her, he remained quiet, unmoved.

"Please… talk to me," she pleaded again. She heard him sigh, and his beautiful velvety voice caressed her ears.

"Arielle, I think that you are tired of me, and I'm devastated," he murmured. She cleared her throat, lifted his chin and leaned in. Her tongue circled his mouth, and parting his lips, she pressed in with clear hunger, passion and want. Her hands caressed the planes of his back, pulling him closer, and her kiss became hotter as her heart picked up speed.

"I love you, Darcy," she murmured, without breaking the kiss.

"I need you right now." It took but a short second, and she felt his arms encircling her and pulling her even closer. She heard him moan, and she felt his excitement, and she knew she wanted him more than she ever did before.

"Are you sure?" His voice was completely out of breath.

She reached to the back of her neck and unclipped the necklace, as his eyes watched closely.

"You tell me," she whispered, her lips curved up in a smile full of desire and her eyes filled with longing and anticipation.

She yelped, overwhelmed by his speed. He had risen to his feet with Arielle in his arms, taking her breath away. She found herself on their bed before she could take her next breath. His eyes were intense, his gaze sweltering against her skin, and his smile a perfect conductor of heat. His arms were securely fastened around her body, and her heart was pounding in her chest like a hammer. His mouth was hot and wet, and she could taste his immortal sweet scent. He groaned as their bodies merged together, and she moaned imploringly as his body was pure stimulation. This time, she took over and made him cry out. She looked at his face, and his eyes were closed tightly as his expression showed intense satisfaction. She reached for his mouth, and his tongue tasted like honey. The climax was pure ecstasy that traveled through their bodies at supersonic velocity and created frantic ripples of scorching heat as their lips remained locked in fulfillment.

"How could you ever think that I had a problem with this?" She chuckled, his arms still holding her tightly against his amazing body. His lips curved up to that familiar smile, and she felt complete. His next statement caught her by surprise.

"Arielle, I'm worried that you'll change your mind, and you'll not marry me. I'm warning you that I'll never let that happen. You have accepted my ring, and you have made a commitment."

"Seriously, Sebastian, what is going on with you tonight? Why would I ever change my mind? I love you!"

"I'm warning you...Lizzy." The smile never left his face.

"If you were not smiling, I would think you were serious." She rolled on her back and stretched, and she laughed thinking how unbelievably wild her life had turned out to be. The most astonishing-looking man jealous of her... She chuckled, pulling herself closer to his glorious body. She was unable to sleep any other way but enfolded in his arms. He held her just like he did every night before they drifted off to sleep.

The next few days, they focused, preparing for the upcoming classes. She tried to grasp the reality of a last semester. Why did they even bother to prepare? Conceptually, they had been ready for this for the past four years.

This was the last semester before commencement, before they received their bachelor's degrees! *How wild is that?* But having the end result within their grasp was an adrenaline rush of enormous proportions.

This last week, spending quality time with Gabby was part of their daily activities. They were delighted to see her looking better and better with each day that went by. Troy spent every possible moment he could with Gabrielle. Arielle and Sebastian spent a couple of amazing evenings with Eva, Ian, Loren, and Paul. They went out to some of their favorite restaurants for dinner, saw a couple new films, and visited their usual nightclubs. This was something they hadn't done in a very long time. They wanted to have a little fun before they buckled down. *At least I have to buckle down to get through the last semester. Not Sebastian,* she thought. The gang was thrilled to be together again, but they did miss Troy and Gabby. They all agreed to wait for Gabrielle to completely heal before they dropped the bomb on her about Eva and Ian's transformation.

A soft kiss, a warm squeeze, and a velvety voice were her alarm clock on the first day of school. She turned to her side to face him. Her eyes met a warm deep emerald gaze, and a striking smile.

"Good morning, sleepy face," he greeted, pressing his lips to hers, gently. She stretched sluggishly and sighed as his arms slipped underneath her back, pulling her closer to his warm body.

"Good morning, Darcy," she moaned, moving into him, and she heard him sigh. He leaned in and kissed her again, this time longer and with passion. She pulled back gently, and their gaze locked. Her heartbeat elevated, and every thought in her head came to a screeching stop. She just wanted to stay in his arms forever.

"We need to get moving; you don't want to be late on the first day back to class, do you?" he murmured, still kissing her.

"Okay." She stretched her arms above her head, still holding him to that kiss and moaned provocatively, pressing her body firmly against his.

"Arielle, seriously, you need to get up." She pulled back reluctantly, keeping a frown on her face. Getting out of bed, she walked slowly toward the bathroom. She heard him chuckle with satisfaction. She stopped moving and drawing a deep breath, she turned to face him. He was still sitting on the bed naked, looking gorgeous, hands resting palms down on the bed.

Desire was clear in his eyes, lighting them from beneath. Her heart skipped a beat at the way his lips were parted, waiting for hers to meet them. The surge of heat burned her skin and caused parts of her body to tingle in anticipation. Only a second passed before she sprinted back to him. Jumping onto the bed, she threw herself against him, pushing him flat to the bed.

Her movement shocked Sebastian, but he quickly recovered. The laugh he shouted to the room assured her that she'd made the right decision as he lifted her off the bed. The speed with which he moved left her breathless. His immortal reflexes were beyond the ability of human sense to comprehend.

Before she could blink, she stood in the shower alone, water running, totally stunned. She gulped a mouthful of air, and she stood very still trying to recover. She could still hear his hearty laughter in the bedroom and pursed her lips, wishing that she had a bit more control over her emotions. Fifteen minutes later, she walked out of the shower and put on a pair of jeans and light blue silk blouse. She dried her hair quickly and pulled it up into a ponytail. She took a last look in the mirror and stepped out of the bedroom.

She walked into the kitchen. While she'd been showering, he'd dressed in a pair of jeans that defined his perfection and a light green shirt that highlighted his emerald eyes. He was holding two pieces of buttered toast in his hands and a great big smile that made her weak in the knees. He set the toast on a plate, pulling her so close that her breath hitched. His tongue parted her lips, claiming what he was sure was his.

"You must eat something before we go."

She took a deep breath and cleared her throat, trying and cool off the nerves in her body that his touch had jolted awake in a crashing heat wave. He pulled back giving her room to reach the table, but the smile of deep satisfaction on his face didn't escape her. She knew he loved the power he held over her. He could turn her world upside down with just one finger, and she was fine with that.

"Thank you for breakfast," she said with a smile. She took a piece of toast from the plate and bit into it, chewed, and swallowed.

"Mmm...it's awfully good; where did you learn how to cook?" she asked, amused, before breaking into a blissful laugh. He joined in as she put the rest of the toast in her mouth and held it between her teeth while reaching into the fridge to pour a glass of milk.

Soon, they were on the way to school. His gaze swept over her and his lips curved up to that so familiar smile. He took her hand and placed it on his thigh and held it there by putting his hand on top of hers.

"Maybe you were right," he said. "Maybe we should turn around and go back home. It'll be nearly impossible to sit next to you and not be able to touch you." She laughed quietly with him, but she kept her eyes on the road without responding to his comment. She could see the buildings of the university spread across the land in the near distance. She could see the tall residence buildings reaching towards the gray morning sky. Her thoughts went to Gabby, and she tensed, sighing softly. He felt her tension and pressed her hand, nothing escaped this amazing immortal.

"What is it?" he asked softly. She pursed her lips and turned to gaze at him. His eyes were luminous but curious.

"I was thinking about Gabby and...." She trailed off, feeling a bit stressed.

"What about Gabrielle?" he pressed on, keeping his eyes on her instead of on the road. He always scared her when he did that, but somehow he could drive extremely well even with his eyes closed. She dragged in a deep breath.

"It'll be extremely strange without Gabby at school," she said, her words barely audible. "This will be the first time since primary school that we are not going to be together." She bit her lower lip and smiled bitterly.

"Arielle, you can visit with Gabrielle after class. She is fine!" he said softly. "She'll be back in class before you know it." He pressed her hand again with certainty. He was right, and she needed to snap out of this trivial mood.

The first day back was surreal. They didn't need to have to worry about setting the tone for the rest of the semester. They already knew each professor's course expectations and their standards. The only excitement was seeing and being with their friends. The accident was pretty much the center of discussion, but everyone was extremely pleased that the outcome was good. Gabrielle and Troy were awfully missed, but they would be back in a couple weeks.

Chapter 15

ARIELLE WAS AWARE that school was boring Sebastian to death. But each day she watched him attend classes and take a seat next to her attentively, joyfully, without complaining. She loved him deeply, but she found that type of action disconcerting. Five centuries of matriculating would become dismal. She begged him to skip the last semester, but he wouldn't hear of it.

She was his remedy, his compulsion, and she provided him with a sense of ease that was overpowering. He wanted to protect her and make sure that she was safe.

Arielle wasn't sure if she should feel pleased or unhappy about all the attention, but she didn't try very hard to change his mind. His presence was like the air she needed to be able to breathe. She was exultant to know that he was there only for her. There was nothing in this world that could compare to the feeling of walking through campus next to a man like Sebastian with their fingers intertwined. They had this special connection that ignited passion between them. Every day she rode a perpetual merry- go-round made out of Sebastian's emotions, feelings that tantalized her and filled her with gentleness, thoughtfulness, passion, and adoration.

She was the envy of many females around campus who didn't try to hide their feelings. A few times, his admirers were so blatant in their attention that they begged Sebastian for a date in front of Arielle, as though she were invisible. If he hadn't dismissed each proposal politely while making it obvious that Arielle was his only love, she may have become jealous.

This last semester she was taking chemistry, design & technology, biological science, and physics. She was finished with the other courses that were required for her Bachelor's degree.

Second period was Physics with Professor Mayfield. He was one of her most favorite professors, and she enjoyed his sessions immensely. She walked with Sebastian through the auditorium doors and paused, trying to locate two seats together. She wanted to sit next to Sebastian; unfortunately, nearly every seat was taken. She gazed up at him and pressed her lips together filled with anxiety. He smiled, and she frowned in response. They would have to sit not only in separate seats but also in separate rows. She wasn't happy at all, and she didn't bother to hide her disappointment. Sebastian leaned closer, and she heard his velvety voice filled with mirth.

"If you didn't take your time in bed this morning, this could have end up a little differently."

"I don't regret a moment of it," she muttered. She knew he was right, but she wasn't going to admit it. She leaned closer to him. "I love being in bed with you," she added, squeezing his hand. They climbed the steps of the auditorium and found an aisle seat next to Danielle. She was one of their dear friends Damien Sander's girlfriend.

"You take this seat," Sebastian said, and she nodded.

"Sebastian, Arielle!" They heard a low voice and looking up they saw two more of their friends-- Alex Durand and Robert Gibson-- waving a few rows higher, motioning to Sebastian to take the vacant seat next to them. She waved back with a smile, and Sebastian nodded in agreement. Just before he walked away, he lifted his hand up to trail the side of her face with his warm fingers. Her skin blushed with excitement, and she pressed her lips together, knowing that she was going to miss holding his hand through the class. He smiled softly, gazing over her face. "Miss me!" She sighed as she watched him walk up a few steps and take a seat next to Alex. She turned around and sunk quite unhappy onto her seat.

"He is a real knock out!" she heard a woman in the row behind her say.

"Yeah! He is pretty hot!" another voice whispered. Arielle pressed her lips together in anger, or maybe jealousy.

"Hi, Arielle," Danielle's voice had a pleasant tone.

She turned and smiled, truly pleased to see her. She was a real sweetheart. They had become friends during their first year at the university.

"Hi, Danielle, how are you?"

"Fine," she replied with a soft smile.

"How are you getting along with Damien?"

"Oh, pretty well, we decided to live together. We rented a flat very close to campus, this way we can walk to class and save money on gas," she said.

"That sounds great!" Arielle looked back, meeting Sebastian's gaze, and she felt herself lured toward his warmth. She sent him a wishful smile in return and settled back into her seat. This was going to be a very long session.

"Did you see the new professor?" Danielle voice broke her out of her reverie.

"What?" She averted her gaze swiftly down to the platform in total shock. She narrowed her eyes and racked her fingers through her hair.

"Who is he?"

"I don't know; he must be Professor Mayfield's replacement," Danielle said.

"What do you mean replacement?" Her eyes widened, revealing surprise. "What happened to Professor Mayfield?"

"I heard that he was in a serious accident during our summer break, and he will not be teaching the rest of this year," Danielle confided.

"Oh..." Arielle's expression went blank, and she pursed her lips. "Crap!" Quickly she fished her phone out of her pocket and text Sebastian.

"OMG. Did you hear that Professor Mayfield had an accident?!"

"Yes." he texted back,

"How did you know?"

"I heard Danielle telling you ;)."

Arielle snorted, realizing the idiocy of her question. Sebastian's immortal hearing traveled at a subluminal velocity. He could hear a pin drop on the grass. She turned meeting his gaze. His head cocked to the side, his hand rubbing his chin, and a playful smirk on his beautiful lips. *Will I ever be able to have a private conversation with someone? Of course not!* Not as long as Sebastian was around. She frowned and turned back to face the platform.

She wasn't very good with changes, and she certainly was not happy about this change. She took a deep breath, jaw clenched, and pushed her hair off her face. Her thoughts were drifting into unfamiliar territory. This was one of the most important classes this semester, and it was critical that she had a good rapport with the professor. How could see do that with someone she had never met before, especially if he didn't know anything about her or her qualifications.

She was startled by Danielle's exclamation.

"Jeez! Arielle! Let me see your ring! Gosh it's gorgeous!" she exclaimed with a low gasp. She reached over and gently pulled Arielle's hand closer to take a better look at her engagement ring.

"That's some kind of a rock," she exclaimed. "It sure looks very expensive."

Arielle eyed her ring and winced. She pulled her hand away from Danielle's and placed it on her lap. "Don't talk about that," she said sternly. "I don't care about the monetary value of the ring." Danielle didn't seem to be affected by the harshness in Arielle's voice. There were certain things that got under Arielle's skin, and placing monetary worth on an item was one of them. She didn't like to talk or even think about Sebastian's wealth. "It's the meaning behind the ring, not the price," she muttered, trying to soften the severity in her voice.

"I agree," Danielle asserted. "But you have to admit that this diamond is too darn large!"

Arielle shot a thankful glance at Danielle and concentrated on the new Professor. He was still busy looking down and shuffling papers. Her mind wondered aimlessly for a few minutes. Sebastian's face brought her thoughts to a screeching hold. She couldn't help the brilliant smile that split her face. A smoldering heat traveled like fire across her body, and she tried to control her breathing. How in the world could he have such an astounding affect on her even when he wasn't near? She closed her eyes and her lips kicked up into a dazzling smile. Danielle's voice startled her.

"When is the big day?"

Arielle scoffed…she was sure that Sebastian was listening to every single word of their conversation. That was one of his immortal gifts. *I'll never able to have a private conversation as long as Sebastian is somewhere in the vicinity,* she thought. She could feel the weight of his gaze on her back. She turned and smiled at Danielle, giving her a vague reply.

"We haven't set a date," she said. She closed her eyes and sighed. When she opened them again, she focused at the tall posture of the man that was facing away from them and wondered what he actually looked like. He was holding a book in his left hand, and he was still busy flipping through the pages. She was sure that he was waiting for everyone to settle down before he addressed the class.

"Did you notice the changes on Professor Mayfield's desk?" Arielle's eyes followed where Danielle was pointing to the desk at the corner of the platform. Normally, the surface of Mayfield's desk would be cluttered with physics books, articles, and loose papers that covered every available surface, towering centimeters above the desk in places. But that was not the case today. This desk was perfectly organized, not a single item out of place. Several books were stacked perfectly, one on top of the other, and no loose papers were anywhere to be seen.

A large book was open at the top of the podium, and the stranger continued to stand with his back to the classroom. He didn't have white hair like Professor Mayfield, and he didn't wear a suit. This man was much taller, quite muscular, and dressed in casual attire. He looked more like one of the students than a professor. By the time she finished her thoughts, he had succeeded in completely filling the slate with formulas, mathematical expressions of physical concepts, and symbols.

Leaning forward, she waited to finally see their new professor. When he turned to face them, she was taken aback. He was quite young, in his mid-thirties, and very handsome. His hair was black, falling carelessly over his forehead. His gentle features complemented his full mouth, bowed perfectly in the center. One thing was certain; she hadn't seen him anytime during her four years here.

Though she had long ago adjusted to the perfection of immortal features, she found herself admitting that he was handsome for a professor. The light at the podium reflected his eyes when he shifted ever so slightly and looked up at the auditorium. She was sitting close enough to notice that they were deep, deep blue with a definite appeal that was very hard to ignore. She thought she stared at him for a very long time, and she had some difficulty listening to his instructions.

"Good morning, class." The baritone was just right for an early morning on a Monday.

"My name is Professor Allworth," he said. There was confidence and poise in his voice that was hard to disregard. "I've been assigned to teach this class in Professor Mayfield's absence. He'll be away for the rest of the semester for personal reasons." Walking around the podium, he stood in front of the first row of desks.

"I need for each one of you to touch the screen in front of you and key in your full name. Then, hit send and clear. This will consign your names and positions to my personal screen at the podium. I find this extremely helpful in becoming familiar with your names and faces. If you ever have to change your position, please repeat the same steps so I don't get confused. I'll give you five minutes to complete the task. Starting now."

Arielle keyed her name in and hit send. She looked back at Sebastian, and he had already finished also. Noticing her attention on him, he winked and motioned for her to turn back around.

Professor Allworth's voice brought her to reality.

"I'll not be lecturing and assigning work for you to take home. There'll be actual interaction among all of us in this class, and it will be based on the day's theory or problem. We'll resolve all your concerns before you leave this class." He paced back and forth while he took a couple of deep breaths and continued. "There will be six tests throughout this semester, excluding your final, and they will be administered at my discretion. You can't miss any of those tests or you will fail the class. If you miss two days of this class, you will be dropped a letter grade. I want to make sure that we are clear on my instructions and that there are no misunderstandings." He now looked down at the screen on the podium and paused for a few minutes.

She couldn't believe that he took the time to go around the auditorium and call the name of each and every single person to confirm that his instructions were understood. He then moved to the board and started to discuss the fundamental theories of physics. She happened to be good in physics, and she had been over the quantum physics, relativity theory, and statistical and nonlinear dynamics, so she was losing interest in his lecture fast.

She turned carefully back and looked at Sebastian rolling her eyes, and she could almost hear his silent chuckle. He lifted his eyebrow, as if he was wondering about her state of mind. She was bloody sure that he knew his presence was turning her world upside down, but he was toying with her. He had been her whole world since the day they met on the beach over a year ago. She was trying hard to dismiss his perfect image from her thoughts; it was rousing sizzling sensations across her body.

She was used to some private daydreaming in Professor Mayfield's class. He used a large portion of his time for lectures. He left the total responsibility in their hands to pay attention, absorb, and learn. He concentrated on facts and used part of his time for conceptual questions to make their brains work, searching for answers that were factual recalls from previous discussions. He had called it an excellent way for mind discipline.

She had a system for daydreaming during his lectures, and her mind fell into the old pattern. She pushed away the flood of her classmate's thoughts that invaded her head, some happy and some worried. She successfully placed them in the part of her head that she created for that purpose alone. Now, she moved to her own personal dream world, clearly disconnected from her surroundings in mind and soul. She was in another place, a magical place with only Sebastian. A wide smile had spread across her face, reflecting the wild thoughts that were swirling in her head. She closed her eyes, trying to enjoy the images that were making her skin prickle with sheer excitement.

"Miss Lloyd!" The voice was thunderous. Her eyes snapped open, and she was horrified to see Professor Allworth standing a few centimeters away from her. His blue eyes were glaring into her eyes, and her body began to feel numb, like she was being pulled hard by a strong magnet into that deep, dark blue whirlpool in his eyes. She blinked, shocked, and pressed her lips together in distress.

"Yes?" she managed to say. Her voice came out quivering.

"Am I boring you, Miss Lloyd?" he asked, using the same forceful tone.

She gulped, swallowing a mouthful of air. "No. No, sir..." Her voice trailed. She pulled her book up against her chest and hugged it tightly. She lowered her eyes, unwillingly to meet his gaze. Blood thrashed in her temples, and she prayed that she could get through this without bursting into tears.

His eyes were piercing, making her extremely nervous, and his lips curved into a contemptuous smile. She lowered her gaze, wishing that the humiliation would stop. Rage was slowly replacing her apprehension, and she wanted to strike back.

"Miss Lloyd! Am I boring you?" he pressed on. The whole room went quiet; you could hear a pin drop.

"A little," she replied defiantly, and her voice echoed across the room. She heard quiet mirth move across the auditorium. She lowered the book that she was hugging tightly against her chest and set it on her lap. She lifted her head slowly and glared directly into his eyes.

He had grown completely silent. His gaze had moved from her face to her neckline, and she noticed a hint of shock in his eyes. She knew that her blouse had a low cut in the front, but not low enough to shock or piss off anyone. *What is his problem?* He seemed to be having difficulty expressing whatever he was going to say. There was a resounding silence. Everyone's eyes were now on Allworth, who looked mystified.

She bit her lower lip and kept her gaze fixed on him unwaveringly; she was ready to stand her ground for as long as it took. The short period of silence seemed like a century to her. She heard a soft murmur again moving across the auditorium. It wasn't long before he broke away.

He shook his head, turned around, and walked down the steps to reach the podium in complete silence. He fumbled with his papers for a second. Then, he slowly looked up at her; she noticed the way his expression had changed from mockery to one of surprise.

"Miss Lloyd, please try to pay attention." She could see a concerned expression on his face, but she was sure she was mistaken. She pressed her lips together and dropped her head in her hands. She was so embarrassed and worked to swallow her humiliation. She hauled a huge breath feeling suffocating, trying to get as much air as she could in her lungs. She sighed and leaned back in her seat.

Danielle leaned closer and whispered quietly. "Seriously, what was all that about?"

Arielle shrugged her shoulders, and they both chuckled quietly. It had been a couple of minutes and Professor Allworth was still scanning through his papers. The last time he had said anything was for her to pay attention.

Jane, an old friend since primary school, was sitting directly behind Danielle and leaned forward.

"What in bloody hell is he doing?" Looking directly at Arielle, she nudged her shoulder with her finger and chuckled. "What did you do to him, Arielle? He looks shaken up."

"I'm sure I've no idea what you are talking about," Arielle said, quietly.

Jane leaned closer and whispered in her ear, "Something happened to change his demeanor. Couldn't you see it?" The girl was trying hard to hide her amusement.

Arielle bit her tongue against the overpowering urge to say something unpleasant to Jane, but she fought the words back.

She tried to imagine Sebastian's thoughts. Was he amused or shocked over her ridiculous interaction with Allworth. He was probably amused. She heard professor Allworth clear his throat, and his voice came out sturdy and firm

"I expect you to review the first three chapters. Next class, we will discuss each theory in detail. That's all for today." He collected his papers and moved them from the podium to the desk and took a seat behind it. The room started to clear slowly; Arielle waited for Sebastian to come down to her row before she made an effort to stand up.

"See you later, Arielle," Danielle and Jane called as they made their way down the steps towards the exit. It wasn't long before Sebastian was standing next to her. He leaned down, took her hand, and pulled her up into his arms. The warmth of his embrace brought her senses into the familiar sanctuary that she needed so much right now. She pulled herself even closer, as he bent down and pressed his lips on hers quickly.

"I love that fire in you," he chuckled without breaking the kiss. She pulled back and smiled.

"You got me in trouble. I was daydreaming about you," she said, and he laughed in clear pleasure.

"I wish you could understand how much I love you," he murmured brushing his lips against her ear. They walked down the steps with their arms around each other. She couldn't help gazing up at Professor Allworth, as they walked in front of his desk. She was taken aback again to find him gazing at her with a perplexed look on his face. He then turned to look at Sebastian for a very short second before immediately averting his gaze back to her. She gulped and moved closer to Sebastian, and she felt his arm tightening around her as they walked out the door.

"I wonder what there is about you that made him so bewildered," Sebastian said, face expressing curiosity. He seemed to be thinking and frowned. He couldn't read the professor's mind and that was pretty strange.

"I thought you might tell me," Arielle said, glancing up at him. "Can't you read his mind?" She was now eager for some kind of answer. Sebastian shook his head, brow raised higher, obviously pretty baffled.

"I did try to hear his thoughts, but I all I could get was complete silence." He let out an exasperated sigh. She did notice concern cross his eyes.

"That's weird. I don't understand. How can that be possible?" She took a deep breath and exhaled slowly. "I thought you could read everyone's mind with no exceptions," she murmured keeping her voice soft, gaze focused on his. She noticed tension spreading across his face. He paused and then shook his head completely stumped.

"Arielle, there is something perplexing about Professor Allworth, and I don't like it," he mumbled. "I can't read his mind..." his voice trailed. "And he's not an immortal. The silence of his mind is a huge puzzle for me. I'm not sure what the significance of this could possibly be, but I don't like it," he pressed on, clearly frustrated.

"I'm wondering why he was so bothered by your presence?" he murmured. "It was obvious to everyone in class that something about you got him completely disturbed."

"Well, maybe he finds me irresistible," she chuckled, meeting his gaze. She saw a soft smile lift the corners of his beautiful lips, and he pulled her closer in clear amusement to steal a kiss.

"I don't find that hard to believe. There are a lot of guys in this university that would love to have a chance with you."

"Oh...please! Be serious," she remarked and rolled her eyes, refusing to believe a word of it. "Nobody is proposing to me in front of you; however, I can't say the same thing about you and the females on this campus."

"Arielle," he turned her to him, still in his arms and gazed deep into her eyes. "I don't care about any other female but you. I'm also pretty serious about the guys here and their desires about you. Remember that I can read their minds. If I wasn't with you, the picture would be completely different." She didn't comment, instead she closed her eyes, enjoying his embrace. They walked quietly for a short way.

"Sebastian, the thing is that Professor Allworth makes me a little nervous," she whispered.

"Well, I must say there's something very peculiar about him, but I don't want you to worry. I'll be right here with you," he reassured her.

"I know," she reached up and pressed her lips to his. However, she was still a little troubled. Sebastian kept watching her; nothing escaped him when it came to her moods. He squeezed her softly and tried to change the conversation.

"I'm glad you were daydreaming about me," he whispered in her ear. "I wish I could dream. I would spend a large part of my time dreaming about you, if not all of my time." He pulled her tightly against him and locked them in a hot kiss right in the middle of campus. She was sure that there were a lot of people watching them, but she didn't mind. Many girls among the watchers would love to trade places with her right now. Sebastian, Troy and Ian stirred incredible desires in the female world at this university. She smiled, utterly content, and stayed in his embrace as they made their way toward the cafeteria to meet Ian, Eva, Paul, and Loren. Arielle and Paul would be the only ones purchasing lunch. She was sure the immortals would have a drink, trying to blend with the rest of the students. She chuckled at the thought. They had classes in the afternoon, so they all decided to kill time, the same way they did each and every time, socializing at the cafeteria pavilion located by a beautiful manmade lake.

Chapter 16

AT THE PAVILION, their group was already seated and deep into a conversation. She hadn't seen Paul for a few weeks, and she realized she had missed him a lot. He stood up when he saw them approaching, and reaching out, he picked her up and twirled her around with sheer pleasure.

"Arielle, I missed you," Paul said. The hug was equally happy on both sides.

"I missed you, too," she said with a smile on her face. Sebastian took a seat next to Ian, and she took a seat next to Eva. Sebastian proceeded to describe in detail her unfortunate episode with Professor Allworth.

"You told him that he was boring you?" Eva exclaimed. She held a serious face for just a short second, and then hilarious laughter surged up her throat and she couldn't stop. Arielle pressed her hands to her face as the laughter became contagious.

"Well...well...well, look who is coming," Ian said, chuckling quietly. Every head whirled attentively, following Ian's gaze. Abruptly the laughter stopped, and a palpable silence fell around the table. Professor Allworth and two other men were walking into the pavilion carrying food trays. They were engaged in a lively conversation, and they took a seat a few tables away from theirs. Arielle was in a perfect position to have a full view of their table, and she felt quite uncomfortable. Their conversation slowed down as they dug into their lunch. She took a sip of her drink, and she noticed Colt Allworth leaning over the table, talking in an inaudible voice.

She tried to get Sebastian's attention, but he was in deep conversation with Ian and Eva. Paul and Loren were whispering sweet nothings to each other, holding hands affectionately, lost in their own world. She sighed, and turned her gaze back on Allworth, stunned to find him watching her, scrutinizing her. She pursed her lips and kept her gaze level with his. Her internal gauge was rising to a frantic level. *What in bloody hell does he want from me?* It took but a short second and Allworth's blue eyes narrowed while his jaw tensed. She struggled to remain calm. She could still feel the earlier humiliation at the auditorium. *How dare he!* she thought again, clenching her teeth.

Allworth stopped talking, leaned back at his chair, eyes fixed on her, and silence seemed to descend at their table. Both men turned slowly and followed his stare directly to her. She was sure that they had been talking about her.

Anxiety flooded over her as the professor and the two men practically hovered over the table, faces close together as they whispered again. Both men turned once again to gaze at her with obvious interest. She was wondering why they were so disturbed by her very existence. They did seem to stare at her, but it was clear to her that their gazes were fixed on her neckline, not her face. Instantaneously, she reached up and clasped the amulet that was nestled at the opening of her blouse tightly. Her movement startled the three of them, and they fell silent. She noticed their eyebrows lifting in wonder, and eventually they turned to face each other.

Could they be interested in my necklace? she wondered. *They did look startled when I covered it with my hand.* She picked up her sandwich, filled with more questions than answers, and took a large bite. She held it up close to her face, staring at the teeth marks left on the bread. *It's not as tasty as it looks.* She was really hungry, though.

Allworth was watching her again, his mouth pressed into a hard line. She took a sip from her soda and hid her frustration behind the can. An inaudible oath left her lips, unable to hold her frustration in check. She tapped her fingers on the table and annoyance tightened Arielle's face. "Bloody hell!" she mumbled, this time out loud. Here she was again with more questions unanswered than she had before.

She sighed heavily, closed her eyes, and silence descended again in her head. The moment drew out while her mind had shut out every sound around her. A cool breeze blew across her face, sending a wonderful feeling coursing through her body. She leaned back on her seat and, opening her eyes, she gazed at the clear blue sky. The air felt fresh and clean this afternoon, spreading calm over the issues in her head. She smiled and lowered her gaze to find all of her friends watching her carefully. They looked as if she was to make an important announcement, but she didn't say a word. She was back in her own thoughts.

She knew that neither one of the three men at Allworth's table belonged to that special group of people in her head, because she had no idea what they were thinking.

"What is it, baby?" Sebastian's velvety voice startled her. Her gaze rested on his beautiful face, and she smiled. He was reaching across the table, seeking her hand. She took a deep breath, but instead of sliding her hand to meet his, she hugged herself tightly. She was frustrated with her inability to hear Professor Allworth's conversation.

"What is it?" Eva asked, glancing between Sebastian and Arielle. Her interest was evident, but Arielle kept her mouth shut. She stared straight ahead, gazing between the three men that were huddled over the table, wishing she could hear their discussion. She was sure they were talking about her.

"How strange!" Sebastian murmured. She flicked her gaze on him, hoping that he had caught part of their conversation. Immortal hearing was a thousand times stronger than human.

"What's so strange?" Paul asked casually, taking the sandwich from his plate and biting down on a mouthful while darting his eyes between Sebastian and Arielle.

"I can't read their minds," Sebastian continued, motioning toward the professor's table. He had forgotten all about Paul's presence. "That's very unusual," Sebastian muttered, drumming his fingers on the table apprehensively.

"What do you mean you can't read their minds?" Paul asked, his voice elevated to a higher pitch. He had stopped chewing in sheer shock. "You can read people's minds?" Paul swallowed the food in his mouth too fast, nearly choking. He cleared his throat, his eyes wide open, unable to comprehend Sebastian's words. He started shrinking back in his seat, face turning bright red. Arielle was sure he was worried about Sebastian reading the hot thoughts in his head about Loren. She couldn't help chuckling under her breath. Paul pressed his lips together in utter stress.

"Are you a psychic?" Paul asked, watching Sebastian with a thoughtful frown. He was definitely feeling uncomfortable.

"What?" Sebastian asked, absentmindedly.

"Are you a psychic?" Paul repeated the question. "You said you couldn't read their minds. What do you mean by that?"

"Oh, that..." Sebastian's voice trailed. He shrugged and tried to find the right words to use to ease Paul's mind. "I have a gift like Eva does. Sometimes I can read people's minds, but not all the time," he said, in a nonchalant tone.

"Astonishing!" Paul murmured. "Bloody astonishing!"

"Don't worry, Paul," Sebastian said with a smile. "I'm not concerned about your thoughts." Paul looked extremely embarrassed.

Sebastian said something to Loren in that immortal way that was inaudible to Paul and Arielle. A few minutes later, Loren leaned closer to Paul and whispered something making him smile. They pushed away from the table, and Paul announced that they had to go. They waved as they started to make their way out of the pavilion.

When they were out of sight, Eva turned to Sebastian. "What are you trying to say?" Eva insisted staring at Sebastian.

"If I can't read their thoughts, there has to be another explanation," he was muttering thoughtfully.

"What kind of explanation?" Ian asked, extremely curious.

"They must have something in their possession that prevents me from reading their minds," he said. "For example, I can't read Arielle's thoughts as long as she wears the amulet. So I'm thinking that there has to be something to that effect that keeps their thoughts safe from outside invaders like me." He looked completely unruffled, but Arielle knew he was pretty stressed. He was pinching the tip of his nose, and he only did that when he was totally bothered.

"Are you sure about that?" Arielle asked, gazing in his eyes, completely transfixed by his words.

"Absolutely," he nodded. She flinched and averted her gaze back toward Professor Allworth. She finally leaned across the table, lowering her voice to a bare whisper.

"Can you hear their conversation?" she asked, boring into Sebastian's eyes. She could see them still engaged in deep conversation, hovering over the table, and she could sense that Colt Allworth was watching her.

"No, I can't," Sebastian, said utterly frustrated. He was able to ready every human's thoughts with no exception. The only explanation was that they were immortals, but he didn't want to bring this up and increase Arielle's fears. He would just keep an eye on them.

"What does he want with me?" she mumbled in exasperation, shaking her head. "Eva, can you see anything about these men? I am going out of my mind," she said, and bit hard down on her lower lip.

"There is something very interesting about them," Eva murmured.

"All right!" Arielle exclaimed. "Now we are getting somewhere. What's so interesting about them?" Her eyes fixed on Eva. "Do you get any weird vibrations?"

"There is something quite odd about them," her voice thoughtful. "I get a lot of strange visions about them." Arielle leaned in and touched Eva's arm, making her look at her.

"What kind of visions?" she whispered anxiously. Eva shook her head and looked as if she was ready to say something, but she didn't.

"Arielle," Sebastian called out. She gave him a quick look, waving her hand dismissively, and immediately she averted her gaze back to Eva.

"Eva, wh…" she stopped mid-sentence as she heard Sebastian's unyielding voice.

"Arielle, we have to go, now."

"Why?" she asked, obviously annoyed at not being able to get any answers to her question.

Sebastian dismissed the tone of her voice. "We'll be late for class," he added softly, staring at her now. "You can talk with Eva later." He rose to his feet, and walking around the table, he stopped next to her chair.

"Arielle, we'll talk tonight. We have to go as well," Eva said and stood up. If there was one thing that she had trusted ever since she was a young child, it was Eva's premonitions. Eva leaned closer and hugged her, reassuring her that everything was going to be all right. She loved Eva very much! There was a short silence, and Sebastian's voice snapped her out of my trivial thoughts.

"We have to go," he said, checking his watch. He slipped his arm around her waist and pulled her up, holding her close to him. He bent down and pressed his lips on hers. She picked up her tray to return it inside, leaving most of her sandwich untouched.

"You didn't finish your lunch," Sebastian murmured, pressing his lips again this time on her cheek.

"It tastes like cardboard," she replied, loud enough for her friends to break out into a hearty laugh.

"Later..." she said looking at her friends. Eva and Ian were already walking ahead of them. She decided to take a last quick look at Professor Allworth's table, and she wasn't surprised this time to find that all three men were watching Sebastian and her with undisguised interest. She pursed her lips and moved closer to Sebastian, looking up at him. Sebastian looked totally unruffled, making her feel secure.

"Let's go, baby," he whispered in her ear and pulled her toward the exit of the pavilion.

Dr. Walker, the design and technology professor, was of medium height and in his mid-50s with a very kind face. When they entered the classroom, he was standing behind his desk with a small smile on his face. This was a must-have class for graduation, but not Arielle's favorite.

"Good day, Miss Lloyd. Good day, Mr. Gaulle," he said. This was something he did each and every day they entered his class. He addressed every student with his or her last name. He always looked utterly pleased for his excellent memory. They both chuckled quietly; he was a very likable individual. It was not long before the room was full, and everyone had been seated. Professor Walker opened his notes and stood up. He walked slowly around his desk, and standing right in front of it, he started his lecture. He had been speaking for over twenty minutes, and Arielle was bored to death. Occasionally she took a few notes, but for the most part she couldn't wait until the hour was over. She looked at Sebastian; he looked just as beautiful as ever. She smiled, totally amazed by his endurance and patience, just so he can be with her. *How incredible is that?* she thought.

Professor Walker paused, he gazed around the room, and continued.

"Each one of you will have to design a prototype product that will be manufactured in the workshop. The product will be forty percent of your final grade," he said, and paused again. Then he continued with his instruction on how they were going to accomplish that part of their grade. There was silence as he finished his instructions, and no hands were raised when he asked if they had any questions. "Very well," he said. "That's all for today." He closed the book in his hands, and walking around his desk, he took a seat. He didn't bother to look up as they began to leave.

In the car, Sebastian gazed at her warmly, and a teasing smile curved his luscious lips upward. He pressed the start button, starting the ignition, and he pushed on the gas. The car purred and swiftly left the parking lot.

He turned the stereo on, gazing at her, looking for her approval and she nodded. Bon Jovi's *"I'll be there for you"* filled the air, and she sighed with a smile.

"What is it?" Sebastian asked, turning to look at her.

"Oh! Parts of this song remind me a lot about things you say," she murmured.

His eyes narrowed, and he looked a little surprised.

"But this song is mostly about leaving someone you love. How can that possibly remind you of me?" he asked, truly surprised. First, she was amazed that he knew the words, but then she knew she had to hurry and explain what she meant.

"No…" Her voice trailed, and she shook her head chuckling softly. "There are a few verses that remind me a lot of you," she murmured, gazing in his eyes.

"Such as?" he pressed on.

"Such as 'When you breathe, I want to be the air for you.' You do say that a lot," she said, chuckling.

He paused for a few seconds, and then he laughed softly.

"Yes, you're right. I do say that, and I mean it every time I say it." He reached over, and taking her hand, he traced the skin with his thumb, sending heat across her body. She turned toward him, her eyes grazing over his face. He met her eyes, and leaning in to press his lips on hers.

"Arielle," he murmured softly. "I love you so much!"

"*Je vous adore*," she whispered, leaning close to his ear, tracing his jaw line with the tip of her tongue. He gasped, and she felt his hand shiver. She smiled and hummed softly to the Bon Jovi tune as she stared out the window. She was startled when her phone rang.

"Hi, Eva, long time no talk," she laughed out loud.

"Yea! I know, but Ian and I wanted to know if you guys want to meet at the Rock pub in Hove."

"When?"

"How about eight o'clock tonight?"

"Let me ask Sebastian," she said. She turned to face Sebastian, and he was nodding in agreement. He had already heard their conversation.

"Yes, he said yes. We'll see you there at eight," she said and shut her phone. She heard Sebastian whistling to a song on the radio, and she went back to her thoughts about Professor Allworth. She moved her right hand away from the window and clenched her necklace, tracing the amulet with her fingers. She closed her eyes, and her mind stuttered to a halt as the vivid image of three pairs of eyes glaring at the amulet filled her head. She kept her right hand on the amulet nervously, and suddenly she realized that her amulet was the center of their attention.

I wonder why? she thought to herself.

"What are you whispering?"

"Nothing," she said quickly.

"Arielle, I heard you clearly saying that you are wondering about something," he persisted. She sighed deeply and turned to look at his face.

"I was wondering why these men are interested in my amulet," she said skeptically.

"You think they were interested in the amulet?" he asked, clearly amazed.

"Of course I am!" she said. Sebastian remained quiet for a short moment.

"Well," he said in a quiet voice. "I suppose it's possible...But how can we be sure?"

"It'll be difficult, but I'm determined to find out."

Sebastian pressed her hand softly. "The amulet is connected to a very old and very elite group of royals," he murmured. "It's hard to believe that anyone in this century would be familiar with its existence..." His voice trailed. She was sure he was right, but what had Colt Allworth been talking about to his two friends.

"Maybe he was upset with me being disrespectful on the first day in class," she said, pressing her lips together. "Maybe I embarrassed him in front of the class, and he is planning on making my life miserable." She was growing anxious. "Oh, Sebastian, I hope he doesn't make it difficult for me to graduate."

"Arielle, I think you are extending your imagination way out there. He can't alter the tests. You are so smart that even if you don't listen to a word he says during his lectures, you will ace your tests." He was right again. Physics was her strength, and she was going to get through this. When they arrived at home, she fell in his arms, and he held her tightly, providing that sanctuary that she loved.

Chapter 17

THAT SAME EVENING, they met Eva and Ian for drinks at the Rock Pub in Hove. Arielle was anxious to continue her conversation with Eva and hear what she had to say about Professor Allworth.

Eva's gift to exert her psychic powers and her incredible premonitions about the future was so potent, it bordered insanity, especially now that she was an immortal. Eva and Arielle had had a special spiritual bond ever since they were very young. Their minds moved around the physical and spiritual dimension, beyond the barriers of time and space. They became clairvoyant as children and reached each other mentally. They knew if one of them were in trouble by simply sensing each other's emotions.

Arielle also knew Eva's protective nature. Eva would warn her if something bad were coming her way, just as she had done in the past. But right now, Allworth was on the top of her list. She had too many questions, and no answers at all.

When they entered the club, the crowd was cheerful, and the atmosphere enthusiastic. They chose a table away from the stage, and when the waitress arrived, they ordered drinks. They watched people attempting to sing-along with the mediocre, five member band. This band unfortunately seemed to be the only one performing tonight. They were not unique or fascinating, but everyone seemed to be enjoying their music. Many of the women in the club kept their eyes intently on Sebastian and Ian. What Eva and Arielle found comical was that despite the fact that the women were brazen, obvious, and shameless,

Sebastian and Ian were oblivious to their blatant attempts to draw their attention.

Arielle was happy to be there, spending time with Ian and Eva. They chatted about Italy and about Ian and Eva's transformation. Arielle was mesmerized by the details. Dancing was the highlight of the evening. Arielle loved dancing with Sebastian, and they danced until the crowd started to thin, and the band announced that they had to take a break.

"Are you tired, baby?" Sebastian asked, and his lips quirked into a smile.

"I'm not tired," she murmured, and wrinkled her nose playfully. "I love dancing with you."

Sebastian cupped her chin and lifted her face to his. His mouth came down on hers, and the kiss was deep, intense, and thrilling. Ripples of pleasure coursed through her body, rattling her wits. She heard his soft chuckle and reluctantly, she pulled back, her breath caught in her throat. "Mmmm..." he murmured, and she stammered, trying to gather her wits that were flung into oblivion.

Sebastian pulled her into his arms and gave her a soft squeeze. Then, they walked back to their table. Eva and Ian were still standing in the middle of the dance floor, caught in some kind of intense discussion.

The waitressed appeared again and Sebastian ordered another round for the four of them; by that time, Ian and Eva were back at the table. Arielle noticed the look on Ian's face. "Is something wrong?" she asked, glancing between Eva and Ian.

"Oh, nothing of importance," Eva inserted quickly.

"What?" Ian said, glaring at Eva. Anger was evident in the tone of his voice.

"What's wrong?" Sebastian asked, directing his question to Ian.

But before Ian had a chance to reply, Eva's stern voice interrupted, as if she were considering doing battle. "Ian!" she shouted.

Ian didn't meet her gaze, his lips pressed into a thin line.

Arielle glanced between them once again, and leaning closer to Eva, she hissed. "What in bloody hell is wrong with you two?"

"Nothing,"

"No?" Arielle replied, her eyebrows lifting.

"No."

Arielle glanced at Sebastian, utterly frustrated, and he gave a shrug of his shoulders.

Her gaze turned to Eva once again. "Eva, you know darn well I'm not going to drop this, so spit it out."

Eva huffed. "Alright. Some guy out there was drunk and propositioned me in front of Ian."

"Ohhh, what happened?"

"I wanted to kill him," Ian snapped.

Eva's voice dropped to a whisper. "Can you even envision Ian getting into a fight with a drunken human?" Eva sighed, deeply. "How would we explain an outcome like that?"

"Oh God," Arielle murmured. "You're right."

"I still think I should have taught him a lesson," Ian grumbled.

Eva gave a loud frustrated huff. "That is exactly what we have been arguing about. Me trying to convince him that he can't do that anymore. Not with humans and not in public."

Arielle gazed at Ian and shuddered at the thought of what the outcome of such a fight could have been. "Ian, she's right, don't you think?"

Ian swallowed hard and nodded apologetically, but the defiant expressing didn't leave his beautiful face. "I don't like other man touching Eva," he complained. "If this happens again, it will become an issue."

"I don't disagree with you," Sebastian jumped into the conversation.

"Sebastian, you don't need to add fuel to the fire," Arielle admonished him.

She looked at Sebastian a second longer; then, she turned back to Ian.

"Ian, you can't fight these guys. They are human, and the fight will definitely not be on an even scale. You can really kill someone with the strength that you now hold. Do you think that you can live with that? I know you're now an immortal, but you have feelings, and I'm sure you would never want to do something like that."

"That is exactly what I told him," Eva said.

Ian ran a hand through his hair, utterly frustrated. "I'm sorry," Ian said and meant it. Leaning in, he pulled Eva into his arms. "I'm crazy jealous of you," he murmured, and locked them into a scorching kiss. Eva sighed and pulled herself even closer, pressing deeper into the kiss.

Finally, Ian lifted his head, and meeting her eyes, they grinned at each other.

"Is everything okay?" Arielle asked.

They both turned to look at her and nodded, still holding a soft smile on their faces.

It wasn't long before Sebastian and Ian were engaged in a conversation about sports.

Arielle's thoughts turned to Colt Allworth and Eva's premonitions.

"Eva," she said looking in her eyes. "Can we talk about Allworth?"

"What do you want to know?"

"Please tell me what you saw at the pavilion."

"First off let me say that you shouldn't worry. There are no ill thoughts around you," she said in a soft warm voice.

"Eva --- what exactly do you mean by no ill thoughts? What did you see?" She asked a little puzzled.

Eva paused, propped her chin up with one hand, her eyes gazing down at the glass and swallowed hard. She looked as if she was pondering her thoughts carefully, and then the words streamed out of her mouth. "I had a vivid view of a very old building. I was standing at the front of a wide open door, and after a short thought, I walked in. I descended a staircase that spiraled down to a dark, long, stone corridor. I saw several dark silhouettes in long dark cloaks walking down that corridor, and I followed. There were open doors on either side, leading into black-draped rooms bearing strange signs." Eva paused for a short moment and hauled a deep breath. "Everyone seemed to disappear behind the door at the very end of the corridor, and that is where I stopped," Eva said, and paused.

"Eva, please, can you go into that room? I needed to know." Ian and Sebastian had stopped talking, and they were listening intently to Eva's words. Ian reached around Eva's shoulders and pulled her closer for a kiss.

"Eva, you don't have to do this if you don't want to. Arielle will understand," he said in a soft voice. Eva turned and looked at Arielle and she nodded, but Arielle was sure her worried look didn't escape Eva.

Eva reached for her hand, and meeting her gaze, she whispered, "I'll do it for you. I love you, Arielle, and I don't want you to worry,"

She paused again, and she seemed to be gathering her thoughts. She finally took another deep breath and continued in a soft quiet voice. "I'm in a very large room, the walls reflect the dull light given off by a few silvery lamps hanging on chains from the stone ceiling. The room is filled with people, but I can't see their faces," she pursed her lips. She seemed to be looking around, but I was sure she was not looking at the clubroom.

"There are coats of armor everywhere, huge tapestries hanging on the walls with strange designs of signs and symbols." Her eyes narrowed. "Wait…wait…I have seen these signs before, but where?" Eva seemed to be talking to herself. She waved her arm as if she was pushing her thought away and continued. "There is a huge platform, like an altar, poorly lit by low burning candles. A man is walking up to the altar; he picks up a large book covered in black leather. I can see a large sign burned into the leather; I can see the man's face…" Her voice trailed, and she looked like she was trying to see something. Suddenly they could hear her breathing getting heavier, and she was inhaling deeply. She seemed extremely distraught.

"Eva…Eva…Are you okay?" Ian shook her lightly. Sebastian and Arielle watched her carefully. Eva reached up and brushed her hair away from her forehead, motioning that she was fine.

"This is so bloody outlandish!" she murmured. "I wonder what this vision is all about." She let out a mystified grunt. Sebastian reached and, grabbing the side of Arielle's chair, pulled her closer to him.

"Arielle, you have to let it go," he murmured close to her ear. "You are not in any danger. If you trust Eva's premonitions as much as you say that you do, then I'm a little perplexed about your obsession." Sebastian's voice was soft and soothing. She leaned in and kissed him, thankful for his understanding. She took a sip of her drink and moved her glass to watch the liquid swaying from one side to the other while thinking about Eva's last words.

"Arielle," Eva's voice snapped her out of her own thoughts. "The pentagon on the black leather book was exactly the same as the one on your book."

"What book?" She was not even sure why she asked something so stupid, but she was not thinking right.

"The book that Olivia Dillon gave you," Eva said. Arielle clutched her glass tightly with both hands, because it was shaking slightly.

"Oh!" She whispered. "Are you sure?"

"This gets even better," Eva said, excitement evident in her voice but no alarm.

"How much better?" Arielle pressed on.

"I saw the face of the man that walked up to the altar and picked up the book," Eva said slowly, dropping her voice to a mere whisper. She looked around to make sure nobody could hear what she was about to say. Arielle's curiosity picked up immensely. She started to ask the obvious question, but Sebastian interrupted her.

"Eva, who did you see?" Sebastian asked pointedly. Eva cleared her throat.

"Colt Allworth," she said, and Arielle clapped her hand to her mouth, trying to prevent herself from crying out loud while she reached out and grabbed Sebastian's arm. She noticed Sebastian and Ian's jaws drop, both completely astonished.

"Fascinating," Sebastian finally said, thoughtfully.

"So do you have any theories?" he asked Eva.

"Sebastian, I'm sure of one thing. While in that room, I was surrounded by gallant souls. I didn't sense anything wicked or sinful," Eva said softly.

"Astonishing!" Sebastian murmured.

Eva reached over and gave Arielle a hug. "Don't worry, Arielle. I stood next to Professor Allworth, and he has a virtuous aura. There has to be a good explanation about today's confrontation. Give it a little time; something will come up," she said, with a soft smile. They all sat in motionless silence for a few minutes.

The band was back after their break and wonderful music filled the room. Sebastian took the chance to move Arielle to the dance floor, and Eva followed with Ian. They had a great time for the rest of the evening, and they stayed away from the earlier conversation.

It was at the parking lot while ready to get in their car that Eva said, "I think Professor Allworth belongs to some kind of magnanimous secret society. And it has something to do with the amulet you possess." She chuckled pleasantly and gave her a hug. "I'll call you tomorrow," she said softly.

Sebastian wrapped his arm around Arielle's waist and pulled her close for a kiss. "Lets go home, baby," he murmured, as they walked to the car.

"I love you, Arielle!" Eva called out while getting in her car. Arielle waved goodbye at both of them and smiled. Sebastian was now holding the passenger door open, waiting for her to get in.

The next couple weeks were uneventful. Professor Allworth continued teaching, not showing any bit of weirdness in class. During the interactions, they addressed each other respectfully, and he was even showing a little favoritism toward her. She was at the point where she had almost gotten over the original episode. Third week of the semester was the focal point of their small group. Troy and Gabby were coming back, and they were elated.

Troy was acting like a two year old that was getting a Christmas present.

"Boy...oh...boy..." Arielle heard Eva's voice filled with laughter "What?" she asked.

"I would like to be a fly on the wall when Troy and Gabrielle get together over the weekend. They have been apart for over two months, and knowing Troy, it will be a wild ride." They both laughed out loud.

On Friday, Ian, Eva, Paul, Loren, Sebastian and Arielle were sitting at the cafeteria's patio in the sunshine conversing about Gabrielle and Troy coming back. They were delighted to see Alex, Robert, Damien, and Andrew walk up and sit down with them. Alex looked around, and he reminded them that their group would be complete once they had Troy and Gabrielle back.

"They will be back on Monday," Paul said. "I think we should celebrate come next weekend." They all agreed, but Arielle saw a quick flash of anxiety cross Loren's eyes, and it disappeared just as fast as it came. Arielle had absolutely no idea what was going on in Loren's head, and she didn't ask.

Chapter 18

MONDAY MORNING, Arielle and Sebastian arrived at the parking lot a bit early and parked right next to Troy and Gabby's car. Arielle's heart skipped a bit thinking of walking next to Gabby again. *Gosh,* she thought, *things are going back to normal.* They approached the physics building and spotted Troy and Gabby close to the entrance. Arielle couldn't hold back, and she called out Gabby's name. Gabby and Troy stopped, and turning around, they saw Arielle and Sebastian approaching quickly.

The embrace between Arielle and Gabrielle was a jubilant one, and they lingered in the same position for a long time. It almost seemed that they hadn't seen each other for ages. Both looked at each other through blurring visions, as tears run down their faces. Troy and Sebastian chuckled and shook their heads. They had been awe-struck by the splendor of the love and friendship that held the three girls together.

"I missed you, Gabby," Arielle said.

"I love you, Arielle," she exclaimed, and she saw tears in her eyes.

"Girls…girls…we need to go in," Troy chuckled giving a soft punch to Sebastian's arm. They both laughed again, and Arielle knew they were happy to be together again. Gabrielle and Arielle walked into class together, beaming in pleasure, while Troy and Sebastian followed close behind. It was early enough to find four seats together. Colt Allworth raised his head and smiled softly.

"Aaa!" he said. "Miss Winters, Mr. Vasser, it's good to see you both in person. How do you feel?" he asked, looking at Gabby.

"I'm fine; thank you for asking," Gabby replied. He didn't bother to look at Arielle; however, she was sure he was watching her. They walked up and took four seats on the fifth row. She felt much better sitting next to Sebastian, knowing that nothing would ever go wrong as long as they were together.

It was at the end of the session as the four of them walked towards the exit making plans for later tonight that Professor Allworth called to her.

"Miss Lloyd!" The entire group stopped and turned around to look at him. The smile on his face didn't show any of the anger or cynicism that he had shown in their first interaction.

"Yes?"

"Can you please stay behind? I need to have a talk with you," he said in a soft voice.

Suddenly, she felt anxiety washing over her as she looked up at Sebastian waiting for his advice. "I'll be right outside." He pressed her hand. "Remember I'm able to hear from meters away, so don't worry," he pressed his lips on the side of her cheek.

"Just you, Miss Lloyd; don't worry. I don't bite," Allworth said. She let go of Sebastian's hand and moved toward his desk while Troy, Gabby, and Sebastian walked out the door; she heard it slam closed behind them. Allworth was silent, and she took a deep breath. Her eyes were burning, and she didn't know what had come over her.

Colt Allworth stood up and walked around his desk and down the platform to stand right in front of her. He was even taller that she thought, and his eyes were a much bluer color than she first saw. His face was soft and a smile was lingering at the corner of his mouth.

"Please, don't be nervous."

"I'm not nervous," she said defiantly. She was sure that she was trying to convince herself more than Colt Allworth.

"Please come and sit down for a minute." He pointed to a couple of seats in the front row. She walked over and reluctantly took the offered seat. He stared at her for a long moment, as though he was trying to gauge her. She kept her lips pursed, waiting for his next statement. His gaze moved from her face to her neckline and unease spread through her body. Instantaneously, she moved her numb hand and clutched tightly the amulet. He followed her movement but remained motionless as an eerie silence fell between them. It was not long and she heard his voice very calm, very warm.

"May I call you by your first name?" he asked.

"Sure," she replied reluctantly. She was still clutching the amulet tightly.

"Thank you," his said calmly.

Arielle remained rigid and silent.

"There's no need to be nervous," he furthered.

"What can I do for you?" she asked, her voice low but steady.

"I want to talk to you about the amulet you have on," he said stiffly.

Arielle flinched. "What about it?" She was now trying to put a barrier between them.

"I would like to know where it came from. Did you find it? And if so, where?"

His eyes moved from her neckline to her face, and her eyes widened. "Why do you want to know?"

He looked as if he was waging some kind of war to find the right words to reply. "Arielle, it's of the utmost importance that I find out the origin of the amulet you have in your possession."

"Why?" she insisted, stubbornly.

He seemed to be losing his patience. He pursed his lips and finally he said. "This amulet can cause you harm if you are not the rightful owner."

She let out a gasp of outrage. "I am the rightful owner. It's a family heirloom that has been passed down for generations."

"I don't believe a word of that," he said firmly.

"Well, you can believe what you will, but it is mine." Getting to her feet, she turned and started to leave the room.

"Arielle!" his voice was tight.

She stopped and turned to look at him. Professor Allworth went quiet for a moment watching her carefully. "Please don't leave. Whether you believe it or not, I'm trying to help you."

"How so?" she asked boldly.

She was sure that Sebastian was able to hear their conversation, so she tried to remain calm.

"Can you at least tell me something about it, anything at all?" he said.

"Why?" she countered again, trying to keep her voice from quivering.

"I can't understand why you are afraid of me," he said quietly holding her gaze. "If this is a family heirloom and you know all about it, then you must know that I can't hurt you."

Her mouth dropped and anxiety swept over her just as she became aware that he knew much more than he was saying. He also seemed to be completely aware that Sebastian was right outside the door. *The truth is that I don't know anything about this amulet except that it keeps me safe from immortals trying to kill me.*

"So you do know that I can't hurt you right?"

"Yes, I know," she replied faintly, trying to say as little as possible.

"Good. Unfortunately, Arielle, I don't believe that this amulet belongs to your family." His voice was serious but nonthreatening. "I know all about this amulet," he said and pointed to her neckline.

Arielle took a step back. "What do you know?" she asked guardedly.

"I know the names of all the rightful owners. The Lloyd family is not one of them, but surely you already know that. Don't you?" Professor Allworth said, eyebrows raised.

"Yes, I did," she said quietly, pursing her lips. "But how do you know the powers of the amulet?"

Allworth raised his eyebrow again with a slightly amused smile. "I know more that you think I do," he said. "But if I tell you what I know about it, will you tell me where you got it from?"

Arielle shifted from one foot to the other. After several quiet minutes, she answered. "Yes, I will."

"Well," he said, "The amulet is a scarab, and it means 'he who is coming into being'. The Ancient Egyptians believed that the scarab beetle was associated with the Egyptian God Khepri. Khepri was the symbol of rebirth. It was Khepri that pushed the sun across the sky. Each day the sun disappeared, always to rise again, and be reborn the following day. The amulets were often buried with the dead, so they can be reborn in the afterlife."

Speechless, she tried to process the information. After several long moments passed, he prompted, "Okay, shoot."

Arielle blinked at his words. She tried to gather her thoughts, but it was so much to take in at once.

"Arielle, you must be aware," he paused and took a deep breath, "that there are people who would go to extreme lengths to return the amulet to its rightful owner. Do you understand that? Do you understand that your life might be in danger, for that reason alone?"

There was a stunned silence, and she swallowed hard. "Yes, I'm aware," she said thoughtfully. She couldn't help noticing that he was waiting for something. But she wasn't ready to say anything more.

"So you're not going to tell me are you?" he said.

"No, I'm sorry sir, but I can't." She thanked him, and walked slowly toward the exit.

"Arielle," he called out once again. She stopped, but she didn't look back.

"I don't know how it fell into your possession, but you must return it to the owner." This time she did turned to look at him, and he was looking more seriously than ever before.

"Professor, I—" She started to say, and she immediately stopped. How can she tell him the truth without divulging Sebastian's identity? She couldn't do that.

"It's mine," she said boldly and walked out. Sebastian, Troy and Gabby were waiting outside patiently.

"What in bloody hell was all that about?" Gabby asked exchanging uncomfortable looks with Sebastian, Troy and Arielle. Before she could open her mouth to respond, she heard the door open behind them, and she caught sight of Professor Allworth coming out of the auditorium. He was clenching a book with his left hand and carrying a black briefcase with the other.

"Good day!" he said giving them a quick glance. He paused for a second and turning he rested his eyes on Arielle. "Arielle, I want you to think seriously about our conversation," he said authoritatively.

"Yes—Yes—I will—" She muttered and bit her lip. Colt Allworth walked a few feet away before he spoke again.

"Indeed, you will," he muttered and kept walking until he disappeared around the corner at the end of the building.

"Well!" She said looking up at Sebastian. "How extraordinary was that!" She was completely mesmerized by the professor's knowledge about the amulet. She cleared her throat, and started to tell Gabby the details of her interaction with the professor. She knew that Troy and Sebastian were eavesdropping, and they heard clearly every word that was said in that auditorium.

Just as she started to speak Sebastian interjected softly, "Professor Allworth seemed to be familiar with the infinite depths of the amulet's origin. Why is he so obsessed about the rightful owner?" he said densely. He put his arm around her and pulled her toward the parking lot with Troy and Gabby at their heels. She gazed up at him and he looked deeply impressed by the discussion between her and Allworth.

"Well!" She heard Gabby's voice breaking the silence that had descended among the four of them. They all turned to look at her and she had a baffled impression painted across her face.

"What?" Arielle asked peering in her eyes. Gabby reached over and grabbed Arielle's arm.

"You can't tell him about the amulet's true origin without opening a can of worms," she said anxiously. Her eyes were darting between Sebastian and Troy.

"Don't worry, Gabby, I'm not going to discuss immortality with Allworth," she said giving her a reassuring smile.

"Okay," she whispered. She threw her arms around Troy and pressed her lips to his with eagerness and warmth. Sebastian and Arielle chuckled softly at her reaction. They walked together until they arrived to their cars.

The sun was already dipping behind the horizon, painting the sky bright orange when they arrived at home; they decided to take a long walk on the beach. She picked up a jacket on her way out the back door and kept close to Sebastian's body heat. A gentle gust of fresh air brushed her face making her smile. The view of the sky was absolutely beautiful, highlighted by the colors of a gorgeous sunset. They climbed down the long walkway until they reached the soft sand and dunked their toes in it, leaving their shoes at the bottom of the wooden steps.

Sebastian wrapped his arm around her and pulled her close, leaning in to steal a kiss. They walked for a long time, content being with each other in total quiet. The silence was broken only by the sound of the waves lapping on the coastline. She was lost in her own thoughts when suddenly she heard Sebastian clearing his throat significantly. She looked up at him and reached to meet his enticing lips in a scorching kiss. He moaned with pleasure and pulled her tighter against his muscular body. He broke the kiss first, chuckling.

"Can we talk a little about Professor Allworth?" he asked with a smile.

She reached up and pulled him back into the kiss, and he gave in. She could feel the hot, piercing power of his emerald eyes, and she went numb. Sebastian broke the kiss. Pulling her down, they sat beside each other on the warm sand. She felt a floating sensation as she wiped every bad thought away, leaving nothing but Sebastian's presence next to her. She bent her legs and wrapped her arms around her knees, laying her head down, completely relaxed.

The tenderness of the moment was broken apart by an instant alert of a vivid image. Professor Allworth's face appeared, and she shivered. Frowning, she gasped out loud, and immediately, Sebastian pulled her in his arms and held her tightly, reminding her of his infinite love.

"What's the matter, baby?"

"I had a sudden vision of Professor Allworth," she murmured, quivering at the thought.

"Hmm…you do realize that we have to talk about this sooner or later," he murmured.

"I would rather not, but I do understand we have to discuss this," she said with clenched teeth.

"I'm sure he knows a lot more than what he said," Sebastian murmured, face expressionless.

"Hmm—I wish we wouldn't talk about this tonight. I just wanted to be with you," she murmured. She was bothered by Colt Allworth's interruption of their tender moment. He bent down and pressed his lips against hers. Her lips moved fervently beneath his, but he pulled back and she heard a faint chuckle.

"We are going to be together for centuries to come," he added, and this time he laughed out loud. "Is that not going to be long enough for you?" he was watching her with a wide smile spread across his face. She shook her head in frustration, knowing that time with Sebastian was treasurable.

"Limitless time with you will not be adequate for me," she said rebelliously.

"Thank you, baby," he whispered. "I feel the same way." Silence fell between them.

"But all this aside, we do need to discuss Colt Allworth," he stated in a firm voice breaking the quiet moment.

"We need to investigate his sources. How does he know that your family isn't the rightful owner of the amulet?" Sebastian looked perplexed. Anxiety started to climb, closing her throat, making it hard to breath. The seconds lengthened, and she sat there staring at his beautiful face, waiting for something more. She needed some kind of reaction, something that would lessen her unease. Sebastian tightened his hold on her and leaned in to hold them in a blistering kiss. Heat spread quickly through her body, making her skin tingle with excitement, thrusting away every distasteful thought and fear that was looming over her. *His is my sanctuary,* she thought to herself, and she felt deep adoration for this amazing person that loved her.

"Let's go home," he said softly. "We've got a bit of a walk back to the house," he laughed, and they started walking back.

"Are you hungry?" he asked concerned.

"Yes, but I'll make me a sandwich when we get home," she replied.

"I think it's absolutely incredible that you don't need any food for your nourishment," she said. She couldn't even fathom the thought; suddenly she couldn't help but laugh out loud. He laughed with her and leaning in he stole another kiss.

"Mmm..." he murmured squeezing her softly. "You taste delicious. I'm getting awfully hungry!" he said, and let out an insinuating chuckle. She leaned closer to his body. His fingers slid under her shirt, exploring eagerly, and she shivered with excitement. She couldn't get enough of Sebastian. His sensuous lips curved to an exciting smile, and his perfect body was inviting. She was sure that bedtime would erase every worrisome thought, leaving time only for the rapture that only he could provide for her.

 *Chapter 19*

BY THE TIME THEY REACHED the house, she was starving. She hadn't had anything to eat since early that morning. The sandwich at the cafeteria had been awful. Sebastian walked to the fridge, poured a glass of salve, and took a seat at the kitchen table. He held a sweet smile on his face and proceeded to watch her prepare her dinner.

Slicing a couple of pieces of bread from the fresh loaf she had purchased yesterday, she toasted it and spread mayonnaise on both sides. She put three pieces of ham on one slice of the bread, a piece of cheese, two slices of tomato, and topped it with another slice of bread. She picked it up and sank her teeth into the thick sandwich with extreme enthusiasm. She chewed and swallowed, letting out small sounds of gratification. She heard Sebastian laughing, but she ignored him knowing he was being humorous.

Holding her sandwich tightly in her left hand, like a priceless piece of jewelry, she opened the fridge and poured a glass of milk with her right hand. She took a large gulp and walked back to the table, setting down the sandwich and the glass. She wiped her fingers on the paper towel and walked to the study, bringing back her laptop and setting it on the table.

She looked at Sebastian, and she saw an inquisitive look in his eyes. She took a seat next to him and proceeded to finish her sandwich, drain her milk, and turn the computer on.

Sebastian stilled and his amazing green eyes showed utter dismay at the quick disappearance of the sandwich.

"It must've been really good," he said with a short laughter. She just smiled without replying. As soon as the power came on, the computer pinged to show that she had new emails. The screen prompted her to input her password, so she slid her hands over the keyboard and typed "Sebastian."

"My name is your password?" he asked humorously.

"You're my everything," she replied, sending him a dazzling smile.

"Ahh! An e-mail from Eva," she called out in clear pleasure. She opened the e-mail, and her eyes fell on the first paragraph. "Crap!" Immediately she jumped up and rushed to the kitchen counter, retrieving her mobile phone.

"What is it, baby?" Sebastian asked.

"Eva has been trying to contact me. She said it's important that I call her." She turned to look at him inquisitively. "Ugh! She's not answering." Her eyes wandered around the room, trying to think of what could be so important. "I just saw Eva at school today. What could have happened between then and now?" She pursed her lips.

"Well…did she leave a voice message on your mobile?" Sebastian's voice broke the silence.

"No, no, no messages, just ten calls one after the other," she whispered, running her hand over her hair, a little confused.

"What did she say in the e-mail?" Sebastian asked again.

"Oh—the e-mail! I forgot the e-mail!" she muttered and ran back to the computer. Her eyes moved down the page, leaving her astonished.

"I don't believe it!" She looked up and met Sebastian's eyes. She was completely dumbfounded. Sebastian used his immortal speed to move. She never saw him leave his seat, but he was standing right next to her, leaning over her shoulder. She felt his lips pressing softly against her cheek while his arms embraced her warmly. He reached out and pressed the up arrow on the computer to move the page to the top and proceeded in reading the e-mail from the beginning.

"Arielle,

Ian and I went to the mall right after class. We were looking for a couple of things for the house. I can almost hear your laughter! I know you are wondering why in bloody hell we even bother going shopping. Why don't we just manifest what we need? Well… believe it or not, both Ian and I are trying to keep our lives a little bit normal, if you can call it that. At least we are making an effort.

It was on our way back to the car that we ran, and I mean literally ran, into Professor Allworth. We were looking back at a group of kids fighting in the parking lot, and when we turned around, we came face-to-face with Allworth and the young woman hanging off of his arm. Pretty snugly if you know what I mean…

Allworth said hello in a dignified voice. We excused ourselves awkwardly, but I was directly in front of the girl. It was hard to miss her exposed neckline. Our faces were only a few centimeters apart. Ian and I were completely astounded at the sight of her necklace. A beautiful antique chain held an amulet identical to the one you own. We lapsed into a stunned silence; how could that be possible? I think Ian and I stood there for what seemed to be forever, completely speechless, staring at this incredibly rare amulet.

The professor looked annoyed and a bit nervous, and I mean undeniably nervous. He immediately asked if he could help us with something. I got the feeling that he knew we were staring at the amulet, but he wasn't aware that we knew anything about its history. I'm sure that his reaction had a lot to do with the fact that he saw us all sitting together at the pavilion.

His eyes traveled from us to the amulet. I've got a very strange, uncomfortable feeling about this, but I wasn't going to say a thing. We couldn't let him know that we were aware of how powerful and mystical the amulet was. It took us a moment to regain our thoughts, and I used the excuse that we thought her necklace was absolutely gorgeous.

He totally avoided looking at us. He looked at the girl, and she beamed excitedly. He ended up dismissing us.

Arielle, the shock of finding that this girl had the same amulet as you has worn off slightly now. The fact that there are deep secrets hidden behind this whole thing has started to sink in. I can feel it deep in my bones.

Maybe Sebastian can talk with his mother and find out if there are more of these amulets out there and who are the owners.

I am sure we'll get to the bottom of this. Colt Allworth intrigues me. I now understand why he was so interested in your amulet and its true owner. I tried to call you but you didn't pick up. Call me when you get back. I love you,

Eva…

When they finished reading, she felt the heat rise in her face, and she could have given easily to the wave of nausea that rose. Stillness fell again, but this time it was stillness so appalling, so bitter you could almost taste it. She turned around and met his gaze.

"What does that mean?"

He opened his mouth to say something, but he decided to remain silent for a few minutes.

"C'est impossible!" he finally muttered with a faraway look in his eyes. He pulled her up and held her tightly against his body.

"I'm very curious to know what this is all about," she murmured and clutched the amulet. "Do you think I should call Eva back?"

"It's half past ten, and you have to get up early tomorrow. Do you think you want to do this tonight?" he said softly, bending down and pressing his lips on hers.

"I'm not sure about anything right now," she said plaintively. She pursed her lips and gazed in his beautiful eyes. He had a heartfelt grin on his face that spread warmth across her body. He was definitely her safety blanket, her private sanctuary. She stayed in his arms and closed her eyes, breathing deeply.

"Don't worry, baby," he whispered. "Tomorrow we will go and talk with Olivia, and I'm sure we will get some answers." He bent down and stole another kiss.

"You will do that for me?" she asked brightly.

"If I could, I would change the earth's orbit for you," he said with a chuckle, making her smile. He picked her up and turned toward the bedroom.

"We are going to bed," he said unyieldingly, while the light curving of his lips upward made her heart skip a beat. His mouth covered hers and locked them in a sizzling kiss. His eyes held her gaze, and she found him incredibly and gloriously irresistible.

"Do you want to go to bed with me?" he purred against her lips, and she could almost hear his silent chuckle. His arms gathered her so close she couldn't breathe. She hesitated, and he narrowed his eyes with amusement. *He knows well enough that I'm not going to resist him, so why does he even bother to ask?*

"Maybe," she said with amusement, and his gaze burned into her eyes. He beamed mischievously, and she found herself trying to catch her breath. His speed was supersonic; before she had a chance to blink, she was in bed, flat on her back, totally naked, locked in his steel embrace. She would never understand how he could transport himself and anyone in his arms with mind-blowing speed. Her human eyes could never follow that type of movement. Every time he did that it took her breath away. Her heart was beating so fast she thought it would burst right out of her chest.

"Mmmm..." he murmured and crushed her lips beneath his. Her body tightened in expectation, and passion enveloped them. She gave all she could give to please him, and he took her with hunger and unrestrained eagerness. They clung to each other as their bodies fused and ecstasy burned every fiber, every vein, leaving them completely spent. Sebastian groaned in pleasure. They stayed in each other's arms, savoring the aftermath of a scorching encounter. It was much later when he lifted himself up, resting on his elbow and holding her gaze for a long moment—so long that she thought he forgot what he was going to say. She giggled and pulled him down for a kiss.

"Do you know how much I love you?" he whispered. She felt his body moving against hers, spreading heat across her skin, and her breath hitched.

"I think I do," she murmured and reached for his lips one more time. After another wild round of lovemaking, he lay back, slid his hand around her, and gathered her close. She splayed her arm over his magnificent chest and rested her head in the crook of his shoulder. She felt her body relaxing into sleep, completely enveloped in his embrace.

She woke to the sun seeping through a small opening of the curtain. Her beautiful dream was asleep with his arms still wrapped around her. She closed her eyes, and she found herself grinning as the events of last night replayed in her mind. She felt him stirring, and her eyes snapped open to find him watching her with that sexy grin that always made her fall apart.

"Good morning, baby," he whispered sluggishly.

"Mmm...good morning to you, too," she murmured.

"Arielle, you need to get ready for class," he said softly, looking down at her.

"Oh…are you saying you are not going to class with me?" she asked, gazing at his perfect face. He was breathtakingly beautiful.

"No, baby, there is a very important board meeting this morning, and I'm a bit in a hurry. As head of the company, I can't miss it. Troy must be present as well," he said firmly. "I should be back around noon, or early afternoon," he continued tipping his head back.

"Hmm…" She frowned a little disappointed.

"What is it?" he asked, his eyes never leaving hers.

"What if I see Allworth?" He paused for a short moment looking down at her, his expression reassuring, unruffled.

"Well—you don't have a class with him today. There should be absolutely no reason for any interaction between you and him," he said, raising a brow.

"Isn't there?" She said. She knew he was right, but she didn't like it.

"Okay then—" She pushed back the covers and sat up on the bed, running her fingers through her hair, pushing it away from her face. She was startled to find herself lifted in his arms swiftly, and deposited into the shower under the warm water. She dragged in a huge gasp, feeling that she had been moved by a tornado. A seductive shiver traveled down her spine as she gazed into his beautiful eyes. "However, I do have enough time for a shower," he said, flashing a grin. He turned the water on and gathered her tightly in his arms.

"Kiss me, baby," he murmured, and leaning in, he brushed his lips across her ear. Her breathing picked up, and she gave in to the man that changed her life.

She dressed slowly while he shaved in front of the mirror, whistling an old song. He was still holding a satisfied grin on his face. She beamed and turned to walk toward the kitchen.

"Your jeans are awfully tight," he called out. She halted in the hallway, quite surprised. Turning to face him, she searched his eyes.

"What?" She glanced down at her jeans in wonder. She had put on the same jeans several times before. Why was he so bothered by the way she looked in them today? Eyes wide, she stared back at him.

"What?" she repeated.

He seemed to ignore her question. His next statement was even more confusing.

"You show a lot of skin with that little shirt on," he pressed on, looking quite amused. She was extremely surprised by his remarks, but she quickly recovered, and she realized that he was joshing her. She raised her brows arrogantly, by now completely unruffled by his teasing.

"Well, you'll not have to look at me, since you are not going to class today," she replied, shrugging her shoulders nonchalantly.

"But I only want you to look like this when I'm with you," he said, moving his hand up and down, pointing at her body with a smile.

"Sebastian Gaulle! Jealous, are you? You—an incredible immortal man—who could have any woman on this earth, and you are jealous of a simple human?" She started to laugh out loud. Turning, she walked to the kitchen. He was in front of her before she reached the counter. He pulled her into his arms tightly and brushed his lips against hers. The yearning for his touch was a constant temptation. Sebastian comprised every little thing that makes a man perfect.

"Arielle, I'm a very jealous man," he murmured while his lips moved against hers. "I want to be the only man in your life." He looked down at her again for a long moment and pulled her tighter in his arms.

"You are joking, right?" she questioned in disbelief.

"I never joke when it comes to you; I want you for my eyes only," he said, and kissing the tip of her nose, he released her.

"Then you'll have to lock me up in this house," she stated.

"Don't tempt me!" he replied, and turning around, he walked back to finish dressing, still whistling an old tune.

"We are going to see Olivia this afternoon," he called out. "I'll call her on my way to the office and set it up."

"All right, I'll meet you here," she replied. She opened the fridge and took out a water bottle. She picked up her books, threw her mobile in her purse, and walked out to the garage.

"Later," she called out, shutting the door behind her. She threw her books and purse on the passenger seat and started to slide into the driver seat. He appeared out of nowhere, arms pulling her back against him, scaring the bloody crap out of her once again.

"Later won't do it for me, baby." His lips brushed against her ear. He pulled her out of the car, and turning her around, he gathered her against his muscular body. She looked up, and before she had a chance to say a word, he crushed her lips beneath his. "I'll miss you," he murmured through the kiss, and she giggled with delight.

"I love you," she whispered. He released her and held the door open for her to get in. He stood by the car while she pressed the ignition and leaning inside the window. He brushed his lips against hers. She smiled as she heard his velvety voice. *"Miss me."* Suddenly, he was out of sight just as fast as he had appeared. She shook her head in disbelief at his ability to move the way he did. She pushed on the gas and laughed with pleasure; it was going to be a long day without him.

Chapter 20

IN THE CAR, she turned the radio up and hummed along to the music. The traffic was heavy, and the streets of Brighton were busy with pedestrians. Some were rushing with the sole purpose of reaching their daily destinations, and others were busy texting or talking on their mobile phones. They seemed to be oblivious to the people around them. She was fascinated by their ignorance of the danger while attempting to cross the road without checking for the upcoming cars. She flinched at each loud horn that blared out when a car barely missing people crossing the street with their phone glued to their ears.

Reaching the end of the main highway, she took a left onto the road that led to the university grounds. The traffic was light, and she relaxed, as she kept her eyes on the road. She still had a bit of a drive to reach the student parking lot.

Her mind whirled around the details of her last encounter with Allworth. She tried to process his words and his concerns, and she frowned. *Why is he so determined to find out the source of the amulet?* She had to admit that he did know a lot about its origin and its powers. Eva also told her that Allworth was a good soul and to not be afraid of him, but she still didn't feel comfortable facing him, especially without Sebastian.

She didn't even like going to school without Sebastian. She chuckled at the thought. He had spoiled her, and she was already missing him desperately. The mental image of Sebastian's flawless face filled her mind, and the music slowly faded away into the background. She shivered as heat coursed through her body, and her mouth went dry. This was the exact same reaction she had every time they were close to each other, and now when she simply thought about him. *How crazy is this?*

There was nothing in this world that could feel more perfect, more complete than sharing her life with Sebastian. He had become the focal point of her existence. She couldn't comprehend the void that enveloped her each and every time they were apart.

She gasped out loud, hitting the break hard as she barely missed colliding with the car in front of her. She immediately came to a complete stop, shaking her head in disbelief. Her heart was beating fast, and her hands were sweating. Jeez! *What in the world is wrong with me?* Every time she thought of Sebastian she seemed to lose time and space. She had to stop thinking about him. She sure didn't want to mess up this beautiful car, and she didn't want to hurt herself. She laughed at the ranking of priorities; car first, hurt second. *Good God, what in the world is happening to me?* she thought again.

The car was last year's birthday present from Sebastian, and she treasured it, but it was more important that she arrived to class in one piece. She still couldn't believe how her life had changed since the first moment she set eyes on Sebastian. She fell deeply and passionately in love with him. She knew that the same thing happened to Gabby. How in the world two simple human girls in Brighton could get drawn into this amazing everlasting world of two stunning immortals? She shook her head to clear the haze, and slowly she pushed on the gas, heading toward campus.

She pulled into the parking lot and parked right next to Ian's car. She had one class with both Eva and Gabby. She walked around the car and, opening the passage door, picked up her books and purse. She threw her purse over her shoulder and closed the door.

She was now looking forward to seeing Eva, and discussing in detail the e-mail she had sent her yesterday. She wanted to hear all about Allworth and the strange girl at the mall.

"Arielle!" The voice was loud and eager. She turned and searched the grounds for the source, but she didn't see anyone. "Over here! Over here!" She turned the opposite way, and her gaze focused on her friend Robert, who was running toward her from the west side of the parking lot.

"How are you?" he asked, a little out of breath, when he reached her. He was grinning.

"Oh...fine," she replied, quite happy to see him. "What's up?" She kept her eyes on his.

"I tried to call you yesterday afternoon, but you didn't answer your phone," he said.

"Hmm... I know—I missed a few calls from Eva as well," she said and pressed her lips together. "Sebastian and I took a walk on the beach."

"Ah! That sounds nice."

"Sorry that I missed your call. Did you need something?"

"No—not really, I just wanted to tell you that some girl was looking for you yesterday afternoon," he said, indifferently.

"Really? Did she say who she was?" she asked, feigning interest.

"No. However, I did ask, but she didn't give me her name. She said she would be back today. She said she wanted to talk with you alone."

"What did she look like?" Arielle asked, and started to walk toward the engineering building with Robert at her heels.

"Arielle, I would love for you to introduce me to that girl! She was absolutely perfect. She was so beautiful that I could hardly gather my thoughts. She reminded me a lot of Loren," he said, and she could hear a soft chuckle in his voice. Arielle stopped dead on her tracks. Her eyes twitched slightly, and the smile faded off of her face. Terror took over every muscle in her body as bile climbed up her throat slowly. Only one name entered her thoughts, and it was making her nauseous.

"Annabel!" she muttered, terrified.

"Arielle, are you all right?" She heard Robert's concerned voice. "Is there something wrong?" She looked directly at Robert, and he was watching her carefully.

"No, no, I'm fine," she said, and waved her hand dismissively. She thoughtfully looked at her watch. "Thanks, Robert. I need to get to class," she murmured, fear creeping up her spine.

"Okay then. I'll see you later in the lab," he said with a wave.

She walked toward class, drowning in her thoughts. She had almost forgotten all about Annabel. *Oh...My...God... that bloody bitch is back!* Anxiety washed over her, closing her throat and making it hard to breathe. She felt her knees go weak, and she leaned against the building wall to support herself. She closed her eyes tightly, concentrating on inhaling and exhaling. Calm was beyond her reach, though. She was trembling at the thought of Annabel showing up.

Trying to collect her thoughts, she rested for several minutes before mentally giving herself a shake. Even if Annabel was stalking her, she just needed to stay close to her immortal friends. She would need their support if the she-devil decided to show up.

She walked into class just a minute before the door closed. She stood still for a short moment and looked around the auditorium, which was already full. Her initial thought was to get out of there and go back home.

"Arielle! Up here!" The voice broke her thoughts, and looking up, she saw Gabby and her other friends gesturing for her to come to them. She didn't hesitate; she smiled wide and dashed up the steps until she reached the top row.

She took a deep breath and exhaled quietly, letting her body relax at the sight of Eva, Ian, and Loren. Three incredible immortals that always made her feel completely safe, and they were now enveloping her with the same comforting sensation. She squeezed by Ian and Eva, who had taken the seats by the aisle, and slid in the empty seat between Gabby and Loren. Paul leaned over and gave her a warm smile. She was unable to hide the relief that was emanating from deep inside. She was happy to be sitting among her amazing friends.

Eva leaned across and whispered, "We need to talk."

"Yes, I can't wait," Arielle murmured back.

"What's going on?" Gabby asked. Arielle knew that Loren and Paul were tuned to the conversation. She set her books in front of her, and her purse dropped on the floor with an inaudible thud.

"Well?" Gabby insisted.

"Oh… Eva and Ian ran into Professor Allworth yesterday at the mall," she murmured dully. "And I want to hear all the details about that meeting."

Arielle wished Allworth was the only concern she had right now. In reality, she was really more worried about Annabel, who wanted to kill her. She was sickened by the thought.

Professor Dewhurst was sitting behind his desk—which harbored piles of chemistry books in various editions--as he waited for everyone to find a seat. He finally stood and walked slowly to a position directly behind the podium. Silence fell in the auditorium, and he proceeded by taking roll call. He then opened the chemistry book in front of him and started reading in a firm voice. He appeared extremely pleased to have them all there to listen to his lecture.

Dewhurst was an older man with silver hair and a very kind face. His class was not the most energetic one, and most of the students would completely disengage halfway through the lecture. However, he was a no-nonsense professor that expected nothing but perfection during finals. She was always very attentive; however, today several things bothered her, and she was not able to focus. She was relieved to hear Professor Dewhurst's voice.

"That's all for today. Have a good day." He snapped his book closed and walked back to take a seat behind his large desk. Within seconds, everyone stood up and started toward the exit. When outside, she walked away from the crowd, followed by her friends. She didn't want to talk about Annabel in front of Paul. He was still completely unaware of the true identity of his immortal friends. The six of them walked toward the cafeteria when they heard Paul's voice.

"Loren and I have another class in five minutes, so we have to go," he said smiling, and they both walked away.

"Well, our next class is not until eleven, so let's go to the pavilion," Ian said. Gabby and Arielle walked to the pavilion after waiting in the cafeteria line to purchase a couple of drinks. They found Eva and Ian sitting at a small table close to the water.

Arielle decided to discuss the e-mail first and then tell them all about Annabel. "Okay, Eva, I'm ready to hear the details. Are there any details?" Arielle asked, taking a seat next to her. "Tell me all about yesterday." She kept her eyes on Eva, eagerly waiting for her to speak.

"What happened yesterday?" Gabby asked, looking oblivious.

"I told you in class." Arielle said affably. "Eva and Ian ran into Professor Allworth at the mall yesterday. A girl was hanging off of his arm, and they looked pretty chummy."

"Oh…" Gabby's voice trailed. Arielle went on to tell her about the content in Eva's e-mail and tried to bring her up to the moment quickly. She then turned back to Eva. "Was the girl young? Did she look more like his girlfriend or family?" Arielle wasn't sure why she was asking such a dumb question.

"Oh, she was no family," Eva chuckled. "The way she was hanging off of his arm and the way they were looking at each other, I can tell you indisputably that she was no family." Eva and Ian were now exchanging amused looks. She leaned forward and added cautiously. "What really surprised us was his reaction when he realized that we were staring at the amulet on the girl's neck."

"What do you mean?" Arielle muttered.

"I mean, he looked extremely upset and in a big hurry to get rid of us," Eva said.

Arielle's eyebrows rose high. "I wonder why?"

"I don't know, but it became obvious to us that he wanted us to go away, and we did." She appeared thoughtful and remained silent for a short time.

"Did you get any vibes from being so close to them?"

"Arielle, I think I told you before; I don't see anything bad around Professor Allworth, and that is why I'm so puzzled with his reaction to us."

"Did the girl say anything?" Arielle asked.

"No, she was glancing between Allworth and us, but she never said a word."

Arielle bit her lower lip and looked noticeably stumped. "I thought this amulet was rare. I can't believe that she had the exact same one. How…? Where…?" Arielle's eyes narrowed to slits.

"I don't know," Eva said. "Maybe Olivia can unravel the mystery of the pendant."

Arielle harrumphed. "Well, I'm going with Sebastian to visit his mother this afternoon. Maybe I'll find out what is going on with this necklace," she said. Her voice was laced with bafflement. She lifted the soda can to her lips and sipped while taking a look around them. Laughter and happy conversations filled the air. Everyone seemed to be enjoying the day.

Ian and Gabrielle engaged in a conversation about their medical vocations. Arielle gazed out toward the lake and winced as Annabel's face flashed before her eyes. Her fingers drummed the top of the table tensely, and she drew in a shaky breath. Eva noticed and, reaching out, she placed her hand over Arielle's to stop the drumming. Arielle blinked, and turning back, she stared at Eva inquisitively. Eva raised a brow and waited.

"What?" Arielle asked.

"What's going on in there?" Eva said, pointing at Arielle's head. "You look extremely nervous and quite upset."

"I..." Arielle started to say, and then she stopped and took a deep breath. She looked troubled and stared once again out in the distance getting lost in her thoughts. It was apparent to Eva that something was disturbing her.

"Arielle, what's bothering you?" Eva's voice brought her abruptly back, and she noticed that Eva was watching her carefully.

"Allworth is not my number one concern right now."

"Oh!" Eva exclaimed, looking completely puzzled. "Then what is it?" She kept her gaze on Arielle's troubled face, waiting for a reply.

Arielle drew a nervous breath and ran her tongue over her dry lips before she began to speak. "I saw Robert in the parking lot this morning, and he told me that a girl was looking for me."

"What's so strange about that?" Eva asked.

"He said she was unbelievably beautiful and she reminded him a lot of Loren," she said, her voice shaking. Silence lingered for a few moments. She took another deep breath. "I think it's Annabel." Her voice was barely audible, and she felt a little sick. The name seemed to draw Gabrielle and Ian's attention.

"Annabel!" exclaimed Eva. "Excellent!" She let out an unforgiving laugh.

"Why excellent?" Arielle asked completely startled by Eva's outburst.

"Well...have you already forgotten that she tried to kill us both at Saint Jean de Luz?"

"No, I haven't forgotten," she said disdainfully as Annabel's face flashed before her eyes.

"Well then, we have a score to settle with her. Don't you think?" Eva asked.

Arielle looked shocked. She crossed her legs nervously and intertwined her fingers around her knees. She had a bad feeling about a meeting between Annabel and Eva.

"I'm looking forward to facing that bloody bitch! And this time things will be on an equal level," Eva said fiercely. "There's payback as they say, and I'm ready to pay her back."

Gabby and Ian were now glancing between Eva and Arielle.

"I was wondering if you can take me home?" Arielle muttered. "I don't want to drive home alone. Sebastian may not get there before me." Her voice was fretful.

Immediately Ian chimed in. "I'll drive your car home," he said. "You can ride with Eva." Gabby reached over and took Arielle's hand, pressing it supportively. The pavilion was crowded, Arielle noticed as she took a quick look around. She couldn't suppress the feeling that Annabel was somewhere nearby, spying on her.

"What are you looking for?" Gabby inquired.

"Nothing, nothing at all," she replied untruthfully.

Eva leaned closer and put her hand of Arielle's shoulder soothingly.

"Arielle, she is not here," Eva said. "Even if she did show up, Ian and I will protect you, so please don't worry." Arielle managed a smile and breathed a sigh of relief.

Chapter 21

IT WAS TIME FOR THEIR NEXT CLASS, so they stood up and left the pavilion. Gabby walked next to her, chatting away cheerfully.

"I need to go shopping for new clothes," she said. "Do you all want to go shopping with me?"

"No, not today, Gabby," Arielle said. "I have to go home and meet Sebastian. We are going to see Olivia."

"Oh, you did say that earlier. All right then, let's make plans for another day."

"I'd like that," Arielle said, and Eva agreed. Ian seemed to be totally disengaged from their girly conversation, and he walked along whistling quietly. Arielle couldn't have visualized a better bunch of friends. They lifted her spirits, and she felt extremely lucky. She and Eva had to attend a biological science lecture, while Ian and Gabby had lab together. Just before they walked away, Ian leaned close to Arielle and whispered warmly, "Don't worry, Arielle."

She looked up at him, and he winked at her. She was struck by how beautiful he really was. She watched him in amazement. The realization that both Ian and Eva were now immortals was a bit hard to swallow but not hard to accept. She loved them dearly, and their friendship was one that she treasured.

She grinned at him, and whispered back, "Thank you, Ian." At the end of the lecture, Professor Caruthers gave them next week's assignments. They were to prepare a paper that should not exceed fifteen hundred words in length, providing an overview of the points that were discussed during the last four lectures.

Undertones of discontent filled the air, and Arielle grunted in displeasure. "Bloody hell," she whispered, "I hate presentations."

Eva chuckled as they gathered their books and left the lecture hall. They met Gabby and Ian at the south tower located near the parking lot. Arielle handed Ian her car keys.

"I appreciate you help, Ian."

"No problem at all," he said grinning. He pulled Eva in his arms and locked in a hot kiss. "Don't be long," he murmured against her lips, and hugged her tightly.

Gabby and Arielle giggled noticeably. Ian held Eva to the kiss for a long moment more, and he finally lifted his head looking pleased with himself.

"Anyone else need a kiss?" he asked, and glanced between the three of them. They stared at him in complete silence. "Well? Ladies? Step up. I'm in a hurry," he added, holding his arms wide open, trying to suppress laughter unsuccessfully. His lips were pressed together, his eyes were shimmering with amusement, and he finally burst out into a hearty laugh. Eva, Arielle, and Gabby stared at him in delight, suddenly caught in his contagious laughter. He eventually turned and started to walk toward her car. "Wait, Ian," Eva called out. "I need to talk to you for a second." She ran to catch up with him.

Gabby turned to Arielle. "Let's go shopping tomorrow afternoon," she proposed.

"I'd love to do that," Arielle replied. "I'll call Loren to check if she can go with us. Do you mind?"

"Oh, no! I love Loren. She has an amazing taste in clothes."

"Yes, I agree," Arielle inserted. "She always looks so stunning, doesn't she?" Gabby nodded. They turned as Eva approached, realizing after a quick look around that Ian was already gone.

"Well, I have to go. Troy should be home soon," Gabby said. "I can't keep my hands off of him." Eva and Arielle laughed out loud, knowing exactly what she was insinuating.

"Call me later tonight, after you get back from seeing Olivia," Gabby called out and waved.

"I will," Arielle replied.

Eva and Arielle walked gradually toward the parking lot. Arielle chuckled out loud when she noticed that her car was already gone.

"I still can't get used to the immortal speed," she said, looking at Eva with, amusement.

"It's quite exciting if you are the one with the ability," Eva said, casually.

"Come off it, Eva, it's more than exciting."

"Okay then, it's exhilarating." Eva muttered lightly.

They had reached Eva's car when the sound of familiar voice jolted both Eva and Arielle to stop. They spun around and came face to face with Annabel's beautiful, cruel expression. Arielle gapped in horror, terror constricting her chest and making it difficult to breathe.

"Jesus!" She felt bile climbing quickly up her throat. Annabel's gaze was fixed on Arielle, and she completely dismissed Eva. The dark light in her eyes boded ill for her intentions. Silence fell between them.

A satisfied smirk crossed Annabel's lips and swiftly vanished.

"Well… what a tender moment! The three of us together again!" Annabel's mocking voice was as icy cold as the look on her face. Arielle heard Eva's furious mutter, but she couldn't understand what she was saying, because every part of her body was completely numb.

She was unable to follow Eva's speed, but her friend was now standing halfway between her and Annabel. Annabel's eyes flicked quickly over Eva, but just as quickly, she dismissed her scornfully. Annabel had eyes only for Arielle, as she enjoyed tormenting her ex-fiancé's new paramour. The ancient immortal took a step closer and realized that Eva was standing unmoving, creating a barrier between her and Arielle. Annabel lifted an eyebrow, and her gaze danced between Arielle and Eva.

She finally set her eyes on Eva and cocking her head to the side. "Do you really think that you can protect your friend?" she asked, her voice filled with contempt. Eva remained silent, watching her carefully. Annabel snorted disgustingly. "Isn't that enchanting, one weak human protecting another? I'm so touched!" Annabel placed her hand over her heart, mockingly.

Eva smiled, enjoying the fact that Annabel was clueless to her immortality.

Annabel now watched Eva curiously. "I must say that you have more guts than your miserable friend," she said and pointed at Arielle. "I can't imagine what Sebastian sees in this feeble human."

"That feeble human is a thousand times better woman than you'll ever be," Eva stated, rage surging through her eyes.

Annabel's mouth dropped in astonishment. She was stunned to find herself being harassed by a weak human. Her resentment, repugnance, and revulsion were palpable. She gazed at Eva and saw rage flooding her eyes.

"Are you kidding me?" Annabel finally spit out, darting her gaze between Eva and Arielle. Her fury was pulsating through her muscles. "Do you want to play with me?" she asked. "It might hurt a little," she added sarcastically.

Eva's voice boomed, unwavering. "Annabel, you have no idea how eagerly I've been waiting for this moment!" Silence answered her words. She was sure that Annabel was shocked speechless by Eva's outburst.

"You are kidding!" Annabel repeated, looking amused.

"Does it look like I'm kidding?" Eva growled through clenched teeth.

"Get out of my way, you insignificant human." The arrogance in her expression would have been visible to anyone.

"Don't even try it," Eva said curtly. Annabel was taken aback again by Eva's defiance. She arched an eyebrow while her eyes shot daggers at Eva.

Arielle saw a wide smile spreading across Eva's face and immediately Annabel lapsed into thoughtful silence. She was obviously confused as to how a feeble human like Eva could dismiss her in such an overconfident way.

Eva was watching her carefully, waiting for her to strike first. Annabel was clueless about Eva's transformation and her immortal powers.

Arielle took a quick look around, and she noticed that most of the cars were already gone, and the parking lot was almost empty. She felt a bit relieved. She prayed that for the next few minutes, nobody would show up. She had a strong feeling that this was going to be a bit messy. Two angry immortals weren't a common occurrence on the Brighton campus.

Annabel's voice snapped her out of her thoughts.

"I have had enough of your nonsense, get out of the way!"

Annabel lifted her hand to thrust Eva aside.

"No, absolutely not!" Eva shrieked, and her hand stretched out and caught Annabel's wrist with her own. She quickly twisted it behind Annabel's back and shoved upward, dislocating the other immortal's shoulder with an audible pop. Annabel staggered, shocked. She paused for a moment and gritted her teeth against the pain as she leaped forward. Eva's used the heel of her palm and slammed it into Annabel's face, throwing the whole weight of her body into the move. Arielle heard bones cracking and her mouth dropped. The sharp blow sent Annabel flying backward; she hit the ground with a loud sound.

She let out a cry of agony as she reached up with her good hand and touched her face. Blood splatter covered her hand, and she was too shocked to move. Her breath hissed through her clenched teeth and she shot Eva a seething look.

Eva knew it would not take long for Annabel to heal, so she darted forward ready to strike, but Annabel was already up on her feet. She whirled and threw herself sideways, out of Eva's path. Her lips were drawn back in a ferocious growl. Eva sailed by her with her arms outstretched. Losing her balance, she plunged toward the ground with a loud thud. A blistering bolt of self-loathing shot through Eva, cursing out loud for missing her target. She scrambled to her feet quickly and caught Annabel across the face, as she was storming toward Eva. The large stone of Eva's ring tore a deep gush across Annabel's cheek, squirting blood in the air.

Annabel shrieked and lunged at Eva's throat, raking her nails across her flesh. Eva's hands clamped around Annabel's wrists once again like steel vises and tightened until she heard her knuckles crack from the force. Annabel screamed and struggled hard to free her trapped hands, but Eva's strength stopped her stone cold, forcing her all the way to the ground. Her skin went white as Eva's grip constricted around Annabel's wrists. Her eyes went wide in horror when she heard the break that shattered nearly every part of her arms. Her breath was puffing out of her mouth in hard gasps.

A deep roar of a car engine somewhere close drew Eva's attention for a short second, but it was long enough for Annabel to free herself and back away from Eva. The car raced by and disappeared at the other end of the parking lot.

Eva's head swiveled back to Annabel who was studying Eva curiously. She just couldn't grasp the change in Eva's strength. She was not the same girl she confronted in St. Jean de Luz. She was definitely a force to reckon with. Suddenly she bolted. Lifting her leg, she landed a hard kick in Eva's stomach. The force lifted Eva off the grass and threw her several meters away, knocking the air out of her for a quick moment. There was a blur of movement and Annabel was now standing over Eva, hands on her heaps a sarcastic smile on her face.

"This isn't about you, you dismal human," she hissed through clenched teeth.

"Oh, but it is," Eva replied in an arctic voice.

Annabel's blue eyes narrowed to slits. A slow smile painted her face, "Something is different about you."

"Why don't you try to find out?" Eva goaded her.

"I'm planning on beating it out of you," Annabel said, "And I will enjoy every minute if it."

Eva's frown deepened. Annabel didn't know that Eva was now an immortal, and that was definitely to Eva's advantage. Eva pretended to struggle upright; *the bitch is going to pay!*

"Having trouble getting up?" Annabel's disgusting laughter boomed in the air.

The next few seconds took Annabel by complete surprise. Eva's speed was startling; she simultaneously threw her foot forward making brutal contact with Annabel's side, while the fingers of one hand tangled in Annabel's hair, yanking her head toward her, and her other fisted hand crashed against Annabel's jaw, shattering it. Annabel grunted in pain and panic took over when Eva's foot made another contact and than another contact and again a third one with Annabel's side, until her body fell limp. Eva let her body plunge to the ground.

Eva stared at Annabel's bloody mess for a moment and then turned and glanced at Arielle's shocked face. She sent her a reassuring smile and started to say something when she noticed Arielle's eyes widening with fear and she shot her an anxious glance. Out of the corner of her eye, Eva showed Annabel already on her feet standing right behind her. She knew she should have kept her eyes on Annabel but it was too late.

Her head whipped around but before she could react, Annabel clamped her steel hands around Eva's neck and her nails bit into her flesh like hot nails. Her eyes flashed with loathing and the promise of death. Her hands tightened and Eva started to lose consciousness. Eva went down on her knees and collapsed on the grass.

Arielle wasn't thinking clearly because if she had, she wouldn't have sprinted up and thrown her full weight against Annabel. Annabel was startled and let go of Eva. What in bloody hell was Arielle thinking? Her body collided with Annabel's and it was as if she was hit by a fierce tornado, knocking the wind out of her. Arielle groaned upon impact, pain tearing through her as her back collided with the ground. Tears blinded her, and she was sure that she tore up her knees and her elbows sliding across the concrete. She gritted her teeth trying to hold back a scream as she felt her skin burning. She sat up, and looked back through the haze. Her stupid decision was not so stupid. She had averted Annabel's attention and had given time to Eva to get on her feet, grinding her teeth in sheer rage.

Eva leaped forward and landed a hard blow in the middle of Annabel's face that sent her flying across the parking lot, landing face down on the concrete. She was screaming in agony, cursing and trying to understand what was happening to her. She stood up, coughing blood, wheezing and gasping as she tried to get some air in her lungs. Annabel's eyes were full of revulsion as she paused for a short moment glaring between Eva and Arielle.

Annabel didn't hesitate; she bolted again with frightening speed, knocking both Eva and Arielle to the ground. Eva was up on her feet, instantly blocking Annabel's way to Arielle. Arielle struggled to get to her feet once again; this time, still dazed, she bit her lower lip so hard she tasted blood. Looking up, she blinked in horror as she noticed that Annabel was now holding a knife. Arielle screamed, and she could feel the blood rushing through her veins. Her nerves were already strained to the breaking point with fretfulness.

"Eva, watch out!" she screamed. "She has a knife!" She was horrified. Annabel was already lashing at Eva with her immortal speed. Arielle's breath held in her throat, and her heart started to hammer her chest uncontrollably.

"I am going to tear your heart out," Annabel screamed. Reaching out, Eva gripped Annabel's armed hand, twisting it upward forcefully, and her forearm jammed into Annabel's throat. Pain exploded in her body.

Annabel's wrist snapped with a sound that made her flesh crawl. She saw the knife on the ground. She wanted to run and pick it up, but she was frozen in place. Eva landed another hard blow on Annabel's chest, sending her flying across the parking lot to land on the hard concrete one more time. She screamed in agony as she tried to get up. Her right arm was hanging awkwardly, but it wouldn't take long before she was healed again.

Eva bent down, her fingers closing around the hilt of the knife. Raising to her full height, she looked livid. Her eyes were wild, and she was focused on Annabel.

"You bloody bitch!" she hissed. "Lets finish this right now. I'm ready to remind you what it feels like to knock on death's door." She darted forward and caught Annabel across the face with the blade. Annabel shrieked as blood splattered, blinding her. Eva positioned herself on top of her and plunged the knife into Annabel's chest. Blood seeped through her shirt, and she looked wild. Her breath was coming out in harsh gasps. She wheezed and squealed in pain, struck by how resilient Eva was. Eva lifted the knife one more time and slammed it into Annabel's chest, ripping into her guts.

Her shriek this time was so guttural that it stunned Eva to an abrupt stop. That was long enough for Annabel to crawl out of the knife's path in supersonic speed. She jumped up, pushed her hair out of her bloody face, and shoved Eva backward. Then, she turned around and vanished in the distance. Eva stood shocked and disgusted, holding the bloody knife in her hand, unable to believe that Annabel had gotten away once again. She felt pretty disappointed. She wanted to finish Annabel for good.

Finally she turned around with a deep frown on her face. She walked back slowly, cursing out loud. "Bloody bitch! You were lucky this time," she snapped. Bending down, she cleaned the blade on the grass and put the knife in her book bag. She gave Arielle a hug as if nothing took place in the last few minutes. Arielle was trembling in total shock unable to believe her eyes.

"I'm sorry, Arielle; she got away again," Eva spit out, clearly frustrated.

"Eva!" Arielle exclaimed, "You were fantastic! You were amazing! Honestly, you were!"

"Let's go home," Eva said with a frown but completely unruffled. "Ian is going to be worried about us."

Arielle gasped in astonishment. This wasn't the Eva she knew. This was a totally fascinating immortal in action. She got into the car and sank into the passenger seat. She was in pain, but she took a deep breath and started to inspect the damage.

"Here," Eva said, reaching in the back seat and handing her a box of tissues.

"Clean up the bloody mess from your elbows and knees, you insignificant human!" she said mirroring Annabel's words. A slight grin grazed her lips. Arielle accepted the tissues and stared into her eyes.

"Seriously, Eva, you were magnificent!" Arielle carefully began wiping the blood off her elbows.

"Filthy bitch!" Eva murmured fuming. "Insignificant humans! Really? Who does she think she is?" She stopped to draw a deep breath, and finally she burst into laughter.

"W— what?" Arielle asked, staring at her.

"Arielle, I'd give everything to know Annabel's thoughts right now," Eva said and snorted.

"She was pretty beat up," Arielle laughed with her.

"Did you see her face when she left?" Eva asked still laughing.

"No— not really," she replied. "I couldn't see her face. There was so much blood gushing out, it was impossible to see her disgusting face." Eva was laughing so hard, she was doubled over the wheel. A few minutes passed, and silence fell between them.

She heard Eva take a deep breath and let out a soft chuckle. Her immortal friend cleared her throat, turned over the engine, and gunned it out of the parking lot. She checked her watch and speed-dialed Ian. Arielle was busy checking her scratches and cleaning the blood from her elbows. She was pretty upset as she noticed fresh blood seeping through her torn jeans.

"She ruined my favorite jeans," Arielle said. Her thoughts turned back to the earlier events, and she bit her lip. "That sick bitch..." she murmured, staring out of the windshield. She shifted in her seat as the pain from the scrapes stung.

"What's the matter, Arielle?" Eva was already off the phone and was staring at her.

"Oh, nothing, really. I was just thinking about Annabel," she said humorously.

Eva was flying through the streets of Brighton, and they were pulling into the driveway in no time at all. She saw Sebastian and Ian standing in front of the garage, engaged in a conversation. They both turned and watched them as Eva pulled up to the house.

Arielle's eyes focused on Sebastian. He was holding an amazing smile on his stunning immortal lips. The warmth of his gaze filled her with thrill and delight. She hurried to pick up all the bloody tissues from the floor and shoved them in her book bag. By the time she threw her purse over her shoulder, he was already standing there, holding the door open for her. He grabbed a hold of her arm and pulled her up into his embrace. Their lips met, and everything faded away from her thoughts.

"I missed you," he murmured through the kiss.

"What took you so long?" Ian questioned anxiously in the background.

"We'll talk about it later," Eva replied, reaching up to kiss him. She looked over at Arielle and gave her a suggestive smile.

It didn't escape Sebastian as he held her at arms' length with curiosity. Suddenly, his face went pale. "Arielle!" he gasped, his eyes moving from her face to her bloody arms and then to her torn jeans. "What happened to you?" He glanced between her and Eva, his eyes narrowed to slits with obvious concern.

"Annabel— that crazy bitch— showed up," Eva calmly explained. Both Ian and Sebastian gasped, and she saw a flash of unease cloud their faces.

"She is still at it?" Ian asked.

"She is never going to go away," Arielle said purposely, taking time to enunciate each and every word. "She'll remain my horrid nightmare until one of us is dead." She pursed her lips and Sebastian moved closer, tracing his finger down the length of her cheek. She took a deep breath and looked up at him. "Unfortunately for Annabel—Eva, the insignificant human, messed up her plans. She had no idea that

Eva's powers were evenly matched with hers." She choked back a laugh. "Eva's first blow broke Annabel's arm, the second blow made her face an absolute bloody mess." The vision of Annabel bloody and miserable, running away in agony, was enough to send her into hysterical laughter, the force of it causing tears to blur her vision.

"What in the world happened?" Ian asked again, nudging Eva for more information.

"Well—she was a bit surprised to say the least," Eva said. A vindictive smile lingered on her face, but when she looked at Arielle, she burst into a hard laugh. "That arrogant bitch. She looked pretty ridiculous running away with a broken arm and a bloody face, didn't she?"

"Your clothes look a bit messy," Ian observed, pulling Eva into his arms and locking them into an intense kiss.

"I ruined my favorite jeans," Arielle murmured, looking down at herself.

"They were too tight anyway," Sebastian said jokingly.

"I did think about you and what you said this morning," Arielle murmured. "I know you didn't like them; however, they were my favorite jeans."

"I never said that I don't like them. I said I didn't want you to wear them when I was not with you."

"Same thing," she replied stubbornly.

"I don't think so," Sebastian said and drew her closer. "How did you ruin them?"

"Annabel knocked Eva down, and I threw myself on Annabel. I'm not sure what I was thinking, but I didn't want her to hurt Eva. God! It was like hitting a moving bus. I flew back, lost my balance, and slid against the concrete, scraping myself to a bloody mess." He snaked his arms around her waist, and she stepped into him. Sebastian bent down and pressed his lips against hers hungrily.

"Arielle, you can't be fighting immortals," he murmured. "What were you thinking?"

"I wasn't thinking; that's the problem," she said, pursing her lips. She heard Ian and Eva laughing; turning, she saw them getting into their car.

"We are going home," Ian announced, unnecessarily.

"Thank you, Eva," Arielle and Sebastian called out simultaneously.

She smiled and waved as they pulled away. Sebastian's arm slipped around her, and they walked in the house.

"Let's go take care of those scrapes," he said and smiled softly.

"I'll do that," she said. "Can you please make me a sandwich?" He nodded, letting go of her. When she walked into the bedroom, she winced as she carefully pilled off her jeans. The pain was agonizing but the need to wash the dirt from the scraped areas of her body was the only thing she could think about. She stepped into the shower and turned on the water and waited until if felt lukewarm to the touch. Under moderate pressure she let it run over the scrapes for a few minutes as pain shot right through every nerve in her body. She took a washcloth and mild soap, and she tried to clean the dirt from the bleeding areas. The pain was unbearable, it made her flesh crawl, and she cried out. Tears were running down her face and she finally succumbed to hard sobbing. She could never remember this kind of pain before.

Sebastian heard the sobbing, and in a flash, he was standing in front of Arielle in the shower, not bothering to remove his clothes. His eyes widened in horror when he saw the amount of scrapes on her naked body. "Oh, baby, please don't cry, let me help you with that." He put his finger under her chin and lifting her head up he locked his gaze with hers. Using his immortal power, he willed Arielle's pain away and waited for a few seconds. "How do you feel?" he asked.

"I feel fine," she replied a bit confused. "I suddenly feel no pain."

"Arielle, I know you don't like me to use my willpower on you, but I think this should be an exception. I must clean your scrapes; they are covered with debris."

As much as she didn't like being willed to do anything, she was thankful about this. The pain had been so severe she thought she was going to die. "Thank you." It was all she could say.

Sebastian smiled gently. He took the washcloth from her hands and bending down, he pressed a soft kiss on her lips. Falling on his knees, he started to clean the scraped areas until all the dirt and debris were gone.

He then took a bath towel, wrapped her lovingly and lifted her into his arms he carried her to the bed. He walked into the bathroom and came back with an ointment tube. He covered all the areas and made sure she was comfortable. She was feeling absolutely no pain and that is what he wanted for her at the moment.

"I made you a sandwich just as you asked," he said.

Arielle feeling absolutely no pain she got off the bed and threw on one of Sebastian's t-shirts that came to her knees. Following Sebastian into the kitchen, she closed her eyes and wondered how long would she have to deal with Annabel. The answer irked her. Perhaps because she knew it would be for the rest of her life.

 *Chapter 22*

"**WHAT TIME ARE WE SUPPOSED** to be at your mother's?" she asked, remembering that they had to go to Olivia's this afternoon.

"Not for a couple of hours," he replied. They walked together to the kitchen.

Sebastian moved over to the other side of the kitchen counter and handed her the sandwich. She sank her teeth into the bread, feeling completely famished. She chewed slowly and swallowed with pleasure.

"Is it good?" he asked with a chuckle.

"Perfect," she muttered. She opened the fridge and took out a water bottle. She twisted the lid and took a large swig, letting out a sigh of satisfaction. She finished her sandwich, taking the water bottle with her as she walked over to Sebastian. She reached up and pressed her lips softly on his. He pulled her tightly in his arms, and bending down he pressed his lips on hers with passion.

"Thank you, baby. I was really hungry."

"Mmm...you are very welcome," he whispered through the kiss. "I'm sorry I wasn't there to protect you from Annabel, but I see that Eva did a great job."

"Yes, she was unbelievable."

In the car on the way to the Dillon estate, she asked the question that was burning in her head. "Sebastian, how do you suppose that Annabel knew that today I was going to school alone?"

There was a pause, then he harrumphed. Arielle turned away from the window and stared at him. He looked as if he was searching for a reasonable answer to her question. "I don't have a good answer," he finally confessed in a voice filled with male frustration. She nodded silently, and the quietness lingered for a long while.

Arielle had no doubt that Annabel would be coming back, filled with fury and ready to strike harder than any time before. She had suffered a very embarrassing defeat in the presence of what she thought were unimportant humans. That had to be a difficult dish to swallow.

"I think she either has someone spying on us or she has been watching us for a while now," she added, bitterly. "I do get a creepy feeling about that." More silence followed her statement. He finally reached over and took her hand. He pulled her closer and pressed his lips softly against her forehead.

"Don't worry, Arielle," he said, voice filled with emotion. Arielle stared out the window, her mind filled with concern. She inhaled mouthfuls of air and exhaled, trying to keep bile that was crashing against her stomach walls from reaching her throat. He pressed her hand anxiously.

"What is it?" he asked, intertwining their fingers together.

"Sebastian, when she comes back and finds me alone, it's not going to be an equal fight! You do understand that?"

He stared at her in disbelief. The rage that had been brewing toward Annabel for all these centuries seemed to erupt like a roaring volcano. His face went pale white, and his fingers tightened around Arielle's in a painful grasp, restricting the blood flow to her hand. Arielle gaped at him and gasped in pain, trying to pull her hand free from his steel grip. Sebastian immediately realized that he was hurting Arielle and released her hand, remorsefully.

"I'm sorry, baby. I didn't mean to hurt you. I hate her so much!" he hissed.

Arielle stared down at her hand and shook it, trying to get rid of the sensation of pins-and-needles that throbbed through the peripheral nerves. She flexed her fingers until the numbness was gone. She leaned in and kissed him on the cheek, and he grinned.

"I understand," she said. "You told me before how much you

hate her."

"Oh, did I?" he said, pretending ignorance. "Arielle, I love you more than life. I would never allow anyone to harm you. Your best friends are now very powerful. They would cover for me when I can't be there for you, just as Eva did this afternoon," he said, and pinched the tip of his nose. "Please trust me, as I don't take your safety lightly."

She thought he was probably right, but the unsettling feeling about Annabel was still making her flesh crawl. She didn't make any comment. She knew that her uneasiness was mostly because much of her life was unraveling in the pretty bizarre world of immortality. Her visits with her parents, school, and her human relationship with Gabby and Paul were the only points that kept her life a bit normal.

"What are you thinking?" he asked. He was watching her carefully. "I don't like that look in your eyes."

She shook her head. "I—I can't help worrying about Annabel showing up," she whispered.

Sebastian didn't answer, but she saw his lips twisting in a faint smile.

"She is evil!" she said irritably.

"That's obvious, but you have to let it go," he said, softly.

"How—How can I let it go? I just can't shake the way she looked at me before she disappeared," she muttered, nervously.

The grin vanished from his face, and he said passionately, "Arielle, really, you must let it go."

She was a bit astonished at his statement. *I can't believe that he expects me to dismiss someone like Annabel,* she thought, but she kept her mouth shut. He was studying her intently, as if he was trying to read her mind.

"What are you thinking?" he asked again, reaching over and cradling her face with the palm of his hand. She looked at him, eyes narrowed, lips pressed together.

"Seriously, Sebastian, you can't guess what I'm thinking about?" He pulled over to the side of the road and turned toward her. He placed his finger under her chin, lifting her face to his.

"Arielle, I love you." His voice dropped to a soft whisper. "Don't let Annabel upset you. There is nothing Annabel can do to change the fact that you and I are linked together forever." He pulled her closer and kissed her eagerly. The kiss started off sweet and then slowly deepened.

"You must let go, baby," he repeated against her lips.

"I just—um…now I just feel like someone is watching us constantly," she murmured as heat spread from his lips to hers.

"Annabel will never become an obstacle between you and me. Do you understand that?" he said. His eyes were grazing over her face.

"Trust me, please, and stop worrying," he murmured. His breath was warm against her face, and she could smell the incredible immortal sweetness. She was completely captivated by him once again.

"Are you compelling me right now? Because I'm unable to resist you," she whispered.

"I'll never do that with you; I love you," he said powerfully.

Arielle was captivated by Sebastian's touch, but she was so fixated with her terrifying thoughts about Annabel that she was struggling to get her mind under control. She drew in a huge breath. Closing her eyes, she sighed deeply.

He wrapped his arm around her shoulders and pulled her closer. "Stop worrying," he murmured against her ear emphatically, but she wasn't listening.

She pulled back meeting his gaze. A deep frown was creasing her beautiful forehead, and a scowl was masking the inner battle she was waging.

"Don't do that," he said firmly. Gripping her upper arm, he shook her lightly.

"Don't do what?"

"Don't scowl. It distorts your beautiful face. I don't like it," he said.

Leaning in, he skated his lips against hers. "And stop fighting me," he whispered, pulling her even closer. His lips were brushing the side of her face. Her breath was coming in gasps, and she was panting as her eyes moved from his incredible face to her hands on her lap.

"Will you stop fighting me?" he asked as he crushed her lips beneath his, and her heart raced into double time.

She harrumphed and gazed into his eyes. "I don't know," she murmured. He pulled back slightly and looked at her in frustration.

"You are so stubborn, but I love you," he muttered, releasing her. Starting the car, he maneuvered back onto the road.

Her mind raced, as immortality and eternity consumed every

thought in her head. She recognized that the limitlessness of those two words had changed the way she viewed life and the world around her. No other person, outside her immediate circle of friends, could understand what she was dealing with.

Sebastian turned the radio up, and the soft music of an old song filled the air. She leaned back against her seat and closed her eyes, trying to calm down. His touch startled her, as he ran his finger across her lips, down the side of her cheek, and continued lower to her breasts. Her breath caught in her throat, and she gasped out loud. His soft chuckle caused her to purse her lips. He was teasing her, and he knew thoughts of him weakened her. She grinned mischievously before leaning in to kiss him.

"I love you," she murmured. He made her feel wonderful.

"That's all that matters to me," he whispered, his tone even and content.

She held him to a kiss, and he struggled to keep his eyes on the road.

"Mmm...that is delightful," he said without breaking the kiss. Pulling back and chuckling, he focused on pulling up to the gate of the Dillon estate.

"We are here," he said. He pushed a code at the panel and waited for the gates to open. Arielle pulled the visor down and took a quick look in the mirror. She ran her fingers through her hair and pinched her cheeks with her fingertips.

"Why do you do that?" he asked curiously.

"Do what?"

"Pinch your cheeks with your fingertips."

"To bring a little color," she said and giggled. "Have you never seen a girl do that before?"

"I don't pay attentions to what girls do. However, when it comes to you, I notice just about everything." His expression clearly held love. "You look beautiful!" She chuckled and leaned in to give him a peck on the cheek.

"Thank you," she murmured. He had now reached the circular drive and stopped right in the front. She never saw him move, but he was suddenly standing outside the car, holding her door open. Taking her hand he pulled her out of the car and into his arms. Their eyes met and locked blue against green. Reaching up on her tippy toes she kissed him softly. He released her reluctantly and taking her hand they climbed together the massive staircase to the front door. Sebastian used his key and a chime played a musical tune as he pushed the door open and they stepped into the foyer. It wasn't long before she saw Olivia appearing at the top of the main staircase.

"Sebastian! Arielle! Welcome...welcome..." she called out as she descended the steps in slow, elegant movements. She was a stunningly beautiful woman, and her smile lit up the foyer. Arielle would never get over the amazing appearances of immortals.

"Hello, Mother." The tenderness in Sebastian's voice was clearer than words that he loved Olivia as though she were truly related to him by blood. His face lit up with delight, and he released Arielle's hand to meet his mother at the base of the staircase. The regal immortal stepped into his embrace, holding him tightly and tenderly patting his back. When they finally parted, she bussed his check.

"I'm so glad to see you!" she exclaimed, cupping his face with both hands. "I wonder why you don't come more often." Sebastian cleared his throat awkwardly.

"Mother, I'm sorry for not visiting more often, but I hope that you do understand," he carefully apologized. "Between work and school, I don't have a lot of spare time, but I do love you."

She nodded. "I just miss seeing you and Loren and spending time together." She appeared as if she was longing for an earlier time and life. She finally released Sebastian and moved to Arielle. She opened her arms and welcomed her with a great smile on her face.

"I'm delighted to see you, Arielle." A grin was painting her beautiful face. "I know you've been taking good care of Sebastian, because he looked extremely happy." She laughed quietly, giving her a peck on both cheeks. "Mm...do I smell freesia?"

"Yes, it's my favorite fragrant flower," Arielle replied. She remembered only too well Sebastian having the same reaction when they first met.

"What a coincidence!" Olivia exclaimed and held her gaze steadily.

"Oh?" it was all Arielle could muster.

"Didn't Sebastian tell you? Freesia is one of my most favorite fragrances as well!"

"Really! No, he never mentioned it." Swallowing quickly, she tried to hide the surprise.

"I'm sorry, Mother; I simply forgot." They heard Sebastian's apologetic velvety voice. Inwardly he grimaced, annoyed that the subject even came up.

Arielle turned to glance at him quizzically. Sebastian raised an eyebrow. She lifted her finger to her mouth and sent a kiss his direction. His lips kicked up, and she felt his warmth envelope her.

"When did you fall in love with freesias?" Olivia's question made her blink, and she turned back to look at her.

"I'm not sure that I can remember the exact time. Freesias were part of my mother's life while I was growing up. They were all over the house and in our garden. The exquisite scent became part of me," she responded with a small grin. "What about you?" Arielle asked. Olivia took her hand and pulled her into the sitting room with Sebastian at their heels.

"I know you will absolutely love to sit on this sofa. It faces the garden," she added, grinning enigmatically. Arielle gazed back at Sebastian, but he shrugged his shoulders, utterly stumped. She turned to Olivia and looked at her enquiringly.

Olivia's lips curved at the corners as she pointed out the window. "Well, what do you think?" Arielle followed her finger, and her jaw dropped. The grounds were covered with flowerbeds, full of life, with no bare spots. The rainbow of colors elegantly intermingled, extending as far as they eye could see. The blossoms gracefully swayed in the mild breeze, creating a moving ocean of freesias. Olivia opened the window and filled the room with the mind-blowing scent that Arielle loved so much. Arielle choked at the sight.

"Oh...my...God..." she gasped. "You really do love freesias!"

"As an immortal, I could never lie," Olivia answered, delighted by Arielle's reaction.

"How did you grow to love them this much?" Arielle asked, still captivated by the sight.

"My husband and I spent a few years during the 1800s in South Africa. Christian, my husband, always loved to surprise me. Every day he brought a new-exotic flower. One morning, he came in with a gorgeous white flower in his hand. I'd never seen anything like it. It wasn't just the beauty of petals but the fragrance that captivated my senses. At that moment, it became my favorite flower. I can't tell you how pleased I am that you love freesias." She turned toward Sebastian and smiled. He diverted his gaze to Arielle, enveloping her with such love that the feeling was palpable.

"Mother, I wish you could come and visit us. The gardens are filled with freesia flowers. I thought it was amazing that she loved the same flower as you do. I just don't know how I failed in mentioning to Arielle your obsession with the same flower." Arielle stared at Sebastian, holding a warm grin on her face. His gaze was so irresistibly exciting that she could almost feel his lips brushing against her skin, making her quiver. She closed her eyes, trying to shake all those thoughts out of her head. She heard him chuckle, and she was sure he knew her thoughts.

"Are you all right, dear?" Olivia asked watching her now intently.

She cleared her throat. "Yes, I'm fine, I'm also happy that we share this amazing love for freesias," she muttered. Olivia took a seat on the sofa; reaching up, she took Arielle's hand and pulled her softly down to sit next to her. Sebastian took a seat in the large armchair across from them.

Olivia drew a deep breath and gazed at Arielle carefully.

"Sebastian told me that you're worried about your professor's obsession about your amulet," she said.

"Yes," Arielle replied. "He makes me feel quite uncomfortable."

"I want you to take your time and tell me everything," she urged in a low, serious voice. Arielle inhaled deeply before gazing in Olivia's eyes and starting to speak.

"Well, the whole thing is a bit peculiar. It all started a couple weeks ago. Professor Mayfield, our regular physics professor, had an accident during the semester break. He couldn't return to class. His replacement is a young man, likely in his mid-thirties. His name is Colt Allworth, and he seems to be very nice, though quite strange." She paused and ran her tongue over her dry lips. "Yesterday, he became very upset with me for not paying attention to his lecture, so he reprimanded me. I was utterly humiliated in front of the class."

"She was magnificent!" Sebastian chimed in and chuckled, making his mother laugh with him. Arielle scolded him with her expression.

"Anyway," Arielle pressed on. "He was almost finished delivering his humiliating speech when his eyes suddenly zeroed on my necklace, and he froze in mid speech. He seemed unable to compose himself. His facial expression changed, and he appeared literally mortified. He was so shaken up that he forgot what he was about to say and stared at me apprehensively." She paused to take a breath. "The whole class seemed transfixed by his bizarre behavior. I couldn't help but feel a lurch of anxiety." She stopped talking and swallowed hard, recalling the moment. "I was sure I had touched a nerve, but I was completely clueless as to why he was so sidetracked. He was breathing intensely, and he remained speechless for a long moment. He finally turned around and walked back to his podium, not saying another word to me for the duration of the lecture."

"At the end of the lecture, he asked me to stay back so we could talk, and that is when he asked me about the amulet. He wanted to know its origin and how I happened to have it on. I told him that it belonged to my ancestors. He shook his head back and forth in clear denial. He told me that my ancestors couldn't possibly be the rightful owners."

"I've no idea why he created such a show and why he was so adamant that I wasn't the rightful owner of the amulet," she said raising her eyebrows. "He told me not to be afraid of him. Why would he even think that I was afraid of him? He told me he wasn't going to hurt me. Why would he hurt me? I guess I have all these questions," she said nervously. "Who is this guy? And why would he warn me to come clean about the amulet?" She looked down and rubbed her hands together uncomfortably.

"Don't be nervous, dear," Olivia said calmly. She put her finger under Arielle's chin and lifted her head to meet her gaze.

"Go on…" she said with a soft smile, patting her hands with hers.

"My best friends Eva and Ian ran into Professor Allworth and a female friend of his at the mall yesterday afternoon. Eva noticed that the girl wore an amulet exactly like mine." She stopped talking and hauled in a deep breath. "I guess I just don't understand what's going on, and it's making me very uncomfortable," she said. She cleared her throat significantly and continued. "I've been struggling to understand

Allworth's involvement with the amulet. You can imagine why I—why I'm so perplexed. I've all these questions but no answers. What's going on? Who is Colt Allworth? And what is his motivation for this intense interest about this amulet?" She clasped her necklace and clenched her teeth. A long silence followed.

The silence in the room was broken by a soft knock at the door, and the butler came in carrying a silver tray with a teapot, three cups, and a plate of crumpets. She was sure that Edwin had likely brought the extra glasses for show, as most immortals preferred not to eat or drink human food. He set the tray carefully on the small table directly in front of them. To Arielle's surprise, he picked up the decanter and poured tea for all three of them. He set it back down, gave a polite smile, and walked out, closing the door softly behind him.

"Have a crumpet, dear," said Olivia, picking up the small plate and moving it closer to Arielle's reach. Arielle took a crumpet and brought it to her mouth. She watched surprised as Olivia took the teacup, lifted it up, and sipped, never averting her eyes from Arielle. Arielle grinned, knowing that the last thing Olivia wanted to do was drink tea. She was certain that Sebastian's mother was trying to make her feel comfortable.

Sebastian picked up a cup of tea, chuckled, and took a sip. He turned to his mother and started to give her his personal view about Professor Allworth. Arielle assumed that they were giving her time to finish her crumpet and drink some tea. At first, she watched them carefully, listening to their conversation. What had begun as a quiet conversation in English had transformed into rapidly spoken French, a language that she couldn't speak. Especially since they seemed to be speaking an older dialect. Suddenly, Sebastian stopped talking and glanced her way. She noticed his mouth twitching for a short moment. He then gave her a quick smile and returned his gaze back to his mother. *What's going on?* she wondered.

The conversation then changed to that now familiar immortal conversation. She was watching them with fascination. Their lips were moving, but she couldn't hear or understand a single word they were saying. Even odder, something was guarded in the way they communicated with each other. She noticed the worried expression on Sebastian's face, and she shifted in her seat as her discomfit grew. They both noticed and immediately stopped talking.

Sebastian stood up and started to pace back and forth, pinching the tip of his nose several times. Arielle finished her crumpet and drained the teacup, looking puzzled. She set her cup down and cleared her throat. They both turned toward her at the same time, but her anxiety didn't seem to be shared by either one of them. They both appeared completely unruffled. *How strange?* she thought, and she blinked. *One minute they are fussing about something, and then they look like the conversation never took place.*

"Is everything all right?" Arielle asked politely, looking between Sebastian and his mother.

"Yes, yes, everything is fine," Sebastian, murmured calmly.

"I was trying to explain the situation with Colt," Olivia said gently.

The fact that she called Professor Allworth with his first name implied that she knew him well.

"Do you know Professor Allworth?" Arielle asked watching Olivia carefully.

"Yes, dear, I know Colt and his family very well," she said in a soft voice. There was a pause in which Olivia looked up at Sebastian, who stared back at her. "Arielle," she started, in a soothing tone. "My acquaintance with Colt and his family was built under very personal and very complicated circumstances. I've never had a reason to discuss this association with Sebastian or Loren."

To Arielle's surprise, Sebastian and Olivia lapsed into a thoughtful silence. Arielle's head was now swirling with wild thoughts. *What kind of complicated circumstances was she talking about? Why did she never discuss this with her children?* She remained silent, but she couldn't hide her unease. She gazed up at Sebastian once again, and he looked intent. She diverted her gaze to Olivia, and she had the same kind of look on her face. Arielle's mind seemed to be struggling to understand yet another serving of dreadful information. Finally, Arielle broke the silence.

"Olivia, I couldn't help overhearing some of what was said between you and Sebastian. I couldn't understand most of it, but it's obvious that you're both upset." Arielle's expression was edgy. Sebastian had fallen silent, and Olivia was trying to find the right words to reply.

"Well?" Arielle pressed on, darting a quizzical look between Olivia and Sebastian.

Olivia looked up and held Sebastian's gaze for a short moment. His jaw was set, and his expression was indecipherable.

Arielle waited patiently, trying to understand what was creating so much intensity between the two of them. They had come to Olivia's home to discuss Colt Allworth, but their visit was turning out to be something completely different. Looking at Olivia, she noticed a flash of pain cross her eyes. Arielle went still. *What in bloody hell is going on?*

The faraway look in Olivia's eyes concerned Arielle, suggesting that the internal battle she fought was a fierce one. Sebastian sat back down, and the armchair sagged beneath his weight. Finally, Olivia shook her head and peered into Arielle's eyes. When she spoke, her voice was barely audible. "Arielle, dear, this is about a painful time in my life that I have sworn to keep secret. I never shared it with my children, because I truly believed that they didn't need to know. However, today, due to the issue at hand, I divulged it to Sebastian, and he is quite upset with me. Sebastian doesn't like secrets, especially between family members."

"Yes, I know," Arielle murmured, thinking to herself that this visit was becoming even more complicated. *What issue at hand?*

Arielle was watching Olivia intently as she continued.

"A very long time ago," she whispered, "I was a viable young woman in my early 30s, crazy in love with the most amazing immortal man. His name was Christian." Arielle raised her eyebrows quizzically. Olivia noticed and understood her unspoken question. "Yes, I was human in those days. Christian and I fell in love in Germany and decided to get married. We went to Paris for our honeymoon and fell in love with its cultural and architectural beauty. And its wonderful nightlife. So we built a beautiful home in the borough of Auteuil-Neuilly-Passy and establish residency there for the next several years. Christian was a remarkable husband, and we were deeply in love. He had acquired several businesses in London, and he had to leave me for two to three weeks a couple of times a year to handle his company's needs. We drew a large circle of friends, so I was never alone. My parents lived in Germany, and we visited as often as possible. During one of those times that Christian was in London, I had to attend the engagement party of my best friend without him. Going to parties alone wasn't so unusual in those days, however, that particular day was a turning point in my life." Olivia paused. She drew in a deep breath and gazed at Sebastian, who was listening without saying a word.

"I left the party long after midnight. Halfway to our home, highwaymen confronted my carriage. They shot my driver and dragged me out of the carriage. They robbed me, raped me, and beat me savagely, leaving me on the side of the road to die." She paused again and took a deep breath.

Arielle gasped at the word rape. Matt flashed before her eyes, and she looked horrified. She looked at Sebastian, and he was watching her nervously. He thought he understood Arielle's reaction to his mother's statement about rape. Arielle pressed her lips together and turned her attention once again to Olivia, just as she had started to speak again.

"I was 34 years old," she continued in a barely audible voice. "I was sure that I was going to die, and I cried bitterly thinking that I would never see Christian and my family again. I'd been drifting in and out of consciousness when I heard someone speaking to me. Unable to tell if it was a woman or man, I actually thought I was hallucinating. I felt someone lifting me up into his or her arms, and that was the last thing I remembered until much later when I opened my eyes to see a young man sitting next to my bed, watching me carefully. I didn't recognize him, and I had no idea where I was. Nothing in the room was familiar. To make a long story shorter, he had taken me into his home and took care of me. I had been there for three days, and he assured me that I was fine and ready to go home. How could I be fine only three days later? How could that be possible? How could I be fine after a savage, nearly fatal beating? I remember sitting up on the bed utterly confused and in shock. He was absolutely correct. My body revealed no sign of a brutal attack. I was completely healed, and I couldn't explain any of it."

"Oh...my...God!" Arielle mumbled, and her eyebrows flew upward. "I think I know what you are going to say." Olivia nodded.

"He told me that he couldn't have let me die." She pursed her lips and raked her fingers through her hair. "Even though I was familiar with immortality, I went through all the emotions, all the fright, all the agony, that a person would go through, when they find out that they are not human any longer. I wanted to cry, but I couldn't. I wanted to run away, but I didn't have the strength. There was a man in my life who I loved deeply. Christian was coming home in a couple of weeks, and I was alive. It was hard to accept the transformation, but I was very thankful to the man for saving my life. I went home and sulked for the next few days. The young man visited several times helping me go through the changes. It was only two days before Christian arrived home, and I was as ready to face the world with my new identity as I could be."

"What happened when Mr. Dillon came home?" Arielle asked.

"When I finally found the strength to divulge the details of my horrible experience and my new identity, Christian was fuming with rage. He wanted to find them and kill them, but I couldn't remember what they looked like or who they were. It had been dark, and I hadn't clearly seen their faces. He was sad about the loss of Jack, our carriage driver, who had been with us for six years, but thrilled that I was alive."

"What did he say about your immortality?"

"He was elated! He had told me over and over again that he was never going to let me die. He was never going to move through eternity without me by his side." She drew in a breath and smiled wide.

Arielle turned her gaze to Sebastian. The sight of him sent a sudden rush of emotions surging through her body. Christian's words were Sebastian's words to Arielle each and every time she worried about dying and leaving him behind to move on through eternity without her.

"I have never regretted one day spent with my amazing husband." Olivia's words snapped her back to the here and now.

"Oh! God! What about the man that saved your life?"

"Christian invited him to our home, and he became one of our best friends," she said. Arielle was amazed with Olivia's story, and reaching out, she took the immortal woman's hands and smiled warmly.

"I'm so sorry about the ordeal you had to go through, but I'm extremely happy that you're alive," she said genuinely. Olivia hugged her and gave her a quick peck on the cheek.

"So that was my whole conversation with Sebastian. He is upset, because I hadn't told him. However, that's not a story I like to recall."

"I understand," Arielle whispered, thinking about her own ordeal with Matt and how much she wished that she could make the incident vanish from her life. There was a long silence. Sebastian's gaze was fixed on Arielle. Arielle cleared her throat and looked at Olivia.

"So how do you know Professor Allworth?" she asked, returning to her original question. Olivia squeezed her hand reassuringly.

"Colt was the young man that saved my life."

Arielle blinked in astonishment. "Professor Allworth is an immortal?" She now turned to Sebastian once again. "But...you thought he wasn't. How can you make a mistake like that?" she asked, curiously.

"Arielle, he's wearing an amulet, and it prevents me from seeing anything about him. That is why I couldn't read his thoughts."

"Oh..." Sebastian rose to his feet and approached the sofa; he pulled Arielle up and held her tightly in his embrace.

"Are you all right?" he murmured.

"Perfectly," she said. "I'm now quite intrigued by Professor Allworth, I never realized he was an immortal either," she added, thoughtfully.

"No more worries?" he persisted.

"No, not at all. Professor Allworth is a wonderful man. Another big plus is the fact that he is an immortal. How much better can it get?" she chuckled blissfully. "All I have to do now is clear up the issue about my amulet with him."

"I'll do that for you," Olivia chimed in.

"Sebastian, do you think that the other two professors are immortals?"

"I would put a wager on that."

Pulling away from Sebastian's embrace, she sat back down next to Olivia while he walked toward the window and stared out into the open.

"Thank you, Olivia," Arielle whispered. "Can you tell me more about the secret society? I want to learn everything about it."

"I love to," she replied. "I'm a member of the Veneti Society, which was established in September of the year 63 BC. Royals have passed the secret code for membership to their successors. Families of higher status did the same thing with their heirs. There are countless mortals and immortals throughout the world who are members and have been members since the very beginning.

"Our society has been built on firm ground that can sustain the wrath of evil. We are sworn to annihilate those who try to harm innocent people. We're sworn to a life of obedience and insistence on secrecy. As a member of this society, I have the right to protect my family by using the amulet as a shield. You are part of my family now, and I've made you the rightful owner of the amulet." A smile tagged Olivia's lips as she continued.

"The amulets are sacred, and they keep the owners safe from any type of harm. Colt and his family belong to the society. We are all very devoted, and we have created very strong bonds between us through the centuries." She paused for a short moment. "The book that came along with the amulet is an amazing book. It holds powers of which the human mind could not even conceive." Olivia kissed Arielle's cheek.

"I never had to give this to my children, because--as you are well aware-- they have their own powers; therefore, they are in no need of the amulet protection." She gave Sebastian a speaking glance. "Our functions and secret rituals were concealed from the non-members and thus solidified our society. There are monthly meetings, and the rules and codes are read and sworn by all the members. If you wish to attend with me, you'll learn all about the contents of the little black book. You'll understand the meaning of the society, and you'll learn how you can benefit from those powers."

Arielle nodded as Olivia continued. "All the members have a list revealing the family names that belong to the society. This is how Colt knew that your family was not on the list. I never knew that he took the job at the university or, more importantly, that he would be your professor," she said. Arielle was so fascinated that she was sure she hadn't blinked for the past twenty minutes. Olivia reached up and ran her finger across her cheek with tenderness. "Arielle, I don't want you to worry. I'll talk to Colt this evening. There should be no more problems between you and your professor."

One thing confused Arielle. "Why does he have to wear an amulet if he is an immortal?"

"He is a member of the society, and everyone that attends the meetings has to wear the amulet."

"Am I allowed—to—" Arielle began, then stopped, apparently lost for words.

"Allowed to do what, dear?" Olivia asked.

Arielle ran her hand over her hair and hauling in a deep breath she said, "Am I allowed to have the amulet on if I'm not a member of that society?" she asked incredulously.

"Yes, dear," Olivia replied. "You are part of this family now and a human in need of protection."

"I would love to come with you to one of those meetings," she said, and she saw a stunned look on Sebastian's face. Olivia was taken aback, but she recovered immediately.

"All right then, I'll arrange for that. Attending the ceremonies will teach you a lot and help you use your little black book wisely," she said. Her voice was serious. Arielle remained silent for a short time.

"That will be unbelievable! I would love to come with you," Arielle finally exclaimed.

Olivia looked extremely pleased. Sebastian was excited to witness an awesome relationship developing before his eyes between his mother and the girl that captured his very soul.

Arielle felt a wonderful sensation of ease taking over her. Allworth was no longer a mystery. His intense interest regarding the amulet was clearly understood. She felt her spirit lift a few notches higher, and a smiled lifted the corners of her mouth.

"So...what do you think?" Olivia asked Arielle.

"About what?"

"About Colt."

Arielle drew breath as she started to speak. "I... understand Allworth's concerns about the amulet."

"It's a lot to absorb but—you know, it answered all my concerns about Allworth."

Olivia smiled, pleased with the outcome.

"I think we should be going," Sebastian said, glancing at his mother.

Just before Olivia had a chance to reply, Arielle's phone rang. She pulled it out of her purse smiled as she glanced at the screen.

"Excuse me," she said glancing between Sebastian and Olivia. "It's my mum, and I need to take this." She flipped the phone open. Placing it against her ear, she walked away and stood in front of the large window. The conversation was short and ended with Arielle telling her mum that she was going shopping with Gabby, Eva, and Loren tomorrow, but she would be stopping by the house the day after that. She slipped the phone into her pocket and returned to Sebastian.

"Thank you for everything," she said, hugging Olivia affectionately. She noticed the pleased expression on Sebastian's face as they parted.

"Thank you, Mother," he said lovingly. "I'm sorry about the misunderstanding earlier." Olivia made a dismissive gesture with her hand. Sebastian linked his fingers with Arielle's and pulled her toward the door.

"It was lovely seeing you again, Arielle. Please come back soon," Olivia called out.

"I promise, I will," she called, glancing back. "I'm going to those meetings with you, remember?"

They had spent over two hours visiting Olivia, and they were ready to go home. The sun was disappearing below the horizon, and twilight was enveloping the earth. A gentle breeze brushed their faces as they stepped outside, causing Arielle to lift her face to the wind. She was feeling exuberant following the meeting with Olivia. She looked up at Sebastian, and he bent down and brushed his lips against hers softly. She knew she was being silly, but she couldn't help the extraordinary feelings she was holding for this immortal man. She literally ached for him. She felt overwhelmed with pleasure.

In the car, she was extremely quiet.

"What's on your mind?" Sebastian asked.

"I was just thinking about your mother's horrible experience."

"I know. It was hard for me to hear. I also understand why she would want to keep it a secret."

"Oh, you do?"

"Of course I do."

"How come you didn't understand about me keeping Matt's attack a secret?"

Sebastian inwardly cursed. "*You* are a different story. I have to know everything about you since the day we first met, and even before that," he said firmly.

"Oh?"

"Do you have a problem with that?" he asked anxiously.

"No, not at all. I was just curious."

He pulled her close for a quick kiss.

The remaining ride home was quiet. He held her hand as he always did, making her feel safe, happy to be alive, and in love with a perfect man.

At home, Sebastian poured himself a glass of salve and sat at the kitchen counter. He picked up the newspaper and flipped though it while sipping slowly. Arielle walked into the bedroom and pulled her dresser drawer open. She took out the little black leather book and walked back, clenching it tightly in her hand. She set it on the top of the counter and ran her fingers over the leather cover several times.

Sebastian lifted his head and watched her carefully but kept quiet. She finally sat down and flicked through the pages slowly, stopping every so often to trace over the strange symbols and signs with her fingers. She stared bleakly at the pages, unable to decipher the meaning behind all the ancient symbols. They belonged to so many secret societies, written in various dialects such as Etruscan, Shinto, and Roman. She shook her head and let out a discouraging sigh.

"What are you doing?" Sebastian asked softly. The question pulled Arielle from her fascination. She lifted her head and met his eyes. She let out a soft chuckle and resisted the impulse to tell him not to worry about it.

"I wanted to see if I could translate some of these symbols on my own. Eva seems to know and understand all about these books; not me, however."

"You sound angry, are you?"

She looked up at him and a smile spread across her face.

"I'm sorry, I didn't mean to sound aggravated," she replied. "How surprised were you to find out about your mother and Colt Allworth?"

"I was more surprised than you were. I absolutely had no idea how she became an immortal; I knew nothing about the Veneti society or my mother's involvement. I guess I can understand why she didn't find it important enough to talk about any of it to Loren or myself.

As immortals, we have absolutely no need of the amulet protection or the power book," he said with a soft chuckle. "So what are you looking for in that book?"

"I'm not sure. Mostly, just curious. "

"Well then, why don't you let my mother help you? She'll teach you everything you want to know about the powers held in that little book." He put down the paper, stood up, walked around the counter, and stopped directly behind her. Leaning down, he pressed his lips on the back of her neck. Her nerves leapt; she sucked a tight breath as she felt the heat spreading across her flesh. Lifting her chin, she stared up into his eyes. He held her gaze and his lips slowly curved to that amazing smile.

"Let's go to bed," he whispered. Sliding her hand into his she drew enough breath to keep herself from falling apart.

"Tomorrow will be another grueling day in Chemistry."

"I'm sure you'll endure," he said, chuckling.

While getting ready for bed, an unwelcome twinge ran through her mind, and her heart sank as she latched onto one horrible name: *Annabel*. "I wonder when Annabel will decide to come for me again?" she asked Sebastian. A ghost of a frown flickered on his face. "Arielle you have to stop thinking about Annabel."

She humphed. "Easy for you to say." She couldn't let her thoughts run wild, but the truth was clear. Annabel was coming for her. It was not if she would be coming, but when. She vividly recalled their last meeting at the university parking lot. Eva had been there to protect her. Venom dripped from Annabel's bloody lips when she'd said. *"I'm coming back for you and I'll kill you, you miserable human."* Arielle didn't miss the deadly promise that flashed in Annabel's eyes. Her mouth twisted at the thought and she bit back a groan. There would have to be a final confrontation, but when? This was a sheer nightmare and there was no end in sight.

In bed Sebastian drew her in his arms, and pressed his lips to her nape. She stared into the blackness, and inhaled his sweet immortal scent. Enveloped in the sanctuary of his embrace, all tension fell away, and relief slid through her. She sensed his smile, as sleep drifted in and pulled her down.

A sneak peek at the fifth book in the Immortal Rapture Series, *Arielle Immortal Journey*

THE DAY DAWNED cool and clear, perfect weather for Brighton and beautiful for horseback riding. Arielle didn't have to work hard to lure Sebastian—her own Mr. Darcy—into an afternoon ride. As was normal, her thoughts swirled around her lover and their life together while her eyes enjoyed the scenery. Only four days had passed since the revelations about Professor Allworth's involvement in the Veneti society and their interest in Arielle's magical amulet, but little actually changed in Arielle and Sebastian's daily routine.

Every morning, Sebastian and his business partner Troy left for the office and returned home around mid-afternoon. Then Sebastian spent time reading the paper or watching the telly while Arielle completed her homework. As the sun set, the couple enjoyed time together by walking the beach and discussing their plans for the future. Once home, Sebastian accompanied her as she ate dinner, and the discussed news about school and their friends. Sometimes, Arielle chitchatted nonstop, drawing a laugh from her love.

However, the merry mood always dispersed late in the evenings when he and Troy conferenced regarding work. The two immortals spoke in their strange, fast speech that made it impossible for a human like Arielle to understand. However, she couldn't miss Sebastian's facial expressions throughout the calls. Though she wondered each evening what upset him, Arielle didn't want to ask, because as soon as he hung up, she again became the center of his attention. Her beautiful man would take her to bed, making her writhe in his arms and causing her to forget any thoughts or concerns she had.

Each morning when he left, though, she was reminded that she had never visited Sebastian's office. In her mind, she had created an image of this enormous building located in the middle of London. His business completely intrigued her. She wanted to know what his secretary looked like, what kind of people worked for him, and what he did when he was there. As the horses stepped onto the beach, Arielle decided she was going to surprise him one day with an unexpected visit. She shook her head imperceptibly and smiled as she considered how surprised he would be when she entered his office unannounced.

She looked over at Sebastian. He was watching her carefully, his gaze locked on hers and eyes inviting her to speak her mind.

"What are you thinking?" he asked curiously.

She snorted. "About you, of course. Do I ever think about anything else?"

"I'm happy to hear that. But you look perplexed, so what are you really thinking about?" he asked again, a light smile touching his lips.

"Oh..." her voice trailed. There was a long pause. "I was thinking about the telephone calls you have been making to Troy for the past three nights," she said, meeting his gaze. Sebastian narrowed his eyes at her.

"What about the calls?" he asked, surprised.

Arielle cleared her throat. "Sebastian, you look agitated during those discussions. I do hope that everything at work is going well," she said, keeping her expression as calm as possible.

Sebastian moved his horse closer to hers, met her gaze, and held it. "Arielle, why do you feel that you can't ask me about something that's bothering you? Have I ever given you a reason to think that you can't?" He smiled gently.

"No, you haven't, but I don't like to intrude in your private affairs." She returned his smile.

"You're going to be my wife. I can't read your mind while you wear the amulet, and we don't have private affairs," he said, his voice low and velvety soft. He studied her face carefully while waiting for her reply.

She drew in a breath. "Okay then, what's going on at work that has you so worried?"

Sebastian's brows furrowed. He paused for a short moment. Arielle flicked him a quizzical glance.

"Do I look worried?"

"No, not now, but during those calls, you do look anxious," she answered firmly.

"Hmm, I didn't realize that, I'm sorry. We have had a few issues at the office with a security breach," he said and frowned.

"There…you are doing it again," she accused, pointing at his face.

"What?"

"You're frowning."

Sebastian blinked in surprise. He looked uncomfortable and shifted lightly on the saddle. "Sorry," he said.

"Do you have a spy inside the company?" she asked, her eyes sweeping over him.

"No, no, we don't believe that we do. We took care of that problem last year. This has something to do with our company systems."

"Oh…" her voice trailed again. "What are you doing about that?"

"Well, we are very close to a solution."

"I hope this solution doesn't include you leaving the country like you did last year," she admitted worriedly.

Sebastian appeared to notice her uneasiness. "Don't worry, baby. I'm not going anywhere."

"How are you going to fix it?"

"Our engineers have developed, and are ready to introduce, new security products that can be used globally. We are previewing the designs this week, and hopefully, we'll approve their development and distribution." Sebastian's excitement about the new products was evident. Arielle relaxed, and as they started to ride again, she was drawn into his enthusiasm. She enjoyed listening to him discussing the details.

By the time they reached the stables, the sun was slowly disappearing below the horizon, painting the surrounding sky with an intense orange and red glow. Sebastian helped her off her horse and pulled her into his embrace. He held her for a very long time.

"I love you, Arielle; please don't worry."

Arielle reached up and cupped his face with both hands. She pulled him down to her for a searing kiss. His arms locked about her, and he drew her flush against him. She moaned softly, and the kiss grew more demanding. Sebastian finally lifted his head reluctantly and hauled in a deep breath.

"Let's go home, baby," he whispered against her lips. "We don't want to make a scene in front of the stable boys, do we now?"

Her eyes lit up with excitement. She nodded in agreement, a wide smile spreading across her face. She took a quick look around. Several young men were moving about the grounds, but nobody was looking their way.

She grinned and, standing on her tippy toes, pressed another quick kiss on his lips. "Nobody is looking," she said, pulling out of his arms.

He nodded in agreement and reached out to clasp her hand. "Let's go," he said softly and led her towards the car.

On the way home, he held her hand as she whined about having to go to school without him.

"It's only for this week, love," he said, clearly happy that she was missing him.

She humphed and mumbled something inaudible. He glanced at her and their gaze locked. "I'll try to survive without you," she said gloomily, wondering what he was thinking.

Sebastian's happy laughter was contagious. Arielle had to admit that it had been a wonderful afternoon.

Every time Sebastian and Troy couldn't go to class, Arielle rode with her best friend Gabrielle. The two of them spent lunchtime pouring over books at the cafeteria pavilion with their group of friends. Afterwards, she visited the library with Gabby and Eva to research information for their classes. Today, Arielle used the time alone with her best friends to catch them up on her visit to Olivia's house. When she revealed that Professor Colt Allworth had saved the life of Sebastian's mom Olivia Dillon when she was still mortal, they looked stunned. The three women sat close to one another and discussed all she had learned from Olivia about the secret society.

"Are you going to one of the meetings with her?" Gabby asked, her eyes full of interest. Arielle struggled hard to keep a straight face, seeing the eagerness in Gabby's eyes.

Before she had a chance to open her mouth, she heard Eva reply briskly, "Of course, she will. She has to learn how to use the spells in the book; it's very important, right, Arielle?"

"Yes, I have agreed to attend the next meeting with Olivia, and I'm quite excited about it," she said, glancing between Gabby and Eva.

"Well, there you are!" Eva said excitingly.

"Is that the little black book with spells and magic?" Gabby asked.

"None other," Eva said, staring at Gabby. "I remember how eager you were to find out about my books and spells back in secondary school. Do you remember that?" Eva asked and smiled. Arielle thought that she must be reliving memories of her best friend's curiosity about magic.

Gabby frowned. She didn't look happy about the situation at all. Arielle saw a sudden mental image of Marcus flash in Gabrielle's mind and felt her fear. He had been the boyfriend from hell for Gabby and her friend's lips trembled. In that moment, Arielle wished she could not read the minds of some people.

"What's got you all upset?" Eva asked, gazing at Gabby.

"I— I don't know," she said looking down at her hands. "The thing is, I seem to remember all the bad outcomes of practicing spells, and it just gives me the creeps."

"Gabby, this book has everything to do with protecting Arielle from that crazy immortal who is trying to kill her," Eva said. There was a lengthy pause.

Gabby looked over at Arielle and said, worryingly, "Fine, but I don't want you to do anything that might put you in danger."

"I'll be all right," said Arielle with a soft smile. She reached over and gave Gabrielle a warm hug. She knew that Gabby was worried about her, and so was Eva. She loved them both so much. She glanced down at her watch and realized that they had been there for a while. She stood up, closed the book in front of her, and chuckled softly. "Well, we didn't get much done today."

"We sure didn't," Gabby said. "Troy will be home soon, and I want to be there, if you know what I mean." She muffled a chuckle.

"We know exactly what you mean," Eva grinned, glancing at Arielle to share her amusement. They picked up their books, put them in their book bags, and walked out quietly. The weather had turned cloudy, and the sky looked like rain. A cool breeze blew across their faces and they looked at each other with blissful smiles.

"I guess I'll go find Ian, so we can go home." Eva said as she started to walk toward the exit.

"Where is he?" Arielle asked.

"When I go to the library to do my research, he attends a discussion forum once a week with other medical students," Eva replied.

"Oh! That sounds really interesting. I didn't know he was doing that," Arielle said. Turning her attention to Gabby, she asked, "Why don't you go with Ian? I thought you guys took the same classes?"

"I really don't have any interest in the forum discussions," she said, holding a soft smile. "I like to interact with Troy rather than the other students." She remained quiet while Arielle and Eva watched her carefully, and she finally broke out into hearty laughter. The three of them laughed wholeheartedly. The hilarity was addicting and brought tears to the eyes of Arielle and Gabrielle. When they finally stopped, Eva was watching them with a wretched look on her face. She reached over and ran her fingers across Gabby and Arielle faces, dabbing the tears on their cheeks.

"Thanks to my immortality, I'll never be able to do this again," she said softly, looking despondent. "I used to enjoy a good cry now and then." Her voice sounded choked, causing Arielle and Gabby to give her a warm hug so she knew that they felt her pain.

The weekend arrived without Arielle's concern of crossing paths with Professor Allworth being realized. Sebastian would be attending class with her again come Monday, so the girls happily welcomed the end of the week.

Friday and Saturday evening, the group of friends watched a couple of new films, visited some new restaurants, and stopped at their favorite nightclub to enjoy the music. Sebastian and Arielle strolled together on the beach, holding hands and discussing plans for the future. She was so in love with this stunningly beautiful man that each and every time they were together she prayed for time to stop.

On Sunday morning, Sebastian planned a game of golf with Troy at the country club. He left the bed early but not before making sure his beautiful girl was happy and sated. Arielle went back to sleep and didn't wake up until noon. She climbed out of bed slowly and took time to enjoy a light breakfast after taking a warm leisurely shower.

It was a beautiful sunny day, so she decided to traipse through her private haven: the garden. A thin jacket warmed her as she walked outside. A light breeze brushed across her face, and her lips curved up blissfully. She breathed deeply, filling her nostrils with the salty scent of the ocean. Every nerve in her body thrummed with joy. She took a seat under her favorite English oak and placed her journal on her lap, letting the pen glide over the empty pages.

September 30th

Hello once again, my silent friend. There is so much going on in my head, and in my life, that I wanted to sit down and put my thoughts on your pages before I start forgetting some of the important things. It seems that my palette is never blank. There is always something lurking around the corner.

Gabrielle came out of the hospital and moved back with her parents. Troy was quite unhappy, because he wanted her at home with him. He acted like a spoiled child. Gabrielle needed help due to her injuries, and her mother was the best choice until Gabby could do things for herself.

Ian and Eva came back from their recuperating--or should I say life-altering?--holiday in Italy. I nearly choked when I saw them walk off the plane. They looked stunning: flawless features, amazing bodies, and seamless walks. I couldn't peel my eyes away from them. On the outside, they are different from the old Eva and Ian. However, I know that inside nothing has changed. They are exactly the same two people that I adore. I know that it will take time to get used to their immortal looks, but I'm willing to wait. I often wonder how long it will take for our lives to get back to normal following that horrible accident.

Colt Allworth is our new chemistry professor. I was quite concerned about him because of his weird reaction to the amulet I wear as a necklace. As it turns out, he is a close acquaintance of Olivia Dillon and a member of Olivia's secret society. He is very familiar with the list that holds the names of the true keepers of important things such as the amulet and the little black books. My name wasn't on that list, and it gave him great concern as to how I acquired it. He now knows that it was a gift from Olivia, and we have a friendly understanding.

And, oh...my...gosh... I can't forget to tell you about Annabel. She showed up at my campus parking lot on a day that Sebastian didn't attend classes with me. Eva was with me, and the moment their eyes locked, I thought the earth's axis tilted. Eva was furious. She had sworn to make Annabel pay for trying to kill us at St. Jean. I was happy that most of the students had left the parking lot, because I knew it was going to be bad. And it was. Annabel was caught by surprise, unable to understand the changes in Eva's powers. It was a bloody fight that left me dumbstruck and Annabel horrified. She was a bloody mess when she left. Eva prevailed, and Annabel was lucky to be alive. We knew that she would heal in a short time, so Eva was ready for her, but she didn't come back. I hate living with the fear of her showing up unexpectedly and trying to kill me, but I accepted the burden when I fell in love with Sebastian.

Arielle closed the journal. Her eyes wandered across the ocean as she listened to the waves crest in silence. Standing slowly, she started to walk back toward the house. She enjoyed each step she took in her private utopia. The splendor of the garden took her breath away. The fragrance of the winter flowers soothed her senses, and she smiled wide. Once inside, she picked up her mobile and rang Gabrielle and Eva to make plans for the afternoon. The guys would be late coming back from golf. There was no reason for the girls to wait around, Arielle thought.

Note to Readers

Thank you to my fans for inspiring me with your amazing and surreal feedback to continue reaching for my goal. It is the most rewarding experience to receive your wonderful notes after reading my books. To the future readers, thank you for loving books and making my book your choice. This is the fourth novel in my Immortal Rapture Series. *I hope you will enjoy it.*

ALSO BY LILIAN ROBERTS

Arielle Immortal Awakening
Arielle Immortal Seduction
Arielle Immortal Passion

Contact Information
My website: lilianroberts.com
My Twitter: @lilian3roberts
My Blog: lilianroberts.blogspot.com